# COFFIN

# LIGHT

# COFFIN LIGHT

## DOUGLAS K. PEARSON

Coffin Light
© 2010 Douglas K. Pearson
Storymakers, LLC

Edited by David Egner
Cover design by AUXILIARY Advertising & Design
Book design and layout: Dave Gilman

Printed in the United States of America
10 11 12 13 /CS/ 10 9 8 7 6 5 4 3 2 1

Water is the stuff between heaven and earth.
It teaches us who we are and who we can become.
It is the whispering voice of Sailors past
that challenges us to discover.

-Captain Douglas K. Pearson

Derecho:
   A severe gust front or straight line wind with
   high devastation levels. It forms from a bow
   line or bow echo of colliding supercells up to
   a thousand miles away.
   http://www.spc.noaa.gov/misc/AbtDerechos/derechofacts.htm

# LOG ENTRY 1

abaft Morguetowns Coffin Light
East winds to 15 knots.
Waves 0-1. Northbound at 8 knots.
Running full sail.

I now write in my logbook what I couldn't say then. Then was a long time ago. Two decades? Or was it two hours?

I may never know. All time is the same when your son has been murdered.

To my town, I'm the miser recluse, maybe dead and gone.

For my community, I was but the shell of a lifeless man until today. Today I was their leader on a ladder!

As to the murderers? They want to forget, but they cannot. Some of them sense the time is near; others have lost all sensation.

But I have been among them!

They are blind to me but I can see them.

I feel the reckoning! It is starting to ache in my joints and in the bones that I have broken along the way.

So read my log entries and know that it is my story. The young ones might try to take it away from me because they are braver, stronger and better looking.

But they won't.

No one can take anything from me anymore. For the only thing I have left to give has no value.

A black coffin lid had been bolted over the red light-house door some seventeen years ago, sending the message that something was terribly wrong in the harbor. It still covers the door today. Maybe that's why the beacon rises against the sky like a lone, middle finger, telling all that some shelters are not havens. Above the crumbling pier it stands, just west of a gray, frumpy, Michigander town.

Area folk call the lighthouse *Coffin Light*.

Saliva-like fog thrives at Coffin Light because the harbor water is shallow, warm and swampy. When the current oozes into Lake Michigan, it always seems to whip up a phlegmy vapor around the lighthouse like a fog machine. Sometimes the white mist gets carried far out over the blue waters by east winds.

They are the ill winds that create currents in Lake Michigan and rotate the cold, bone-gnawing waters from the depths to the surface. The old-timers refer to it as "turning over".

Eric Nelson sat among the cold, sweating rocks by Coffin Light. He was a black-haired, knobby-kneed and callused-handed seventeen-year-old, not unlike the hundred or so other teens whom the farm region of West Michigan raised. But *he had* come to the water to see *her*, and that did set him apart.

He smelled the stank of land and watched his breath go white as it drifted along the seagull-stained quarry boulders of the pier. He turned his torso to the walkway above and behind him, stretching his faded, cotton T-shirt with some muscle heft. The fog transformed the pier rocks into frozen chunks of curds in chocolate milk.

He gave another long, level look to the north, as if a mere gaze could cut the fog on the channel. He scowled. Turning east he felt the breeze on his face and squinted at the blue sky above town. He then looked west, saw only fog, but sensed the expanse and power of the great lake beyond the white curtain.

Turning north, he tried again to see across the channel. Nobody much gave mind to the poor missies of Mexico North or what they did on their side of the channel. Only a mere handful of those people, the T-benders, stained the edges of the town like scald on a pancake. But they didn't count for much around here.

Folk in these parts weren't Cozy-Cans like in other towns.

Eric frowned at the fog because it wouldn't showcase her white swimsuit as she walked on the far pier. Maybe she was out there; maybe she wasn't. And maybe his eyes *had* strayed. Maybe it was natural to scope an alpha LBG in a white bathing suit.

Maybe not.

Floating trash caught his eye. It swirled in the dark water by his feet, surfing the back ebb, seeking the channel current and open water.

Eric frowned.

They had come.

The fog had kept her away, but *they* had come.

He hard-raked fingers through his hair, narrowed his eyes and faced Coffin Light. Then he stepped up onto the pier walkway. Water hissed beneath him as surge pressed it through the small cracks between big rocks. He glimpsed the white of a bloated carp, bobbing belly-up in a triangle of brown water far below.

Eric kneed his way up onto the pitted concrete pier, stood and walked west into the fog.

Dwight Slash, slouching against a tipped over metal waste drum, ignited another piece of trash and flipped it into the water as the flames licked his fingers. Dwight was a Doverlooking teenager, as pale faced as the cliffs on the other side of the Atlantic. His straw hair had been shaved down to a buzz and his right arm was healing in a cast alongside his chest. White swastikas had been painted on the black cast because he had got himself Latino Licked.

Eric looked down at him. "Quit throwing trash in the water, you moron!"

"Erilick the Derelict," Dwight said.

"Is that real? Don't tell me *that's* real!"

"What?"

Eric pointed at the black swastika tat on Dwight's good shoulder.

Dwight lit another piece of trash, held it up to the white western sky, inspected the yellow flame and dropped it over the edge of the pier.

"Your Grandpa would kill you dead," Eric said.

"Shut up!"

"Your Gramps killed off Nazis and now look at you and your pathetic Neo-Tat!" Eric braced him.

"The gramps are all dead!" Dwight glowed a cigarette from a small green-orange flame of trash that flickered below the black smoke of a melting plastic cup.

"You get Mexed-Up and now you want to be a Skinhead? Skinheads are morons!" Eric said.

Dwight looked past Eric and smiled.

Eric ducked. Too slow. What felt like a hot, blue-flamed knife seemed to pierce the back of his shoulder. He dropped to his knee. Pain pulled his eyes down for a moment. Then he looked up and saw John. "Little John," Eric sneered, managing to stand. He riled John and hoped anger would make the fighter reckless. "Our parents are friends but it comes down to this?"

Eric's right shoulder drooped as he saw a crude driftwood spear in Little John's hands. Trying to lift his hurt arm, Eric winced and stumbled as his shoulder cried out.

Dwight then stood and slid an aerosol can out from his coat. The hand below the cast gripped it. Dwight's other hand opened a lighter and struck flame. "Erilick the Derelict?"

"You crazy?" Eric asked.

"Dear momma, we're all crazy now!" Dwight said. Yellow orange flame burst from the can, driving Eric back.

Blinded, Eric never saw John swing. The stick clubbed the front of his hurt shoulder, bouncing off the collar bone and numbing his arm.

Eric's arm sank lower, tilting his body. Then it started screaming.

"Erilick the Derelict," Dwight shouted and sprayed more fire.

Eric backed to the iron rim of the pier head. He saw John circle right. Dwight's fire can was between him and land. Between the enemies loomed Coffin Light, the coffin lid that had long since been stuck to its door was an unblinking, reptilian eye. Eric opened his good palm. "What is this?"

"There she is." John pointed his weapon to the channel. "You gonna grease off to your greasy little Flipper?"

"Whatta you mean?" Sweat broke on Eric's face from beyond his searing arm. He turned to the channel slow. Weakened by pain, he faced them warily. *They knew about her!* Mist swirled off the tan water and felt cool on his face. The fog horn above Coffin Light burped warning again and Eric knew she was out there.

She was why he came to Coffin Light.

She drew him.

Dwight kicked the trash barrel and rolled the heavy can toward Eric, spilling more debris.

John reached down to the pier and pulled loose some chunks of concrete.

Eric lowered his chin and looked out toward the channel.

Then another burst of Dwight's flame forced him to use up the last inch of pier.

Eric saw the sailboat ghosting in the fog. It flew a head sail and rode the warm, off shore breeze, appearing to be a part of the fog itself.

Eric tilted his head and blinked at the black-haired, brown-eyed, dark-skinned girl who sat in the back of the white sailboat with an old man.

"Two LBGs! A Bag and a Bean!" John sneered.

The sailboat skimmed atop the waxy surface where the brown water met the blue. It sizzled a small bow wake as wind pulled it abeam the lighthouse.

Eric saw a rock bounce off its white hull and he turned back and faced his foes. *And now I'm Can-Klan because I'm with these two!*

John threw more rocks at the sailboat. Dwight saw Eric's eyes linger on the girl and that hesitation clinched it.

Dwight stepped forward. The fingers below his cast depressed the can and aerosol hissed out. He flamed it as John took aim and they flanked. With rock, stick and fire, they drove Eric off the pier and stood at the edge and watched the splash.

Eric resurfaced and screamed from the electric jolt of cold water. His black hair steamed in the icy fog. He looked to the iron wall of the lighthouse platform and saw the emergency ladder, crusted with hundreds of purple, razor sharp Zebra mussels.

John stood high above it and hoisted the fifty-five gallon metal trash barrel over his head and took aim.

Dwight raised his cast in victory.

Above and beyond the attackers, Eric saw the fog-fuzzed Coffin Light.

"Trash him!" Dwight shouted.

Eric's bad arm floated beside him like a dead fish. The frigid water shrink-wrapped his skin in needle-stabbing pain. His eyes flaring, Eric kicked hard away from the ladder where John was taking aim.

Dwight pointed with his good arm. "Erilick the Derelict! Flipping off to his greasy little Flipper!"

Eric's breath vapored white. If he swam toward town, he would strike warmer water. But they would follow him. He saw the metal trashcan in the air and dove. The can concussioned the surface in a splash, stinging his back. In his watery world of silence and cold he struck out, kicking for the far breakwall.

He swam north toward *that* land.

*Her* land.

*Mexiland!*

A rope slapped against his numbed face. He took hold with his good hand and felt it tear into the flesh as it burned through his grip. He clenched harder, the grinding stopped and bubbles gushed around him as his body plowed atop the cold, clear waters of Lake Michigan. He saw his orange Crocs™ bobbing a stone's throw behind him.

He gulped more air and faced the current. Before him boiled the transom of the sailboat. The one *she* was on.

The rush of icy water increased as the sailboat caught more air and the drag pulled him under. *Give up Eric! His heart scolded. Just let go. Swimming to her land would be easier than meeting her like this.*

Then he heard only bubbles. They bounced over his head as if he was plowing through a sea of golf balls. He turned and saw the sailboat again. He was on his back now, facing the nearshore fog that seemed to collect the colors of the sun. He looked ahead, blinked and saw her facing him. The drag of his clothes against the heavy water stretched his face in pain.

His hand weakened and burned down the line until it struck the knot at rope's end. He took hold, but he had no power to pull himself aboard. The drag through the frigid water had ripped his strength. He shook his head, inhaled and told his numb hand to clamp harder.

He was closer to the boat now and his head stayed above water as the angle on his tow inclined. He looked back at his hurt arm, flapping alongside his body like a lamprey and then he looked ahead at the girl. He saw Samantha Lazzair, the one who had Dwight beaten.

Eric tried to release his hand. He didn't want to be *this* close to her. He just wanted to gawk at her from across the channel.

She was a *problema*.

Dwight and Little John were *nada* compared to her.

Now he was in the uncharted waters between the scum and the bait.

The cold went colder. The water turned a rich blue and became very clear.

He was in the Big Lake and still being dragged. The shore was now at too great a distance for him to swim and the cold had too great a start on him. All relief now depended upon his grip and the boat's ladder.

He looked and saw the transom rise in front of him. Water gurgled out from under it and a green shoe appeared on the stainless steel ladder.

Above the shoe was her bare leg. Her skin was dark, as that of a girl who had spent her summer playing beach volleyball.

But Eric knew that Samantha's skin hadn't been tanned dark. It was Spic-skin. He looked up the bare leg, saw beyond the white shorts and focused on her hand reaching down.

She took hold of his shirt and dragged him onto the ladder. Her other hand held a coil of rope and he lowered his face in shame because she had pulled him in like a Cuban would a fish.

He looked back towards land. *I should have just swum the channel*, he thought. He saw the crown of Coffin Light. The sun painted it red. *I should never have come!*

Eric turned back to the girl; her face was hidden by shadows and hair.

She was looking straight into his eyes.

His bare, white foot found the ladder and he helped her lift him.

"Give me your other hand," she spoke from behind a tangle of long, black hair that blew around her face and made her look fierce.

"I can't," he said, surprised at her English. He felt her grip weaken on his shirt as his body got lowered. "It's hurt!" he added in the same breath.

Her frown left and bright teeth appeared in a wide smile.

Eric's good hand, frozen on the rope, bent at the wrist and hooked the stainless steel railing. He boarded the sailboat and nodded to the weathered old Meximan who resembled one of the school's slop mop janitors.

# LOG ENTRY 2

1:50—abeam Montague Light
East winds steady—16 knots.
Waves 0-1.
Northbound—8 knots

I've been silent since the 1981 tragedy. That was the year they tokened me as the first Mexican on the Bay View Town Council and the Chamber of Commerce of Bay View Valley. Back when Bay View was a quaint town of fudge and T-shirts on Michigan's West Coast.

But the hate against me had started long before the '80's. Before the druggies of the '70's. Before the hippies of the sexties. It predated the boom of the '50's when Mighty Mike was born, who later named me Kapin Kirk after his TV space hero.

Before World War II.

Before the Dust.

It started when my father moved his family from Mexico to Michigan.

The 1981 murder of my son didn't start the hate.

Nor did the 1981 bolting of a coffin lid to the lighthouse door seal it.

Coffin Light didn't produce the evil that murdered my son.

If anything, it ended it!

Uohn dropped Dwight at the only grocery store that would cash his mom's check. He gave his friend a gray smile then nodded to the mother.

She flipped him off with her bird brain.

"Come on and help," Dwight pleaded.

"No."

"Come, Johnny Boy! Give Dwighto a hando. I can't get Homer up the ant ramp until the Welfare Wench forks over my new battery!" She leaned over and managed to whack the plastic box under her backside folds. Then she pressed the weak accelerator on her mobility chair and it groaned organically. The electric chair had all but disappeared under the mass of the lady. A dull metal steering column rose between the fat of her thighs and she thumbed the power button.

John froze.

"And stay off the cracks or your poor momma will break your back!" She bellowed.

Dwight rested his hands on the back of his mom's seat. They disappeared under some rolls and he pushed. Nothing. He looked at John.

John left the car to help.

Together, they found traction on Homer's frame.

"Let's go, boys! Giddi-the-yuppi. Gemmee to the top of the ant ramp and I'll be fine. An knock off the nack'n or I'll stall Homer in the rag aisle and holler out your names again."

Dwight and John bent their legs and muscled the under-powered machine up the handicap ramp.

She clubbed the *Entrada* sign on the door with her cane and yapped foul about the meaning.

Dwight was dreading pushing her through the grocery store. It came next.

But at 462 pounds, his mom couldn't shop alone.

He turned around and watched John skip down the ramp and round the corner.

The old janitor steering the sailboat was as grizzled and warty as a reptile in human skin. His sunken eyes mused beyond the half-drowned, shivering teenager, then turned back to the open water as if it were something special. His splotchy, dark-nailed hand turned the sailboat's wheel and more air filled the sail. He was standing, but still small in stature.

After nodding, Eric looked forward too, and squinted into the fog. A stainless steel horn-looking pipe glowed. It seemed to be on the boat's deck so ventilation could go below. He didn't look back at the man because he knew he was a Rag Dragger from his school.

Students called all the Broom Banditos who cleaned the school Mexico Moes. They didn't hassle them much because Spics were supposed to be Mop Pops.

Eric shivered on. As his mind thawed, he recalled how one Mexico Mo did have a sailboat. *Nothing wrong with that!* Eric thought. *He's still in America for jeepers creep! A Mo could buy some stuff if he wanted to!*

Then he looked as his numbed white feet against Mo's dark teak grate on the cockpit floor. He was with that Mexican Mo. He looked again at the withered sailboat captain. *Mexico Mo moored his sailboat on the North Shore!*

The north shore was two miles of pristine, undeveloped land above the slime-grime of Morguetown. The name had been chosen by bonehead city leaders a decade ago in order to schmooze in a factory and its 200 jobs. But above Morguetown and beyond Morguetown Lake was the jewel of the region's Nile: green, lush and undeveloped rolling hills of old growth forest. No people or homes. Just fat cows in knee-deep grass in the cool shade. And somehow, one lone moored sailboat to frame the whole parcel for the town!

Eric wondered if Mexican Mo lived on the Vanderdyke Farm.

"You stay clear of those Vanderdyke Spikes in your high school," Eric's dad had warned when Eric was a mere freshman. "Rumor is that a Mexican Mo knows the one. The one who shined on Vanderdyke himself!"

"What's that mean?"

"They came up here. All the way up here from Mexico they came. A long time ago. But it only took one to be the first," his mother had called out from her recliner in the TV room.

"How old do you think he is? Age has a way of building in them, don't you think?" his dad had said. "It's like it shrinks them back to the tiny tikes they were to begin with!"

"Ain't that right!" the mom yelled out from her chair and above the TV in the converted formal dining room. "The only thing good about them is some of their food! Put me a burrito in the microwave will ya?"

"In a minute!" her husband called out and looked back at Eric. "Back then Vanderdyke was the first to fill his bunkhouses with Downtown Carlos-Browns. Free midget labor! They're all about five foot tall ya know."

"So," Eric had said.

"So? So they helped Vanderdyke buy up the rest of the spreads around him. So that! It was Dyke-Boy who bought out some Hollanders whose pappys drained the swamps from the beginning. The ones that built the first windmills in the region. Back more than a hundred years ago! Back before the D.C. Green Beans claimed windmills were cool! But because of one Spec Mex, Capin Kike, now we got just one big farm up there. And that ain't the half of it!"

"What?"

"What? What nothing!" the mother sang out. "What about Coffin Light? An get to ding-donging my burrito!"

"What?" Eric asked his dad again.

"It was Capin Kike who helped Dyke-Boy get the jump on easy pickings. No farmer around here ever caught up. Then old Mrs. Vanderdyke came under Spic Spill and used her cottage country on the big lake to shanty-town Mexico North! So you stay clear of them! And shy away from any bum who comes off the Mez Rez."

"As to why Texas Tex never stopped her old lady from doing it is beyond us!" Eric's mom had yelled out from around the corner.

"She tried to!" the man's voice went sharp on down the hall. Too sharp for a simple janitor conversation. "Then it all went south. But by then it was too late. The tacos owned the apples."

"Where's my dinner?"

Her husband bounced a frozen beef and beaner into the microwave, slammed the door and pushed a button. "In a minute!" He looked at Eric. "Hey, someone had to open Michigan to the Migrant Hydrants." He whispered this. Some things were too awful to be spoken out loud. "It's just that we don't like Rio Grandville in our back yard trying to teach all the farmers around here that it's better to sell out than to yell out."

"So some of my school janitors live in Mexico North?" Eric had asked.

"That's only part of it."

And then the Microwave dinged and the mother rounded the corner, filling the hallway. "I hope you didn't soggy it!" she scooped out her food with a paper towel, took a beer from the yellow refrigerator and left.

The dad faced the son. "Vanderdyke and Kapin Kike, with their army of free workers, screwed many in this area out of many things. Then Mrs. Dyke up-n-dies and gives all 12,000 acres to Cap'n Spic. Every inch. The old lady was done and dead by the '80's, and her son was killed in Vietnam. But she still had family. She still had her daughter. She still had Texas Tex!"

"No mayor who changes our town from Bay View Valley to Morguetown should be talked about during my dinner!" the mom yelled from her chair.

"Why not!" Mr. Nelson palm-slapped the table, spilling cereal left out from breakfast. "She hates him! That's why she did it! She done done it for all of us! She took a stand!"

"Texas will ruin us all," Mrs. Nelson yelled back.

The dad just looked at his son. "You just pay no mind to those Mexico Moes. Some are old enough to know Kapin Kike himself!" His eyes glassed over as his thick fingers flexed the plastic off a bag of microwave popcorn. The eyes went flat. "What do you want for dinner?"

"I don't know. I'm tired," Eric had said.

Now, from the cockpit of the sailboat, in his ice-water-chilled state, Eric turned and took a quick glance at the sailboat captain. Then he started shivering again. Shivering hard. Almost bone-wrenching. He inhaled deep. The air was a far cry warmer than his body. He hurt when he stretched lungs that the cold seemed to have shrunk to the size of prunes.

The girl appeared before him with a pair of antique scissors. They were long enough to stab through his chest and come out the other side. They opened.

Eric froze colder.

The janitor nodded.

"Nice *amigos*," the girl said. Her voice carried heat. Inferno-Chimy-Chunga heat.

Eric had to admit he felt warmer as she neared. Then the scissors opened and he straightened. He looked at the two towels she had dropped next to his hurt arm. He looked at his fingers on that arm. They were blue. They didn't look good.

She cut off his T-shirt.

It had been one of his good ones; the kind that felt better as it collected dirt.

The boat captain nodded and the girl threw the shirt pieces overboard. She put the scissors into a plastic sleeve on the side of the cockpit that held a winch handle. Between the towels were two white plastic bags. She moved behind Eric and sat up on the wide teak gunwale that kept water from flowing into the seats and served as a backrest for those in the cockpit. Both her knees went around Eric's chicken-skinned torso and she snapped a white bag, allowing the chemicals inside to form dry ice. She put the bag on the bruising of his shoulder, opened one of the towels, and used it to hold the ice in place.

Still numb, Eric didn't flinch.

"Your shoulder is starting to swell." She came around and faced him.

He started shivering again.

She broke a second ice bag and put it on his collar bone.

He felt her fingers on his neck.

They felt good.

Her fingers were long and strong and her nails were thick and painted a soft red. Her face came close to his and he looked into her large, deep-set eyes that hid behind high, strong cheeks. They were eyes that called out to a man and made him feel stronger than he was. Her lips were large and full of life, but not big.

He noticed all this despite the soft wind blowing her hair in front of her face.

She used her elbow to sweep her hair back out of her eyes and adjusted the towel to hold both ice packs.

"I can't feel my fingers," Eric said.

"There's nothing around here for them to feel." She opened the other towel and held the ends in her hands. Flipping the towel up, she caught his head in the middle. Tugging left and right a dozen times she dried his hair and whipped off the towel. "Frodo," she said, nodding to his afro hair.

Eric nodded. "Thank you for helping me," he said, looking at her.

"Thank him," she nodded to the helmsman.

Eric turned to him. "Thank you, sir."

The man nodded. "I saw the flame in the fog, but she threw the line. Thank her."

Eric faced her. "Thank you, Samantha," he said, more to himself than to the girl who was now wrapping him in a towel as if he were a wet cat.

She looked at him as if his words had stung her. She went below and returned with a yellow, waterproof sailing jacket lined with thick, gray fleece. She put it over his shoulders.

It dawned on Eric that a stillness had come among them. A peace. He'd been on the water before, but it was on a boat with a motor that slammed the waves. Now there was only a quiet wind, filled with the warmth of summer and land, stirring around them. It spilled off the sails and swirled across the big lake in silence. And it wasn't pulling the sails any more. He looked around. Off the starboard beam were trees and dune grass. A posse of a dozen or so Vanderdyke Border Bums was horse-riding on the beach.

They waved.

Eric nodded to them like the posse-hater he was, then realized they were waving at her.

She was waving back, giving the gauchos a chance to flex their white smiles.

Two of the Zorros reared their horses.

The sun soon dropped below the horizon, but they sailed close enough to the north shore to escape the blinding fog near the lighthouse. The loud belch of the fog horn had faded to the coo of a lonely bird. Another sail had been raised and both had been sheeted. They hummed along under tight sails in a warm offshore breeze. The sands and dunes glowed gold. Trees and forest were green in the mist.

Eric braced his feet on the far side of the cockpit as the vessel heeled a few degrees and picked up speed where wind funneled between dunes. "I don't think I could pull myself up at this speed," he said to the captain.

"You didn't pull yourself aboard at the slow speed," Samantha said.

Eric swallowed hard. He felt like responding, saying something to defend himself, but he knew any answer would be an inadequate, blame-shifting excuse. Turning toward land and seeing the fog-softened trees and blurred dunes made him think that Pterodactyls should be soaring overhead. The shoreline looked to be from a time long ago.

When all was dark and after the dry ice had been removed, he found himself warm inside the fleece coat. He watched the old man nod and Samantha spring a line off the port winch.

The released headsail luffed as the bow swung toward the looming, dark sand dunes then continued angling back south. Soon the headsail sheet was taut on the starboard winch and they were pointing back south to where Coffin Light was glowing, calling to them from somewhere inside its fogbank.

"I can't see Coffin Light," Eric looked ahead.

The old man looked at him but a second then turned back ahead and faced the darkness as he sailed his boat on faith. Mexico Mo stared to where the sun had fallen below the waves. His face, masked in shadow, became distorted in the soft red light of the binnacle.

Sensing something, Eric shut his mouth. He looked ahead and saw the water glow green as waves refracted one of the boat's bow lights. Dew formed on the sailboat. Eric watched Samantha rub the cold off her dark legs and wished the light was better so he could see her color.

"Do you want the coat?" he offered, knowing it was the only thing between him and bare skin.

"It's not cold," she said.

Eric looked at the old man. "How shall I call you?"

The old man looked at him.

"I mean, when I see you around or somewhere?" Eric asked.

"When I'm on the water, call me Captain," the old janitor said.

"Why did Little John and Dwight throw rocks at your sailboat?" Eric asked.

The old man looked at the girl and she lowered her eyes.

"Because of her?" Eric said, recalling the broken arm Dwight got from the Latin Lads. "That doesn't make any sense. Didn't they throw rocks at this boat before she got involved?" He saw her and felt his words.

She knew that he knew. Samantha inhaled but was forced to hold her breath by Mexican Mo's look.

The old man looked at the boy. Then he stared ahead at the looming, dark lighthouse that strobed a red flash every few seconds against the late evening sky.

Eric adjusted himself on the cockpit cushion. His wet jeans started needling his butt. He watched the janitor give a strange and noticeable nod of understanding to the western sky.

The east wind weakened as they sailed closer to Morgue-town and the captain seemed to smell it as if searching for a scent.

The man swung the wheel, luffed the sails while Samantha went up on deck and hauled them down. He secured the boom to the foredeck by tightening the toping lift and the sheet. He then fired the engine and entered the narrow channel.

Coffin Light was deserted.

In the red flash of the lighthouse strobe, the old man turned to Eric. "Smart boy like you. You should be able to figure when it started. Un chico listo* like you should know why some use sticks and stones to ache people's bones."

Eric turned to watch the pier rocks float by as the captain navigated into the narrow channel, shrewdly keeping to the deepest part of the river.

Eric then saw it!

Dwight and Little John *had* been planning something before he walked up to them.

Eric thought about Dwight and John and their sticks and stones. He wondered why he had not thought of it earlier. He looked to the north wall of the channel and saw the Bean Poppers fishing from perches among the rocks. Their dark, mustached faces reflected light as they baited up around the soft lights of wire-framed, diesel burning lanterns. He shook his head at the F-U-Gs. His shoulders slumped. He thought about his parents. He looked back at that sailboat captain who seemed content and at peace with the fading wind and the swirls upon the water.

---

*a smart boy

The sailboat ghosted up to the docks of Sebastian's Place that a one time used to be a yacht club of sorts. It came in quiet and smooth as if it were the breeze itself. Eric felt it then; he felt Morguetown's hatred for this boat. That it wasn't welcomed down here on the south side of the lake.

He shivered.

"Keep the coat for the night," she said. "You're not warm yet."

He shook his head, unzipped it and dropped it over the teak backrest and stepped down onto Sebastian's warped dock.

You don't borrow things from some people.

# LOG ENTRY 3
Abeam: Stony Lake
East winds to 16 knots. Waves 0–1.
Northbound—8 knots

My story started in 1927. We migrated from Mexico to Michigan to pick apples. We picked a lot of apples and picked them quick. The rancher and his new wife liked us. They liked me. But even at eight I knew certain things didn't mix and I stayed in the fields and orchards with my people.

But over the next decade, I started accepting their invites into the big house.

Every now and then I even had dinner at the big table with Señor Vanderdyke himself. But like I said, some things don't mix and they let me enjoy my kind who eyed me queerly whenever I left the house.

My father died that fall. And Señor Vanderdyke led the prayer at the funeral. Then he made it so the rest of us could stay and help with the winter pruning.

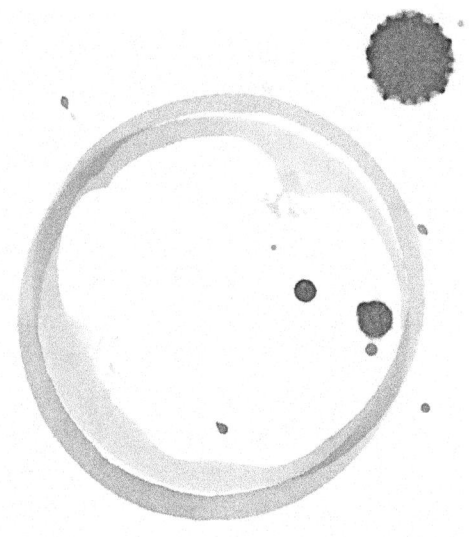

Evert was a homely girl with a pie face and mousy brown hair. At her mother's quarter horse ranch in Wisconsin, she had a walk-in wardrobe the same size as her bedroom, a weekly appointment with the hair stylist and equestrian lessons for her Arabians.

Across Lake Michigan Evert was a member of the Debate Team, Golf Team, Competitive Cheer, 4H, and Leaders for Future America. If her life in Wisconsin was uptown, her life in Morguetown was downtown.

Evert hated uptown. It was bent. So, in defiance of her mother's pressure, she jumped ship to her dad's place at the MTP (Morguetown Trailer Park). At first she had come only to visit her dad after bad fights with her mom. But last summer she just decided to stay over a while and sleep on his couch with the TV remote.

Her life was simple in Morguetown. On the east side of Lake Michigan, wrinkled was right. She could wear a sweatshirt two, maybe three days in a row. No one cared.

She was drawn by the lack of stuff. Evert soon had a life without creating one. She had time. She gained a pound a week, but felt just fine. She was still one of the thinnest around, but the ranks were closing.

In Morguetown, she hung. She be.

As for her dad? He didn't want her to steal anything valued over two hundred dollars because felonies were expensive. He didn't want her to do Crystal Meth because the potency varied too much and made for high dental bills. Marijuana, joints, stem, weed, doobies, and Marlboro Reds were all in the appropriate category.

Morguetown was the van down by the river.

Her Pops bought her the smokes she liked and didn't mind her friends coming into his pad. He liked his life. He had eaten hamburgers at breakfast, lunch and dinner ever since he had to do his own meals. He didn't mess with perfection.

Evert's dad was Bill Thompson. Some of his friends called him Bull Stompson as a reminder of his mean streak when he was young, and when he had community standing because of his wife's money.

"Thanks for letting me come back," she had said to him, seeing him older and more tired as they sat and ordered Chub Tum's from the burger menu at Sebastians. It was his favorite joint.

"I live about twenty bucks on the bad side of broke," he said. "And you can live with that?"

"Ya."

"Your mom's court thing really screwed me up."

"I like how you work," she said. She looked around the place. It seemed that "The System" had taken his will to make money.

"I work the janitor job at the high school with the Mexicantos. You can live with that? Me being a Mexican Mo?"

"What?"

"I'm with the Mexipads," he said. "It's the lowest paying benefit job in town—and that's saying something!"

"I get it. The less you have the more the court can't take." She had always suspected her mom's lawyer had percentage liens against all his earnings.

"I turn down raises so she can't get more. You don't get more either. So maybe we all lose."

"The judge just scared me, you know. That's why," she lowered her head and looked at his feet.

"Hey! Look at me! It takes more than money to bounce trash off the trampoline," he smiled. "But you'll see how Morguetown ain't about money. In fact, except for the Mexican Estancian, nobody in Morguetown seems to have much of anything except after credit card bankruptcy."

"I like it."

"You don't know the best part! There is no way in the jingle of Juice Newton's jazz that your mother will ever come to visit! This place is beneath her. For me this place is the Guel of Hide and Seek!"

Evert looked across her basket of fries. "Can I have the Heinz?"

He pushed it to her. "Heinz is the draw for Sebastian's, Chub-Tum-Burger," he said. "This here's the only joint in town that doesn't cheap away the good stuff."

So who's the Mexican Estancian? What's an estancia?

"It's boarder banglange for a ranch. A big ranch."

"So we got us a high and mighty here in little Morguetown, huh?"

"No one rightly knows. He's been away since…" he motioned for her to pass the ketchup back. He didn't need any, he just liked it in his reach. "He's probably up north of town a ways," he said and went glum like one with Seasonal Affective Disorder.

"What's it like?"

"What?"

"The ranch?"

"It's Vanderdyke land. No one really knows."

"Why's that? Can't nobody drive up there?"

"Nope."

"So how do you get there?"

"Swim the channel or the lake. Or take the main road out of town. But we can no longer take the 143rd, 144th or 145th north because they run smack into his land! You can only go along its borders. Borders everywhere! Even here!" his face flushed red. "They cross ours and then seal theirs!"

"Our roads don't go through it?"

"Kapin Kike bought out the counties' roads way back when he shined on."

"You can do that?" Evert asked. "You mean none of our roads go though his land?"

"They're gated now. Can you believe it? If you got enough you can do whatever. Your mom should've taught you that."

"So just as you're below the Spics on the sliding pay scale, so's the town?"

His lifted his beer. "Welcome to Morguetown! They should re-write your school song for a banjo and make the marching band wear sombreros!"

"And one of his used up dirt farmers is now your boss?"

Bill Thompson lit a cigarette and inhaled deep. No one around him cared. Sebastians was a place without smoke-free seating. "Yup. I work for a Mexican Mo."

Evert watched him shrink his cigarette.

He hadn't said anything since he lit up. But his expression seemed to change. She thought for a moment that she had seen the man his old friends called, Bull Stompson. She liked *that* man.

Samantha Lazzair was a Resident Alien in the United States of America. It said so on her Green Card. She could now start the process of becoming a Naturalized Citizen and she thumbed the thick book about Government and other United States stuff for a test she must someday take to be worthy of citizenship.

She dropped the book on the table, pushed hair out of her eyes and turned off the lamp. She looked around. A light came from the bedroom she shared with her mother. It illuminated the living area, kitchen and the door to the bathroom. It was a small cabin, but warm because of a cast iron stove that now snapped wood as it glowed red in the corner.

Her fingers hovered above the table and she felt the fuzzy air between the wood surface and her fingerprints. She closed her eyes and felt the table stir to the rhythm of the breakers down at the base of the dunes.

She walked to the door, opened it and felt the blast of a hard west wind. She stepped out onto the small deck. Wind as fresh as a breeze off a glacier blew her hair back off her face and she smelled the white foam that flecked atop the dark waters. She sensed the breakers inside her ribcage as the waves dropped on the sand and shook the earth as if more trees needed to be toppled.

Turning her back to the water to stay warm, she looked over the migrant shanty homes, stacked among each other in the dunes. But hers was more like a cottage. It was the farthest west and most exposed to the sheer power and fierce nature of Lake Michigan. Her tongue ran over her teeth. In two weeks she had learned that her father had once worked on this huge farm and that he had drowned in Lake Michigan. And that the small house around her was where it had all started. She could tell it hadn't been lived in for a long time—maybe since his death.

Her mother hadn't spoken much since they had arrived. She cleans and sits in the bedroom and stares. Her eyes fixate on the smallest things.

Samantha knew they had been lured back to Michigan.

"Don't get comfortable here," her mother had said when they arrived. "I'm just visiting some very old and very dear memories."

Samantha now exhaled. Since then she had been enrolled at Morguetown High with a virtual army of other teenagers her age from the ranch. Four of the men who were too old to work the farm were janitors in the school. They sometimes rode the bus with the students. She looked back to the dark, rumbling water and thought over her last four days. She had risen an hour before dawn and was usually asleep at sunset like the others as they tried to weave her into the massive work force. First, an old rancher called Santasa showed off his operations for two days, showing her how the grain gets combined. Nitrogen storage. Fertilizer control. Hormone injections. Disease control. Veterinarian charts and the Veterinarian himself who also doubled as the area's doctor. She learned of barn maintenance. Heating and fuel. Winterizing water lines. Dehorning. Dairy. Trucking lines. Cheese. Sanitation. Retail and wholesale beef prices. Butchering and smoke houses.

They rode horses as he overviewed the systems. "What are you thinking?" he had asked.

"Complicated."

"When you choose tu trabajo, you work aquí! ¿De acuerdo? You escoges choose Santasa? ¿Vale?* Santasa works hard. Always harder than the Señoritas work!"

She smiled at him. He was a stern man. Hands like steel cords, but he was kind.

After Santasa, she went with the farmer called Carlos of Corn. He was younger. Maybe fifty. He was barrel-chested and had hands like bear mitts. If they gripped her thigh, they could snap her femur by flexing. Again they rode horses as they traveled his sections of the farm.

She sat crooked in the saddle, her backsides chaffed by covering so much ground yesterday.

He showed her the orchards. Apples. Pears. Cherries. Blueberries. Fields for strawberries. Peppers. Melons. Pumpkins. Squash. Tomatoes and a six hour trot through fields of sweet corn and field corn. And then they cooled their horses with

---

*"When you choose your job, you work here! Alright? You choose Santasa? okay??

two-hour-long walk along a strip of southern border that had been set aside for pollen bees.

He outlined the harvests tools. Tractors. Trailers. Forklifts. Bulldozers. Backhoes. Cranes. More barns and then more barns. Storage bins. Barns of empty crates. Barns of insulated foam for controlling different storage gases. Water wells. Dikes. Conduits. Pumps. Siphon lines. Ponds. Dams. Crop rotations patterns. Anti-erosion plow patterns.

After two days with Carlos of Corn, her head was as confused as it was with Santasa.

"When you choose where to work, you *trabaja* here! ¿De acuerdo?* You choose Carlos. You don't milk cows all day with Carlos. We grow food. We pick food! Carlos is good. *Carlos nunca grita.*** All want to work with Carlos! No one goes hungry with Carlos of Corn!"

Then Samantha was sent for a day with the shipping foreman.

"Terro!" he said when she asked his name.

"Just Terro. Not Terro of Trucks? Or something?"

He smiled. Wide and full of teeth. "Too many *nombres?*"*** he smiled.

Terro was younger still, maybe forty, and with him she learned of truck lines. Transport readiness. Loading docks. Semi repair garages. DOT regulations. Reefer transport trailers. Shipping and handling. Diesel filling stations and farm fuel management.

The next day, a man in his mid 20's rode up to Samantha's cottage an hour after dawn in a 1964 pick-up truck with no floor or doors and a windshield with many cracks. The window behind the lone seat was completely gone. He knocked

---

*you *work* here! Alright?
**Carlos never shouts
***names

and was waved in by Samantha's mother, who gave him a soft smile and handed him a cup of chicory coffee.

"*¿Está usted lista?*"* he asked.

"*Sí,*" Samantha said.

"Samantha, this is Leñador.** He cuts the wood for us. For everybody."

Samantha looked at the man. He was maybe twenty-five. She looked at his arms, heavy with muscles and noted his quick, strong smile.

They left and he stood next to her as she climbed onto a seat with the springs coming through the fabric.

He came in behind the wheel. "Careful," he pointed at the ground moving under her feet as he drove through the thick sand, heading south. After several stops, the truck bed was filled with others who were going to school.

Three other girls now sat next to Samantha. They were younger. Darker.

"So you're a school bus sometimes?" Samantha asked.

"School truck. One of many." he smiled. "*¿Quiere usted que yo le lleve?***"

She nodded. "It's like home," she said.

The other girls smiled.

They soon left the farm and gravel blurred by underneath. Engine smells and dust seeped up in the breeze. A metal bar had been welded across the rusted opening and they hooked their boot heels on it. Samantha was now nudged against the driver and had to keep moving her knees when he shifted gears.

"*¿Cómo se llama usted?*"**** she asked. "Your real name?"

---

*Are you ready?
**Lumberjack
***I'm awake anyways.
****What's your name?

"Leñador," he said. "No one would know who I am if I use my real name. Leñador is who I am."

She leaned her head back and rested it on a worn axe in a gunrack between bumps. "Where on the farm do you work?"

"I cut wood and take it to the houses," he said. "Do you like your wood?"

"Sí. I like *calor*."*

He smiled. "I haul all the wood in this truck. A very strong truck. Many miles left to ride."

They turned on the tree-lined road and headed east to the big white house which sat in the center of the Vanderdyke complex. The driver veered off before approaching the house or the ten acres or so that had been set aside for some of the finer horses and corralling.

She saw a few fat sheep struggling to keep the grass mowed.

The driver turned south, darted behind the outbuildings and circled the house on a worn, stone-graded road that kept the farm traffic out of view.

They then turned south and soon came to the gate at the border where a few men managed just over a thousand hogs.

Two girls put white cloth to their noses as the north wind carried hog stink down onto the town.

They stopped.

One of the dozen or so boys in the back jumped off the truck bed and opened the gate. His dark, lined face looked hard at the girls in the truck as they passed. He tipped his cowboy hat, then stepped up into the truck after closing the gate.

To their right sat the lake and the town. Ahead was a gravel road and beyond it were a dozen or so sagging, dead buildings that used to be fresh produce stores. Their win-

---

*Warmth

dows had long been broken out. They drove away from the lake and rolled east along a paved rode for a few minutes.

The air cleared of hog stench, and they stopped in front of the high school behind a line of minivans and four school buses.

Samantha felt the truck lurch as the Mexicans jumped or stepped off the truck. She looked at the driver.

"*Que tenga un buen día y buena suerte,*"* Leñador said, looking in the mirror at the blue smoke hazing the car behind them.

It honked.

Samantha gave him a confused look and slid across the seat, avoiding the tips of metal springs so they wouldn't tear or snag her jeans. She turned from the vehicle but noticed an old man was still in the bed of the truck. He was making his way out. "*¿Está bien usted?*"** she walked back and asked.

He turned to her as he made it to his knees, then he dropped a foot down to the pavement. It seemed a long way down.

She took his elbow to stabilize him. "You're a little too *viejo*\*\*\* for school? Go back to your boat!"

"Sailboat," he said. "No boat. Never say boat. Always sailboat!"

With both feet on the ground, he straightened his shoulders to her. "*Muchas gracias,*" he pointed to his chest and his nametag, Mo. "I'm Mexico Mo, here. I'm a *portero*\*\*\*\* here."

"Move it, Bacardi!" a face from the car behind them yelled. Another van honked long and hard.

Mo and Samantha looked at it and stepped out of the way and made it up onto the curb and walkway.

---

*Have a good day and good luck
**Are you okay?
***old

"Can we sail again?" she asked and held out her arm.

"I sail with all who are new to the farm," he said. "This duty has been given to me and I like it."

"Why you? Is it your boat?"

"Sailboat!"

She smiled. "But still nobody on the farm sails but you? I've asked a lot of people. My mother hates it."

"They don't hate it. They just don't like to drag up young boys in the cold!" he winked.

"And get pelted by rocks?"

"And rocks," he said. They reached the main door and she insisted on holding it for him. A half dozen students piled in next and she had to cut in to get away from being a door jam.

She found the old man in the hallway.

"They give you the tour?" he asked.

She rubbed her backsides. "*En caballo\**," she smiled. "*Es una granja inmensa!\*\** She found herself walking with him down the hall.

"I remember when I first came. Back when they *told* us where to work!" He smiled and pointed her to an office for new students and left.

Now, from the cold balcony above the restless cold wind, Samantha turned back and faced Lake Michigan and the roar of wave thunder on the beach. She blinked the tears out of her eyes. Tears caused by the cold west wind blowing up off the dunes. She stared down at the water from the deck of the house, high in the sand where her father had once loved her mother.

---

*custodian
\*\*on horseback
\*\*\*It's a huge farm

## LOG ENTRY 4

4:05 pm—abeam Little Sable Point
East winds to 17 knots.
Waves 0-1.
Northbound—8 knots

I saw the American Dream after a few years. In many ways America was the same as Mexico.

I saw many hollow-eyed men, walking in circles from World War One. A war so terrible that it was to be the one to end all wars.

I found out that America too had ghost towns because of influenza.

I read about America's rich men jumping out of windows because they lost their money.

I learned that their giant ships can hit icebergs and sink.

I despaired over their heroes, ones like Carlos Limburg who flew a plane across the Atlantic only to have his child ransomed and murdered.

All and all I felt sorry for America. It had the makings of greatness, but it had to deal with some bad people and unsettled times.

Just like Mexico.

Officer Belt, beat cop at Morguetown High, sat behind a desk he shared with Cindy who did the school mailings. He motioned Dwight Slash to a chair in the corner as if he needed the Dunce Cap. He pulled out his report form and clicked a pen. Pushing his glasses back up the slope of his oily nose, he lifted his head from the paperwork, grunted and sniffed up some snot. "Since the days of Huckleberry Finn there's been problems between White trash and those that serve them."

"So. What do you want, Belt?" Dwight asked.

"We'll always have Mexicans to mop your slop."

"The point, Belt?"

Belt put both elbows on the table to show the weight of his philosophy. "Dwight, there's Mexi-Cans who mop our slop. We all know the Mexican Moes. Moes are Mexi-Cans! Handy with both the broom and mop. But there's also Mexi-Can'ts. The one's who can't know their place."

Dwight looked at the floor. His good arm rubbed his cast to showcase the pain to Belt.

"I need to know about the Mexi-Can'ts. I'm the one who busts them when they migrate over your personal space boundary. It's my job. Tom Sawyer never mentions Nigger Jim busting up some white kid's arm! Some things just aren't meant to be!"

Dwight shrugged.

"What did you do?" Belt asked.

"Pinch-a-Spic," Dwight said.

"No harm in that. Despite the eye candy, my fingers get tempted to goose a giggle now and again," Officer Belt said. "I'm good at running the school beat and proud of the relative lack of tension between the peanut butter and the bread. Any witness?"

"Yea! Most of Puke's class. I got her good."

"Help me out, Dwighto. You really think I've had you dragged down here because you squeezed a peanut? I'm talking about your beat'n. Anybody witness the Kelp Yelpers who made you yelp for help?"

"Dunno. Maybe Evert. She was with me before it happened."

"You sure?"

Dwight nodded.

"Well that makes sense," he put the pen down and closed the note pad. "There's some things you can do if you want to better yourself," Belt said.

"What?"

"You go eat at Sebastian's Club sometime. The owner heard about your trouble."

"So?"

"So go."

Mexican Mo wheeled a mop bucket with one tire fishtailing a squeak. He shuffled across the glossed-covered wood of the gym floor after reading the Bio-Hazard Cleanup Report that guided him like a carrot hung in front of a donkey. His grey trousers were held up by faded red suspenders and showcased white socks that were snug, inside his worn, black, rubber-soled shoes. His matching grey shirt posted the name, MO, over his right chest.

His free hand held a bottle of bleach. He stopped at the spot, took out two, red 'Bio-Hazard' folding plastic signs and placed them on the court. He then mixed bleach into the bucket and swirled the water with the mop, ready to lather the blood in compliance with the Occupational Safety and Health Administration standards.

"Nacho, Nacho Man! I wanta be . . . a Nacho Man!" one

young man started dancing and chanting the ditty as he walked by with some others.

Another looked over, "Is this floor easier to clean than Mexican tile?"

"Leave 'im be!" the third said. "He's working for change!"

"How'd you buff out the paw prints from the hallway tile?"

Mo turned away and smiled. *¡Qué bueno!* He turned back and saw the one called Eric coming.

"You get overtime for putting up with our crap, Captain?" Eric asked. More laughs.

"Captain? You see a rubber duck in the bucket, Eric?" a teenager asked.

All went quiet then as three Hispanics entered the court, cutting across the gym to another class.

Mexico Mo frowned.

The three looked over at the janitor, stopped and glanced at their worn cowboy boots. They turned tail and left the gym the way they entered.

Mexico Mo frowned harder and drew out the mop, wrang it and slapped it onto the wood. He figure-eighted the blood spill to loosen the stains.

"So this is where Dwight got busted up?" someone asked.

"Ain't right. Not at all. Not for just a Spickle Tickle!" another said and they walked on.

Eric lingered and he and Mexico Mo were soon alone. "Sorry about the hacking," Eric said.

"*¿Entraste en calor* young hombre?"*

Eric smiled. "How do you say cold in Spanish?"

The man's brown eyes were hid behind large wrinkles in his face. "Don't know. It's never cold in Mexico. That's why we can't grow *espárrago***!"

---

*Did you warm up yet?

**Asparagus

"What?"

Mo smiled. He was going to say something else but his voice cracked and went silent.

Eric couldn't put a finger on the emotion. Didn't have to really. He knew the janitor had likely sailed Lake Michigan before. And the lake did funny things to people.

"What do I call you now that we're at school?" Eric asked.

"Call me, Mo." The man dropped the mop back into the water, wrung it out and rinsed off Dwight's blood.

"My name's Eric."

"¡Me llamo El Niño de Espárrago!"*

Eric smiled at him. Whatever.

Mr. Puke, a teacher at Morguetown High who didn't care if his students passed the English portion of the ACT Test, was on probation. Again. He justified this by saying he would rather create a thinking student than a passing one.

He had some creepy issues about closed doors. He kept it secret that his two older brothers were in prison until he made tenure a few years back. The hinges that once hung his doors flapped to the current of students coming and going.

Both doors were long gone despite the Lock Down Code recently handed down by the Department of Homeland Security in case of a terrorism attack. But since he could provide a doctor's phobia note, his class was allowed to join the one across the hall where they could both be slaughtered together if the killers came calling.

His real name used to be Peukerson, but he had it changed to Puke to simplify his life. The official Name Change government document #9821 was framed by his desk, along with the cancelled check to the State of Michigan for $619.79.

---

*My name is Asparagus Boy!

Eric Nelson looked at the clock. It was a school clock, as good as broke because its hands never seemed to move. So he settled into his desk and tried to count the silver bracelets on Samantha Lazzair's wrist. He liked how they clinked on her desk when she moved her hand. They made her skin look darker. Deeper.

"We study any Spanish Americans any time soon?" some kid called Bran asked.

"I hear we're going to dissect one in science next week!" another said.

Eric and several others grunted. Old habit. Tried and true.

Samantha flashed him a look. A cold one.

He felt his blood boil at his insolence. He then willed harm to Bran, just another zit-face who hacked on the petz of Mexico North. Then Eric lowered his chin and willed harm to himself. Even with his eyes on the floor he felt her sting. Swing and another miss.

Mr. Puke wrote something on the board. He moved the chalk slow because he couldn't spell.

"Hey Mr. Puke?" Bran repeated, raising his hand.

"Yes," Puke said.

"Do we have any Mexican writers in our English book? Like is Zorro in it?"

Samantha gave Eric a look that asked, *Are you going to laugh again?*

"What's your name?" Puke asked. It had only been a few weeks.

"Brian," Bran said. "Zorro or Tonto. I'm equally interested in learning about either or."

"You the one the flakes call 'Bran'?"

"It used to be "All Bran". I farted a lot back in 8th grade. But I'm over it. But my real name is Brian Foot, sir. And I'm here and ready, willing and able to learn about Zorro!" He pushed his black glasses back up on his nose.

"So your reality is in Zorroity?" Mr. Puke asked.

"What?"

"Did you just get transferred into this class?"

"No. I've been here."

"You be nice then. There's no need to sell oppression here in Morguetown, Bran. It grows free in the streets. But respect Plato. You know, the one who said that how you learn is a mirror of your soul." Puke went on twisting Bran into that day's lesson, exhaling chloroform. Puke could barf anyone to sleep.

Eric didn't need to know about his soul. By gawking at Samantha, it was pumping enough life to keep him awake for a week. He burned most of her features into his long-term memory.

Evert was learning things too.

Bran sat in front of her.

She watched him scrape zits off his back, then squeeze out white from under his black fingernails. She looked at the clock but didn't know why. She had nowhere to go and nothing to do when she got there. And she had all afternoon to do it.

Leñador drove Captain Kike up to Ludington where they caught the car ferry to Manitowac, Wisconsin. After they drove aboard, they left the truck and went up to the cabin topsides.

The ride across Lake Michigan was calm and cold. They were alone except for a home-school family in a motorhome that was mad because their little children weren't allowed to sleep down below in the camper.

And there was a lone businessman or two. They didn't pay much mind to the dirt farmers. Just a tired old man with a burlap sack and a strong Mexican farm lad.

The homeschool mom brought one of her students over to Leñador. "Can we ask you questions to practice our Spainish.

He smiled.

"Do they have cars in Spain?" she asked.

He looked wistfully over the water.

Once across the lake, Leñador was guided north on Highway 42 and they followed the coast. Stopping only once for Leñador to add some farm oil to his engine from a gallon milk jug. They reached Algoma and headed inland to Euren.

Ms. Boden was waiting for them at the Euren's City Limits next to the welcome sign in her truck. She guided them to her hobby ranch.

Above was the Wisconsin blue sky. Old trees lined her property. She didn't say much as she waved them inside. They all sat at her table and it was quiet and calm with a lot of open windows and air. Canned jars of fruit were on her counters.

"Alfred Bendolly in Euren, Wisconsin," she said, nodding to Leñador but keeping her fire blue eyes on the old man. "How much does he know?"

"All of it," Bendolly said.

"It never sat right with me," her face was weathered and tanned by the outdoors. "What they done to your boy and how you handled it never sat right with me. But I like what you've done to the town. It deserves them."

"They done it themselves," Bendolly said.

"That's why I had to leave. I'll not tolerate watching a town die. And they knew it. What do you need from me? You name it!"

The old Mexican lifted the sack to the table. "I want to buy the sailboat."

"It's true then," Señora Boden said. "My no good husband and my no good daughter…"

The old man didn't say anything for a while. "I'm sure

they'll find their place."

The strong lad looked at the floor.

She got up and returned with a Bill of Sale and signed her name at the bottom and handed it to the man.

The old man took it. "*Muchas gracias.*"

Leñador nodded to her.

"What's the sack for?" she asked.

Cap'n Kike lifted the lip of the burlap, showing her blocks of large bills.

"I don't need your money. You spend it on your plan. Your people."

"I am," he pushed it to her.

She pushed it back. "I want no part of anyone's plans anymore. I'm shut of that town. Now, I know you're doing your best, but don't trust that town. Not a lick. It's in their blood to be rotten!"

He put the Bill of Sale into the burlap sack of money and pulled the lip over it.

She lunged out and grabbed his hand. "I never saw it coming, Alfred! You must believe me! I knew Bull was yeller but I never saw them coming!"

"I do believe you, Señora Boden."

"I thought I was just buying a sailboat," she said. "Back then everyone loved to sail. Back then the lake was good. Are you going to kill them?"

The small, old Mexican lifted a hand to hers. "The weather will change." He squeezed her arm then lifted it from his and lowered his head. He stood. "*Adios,*" he said and walked to the door.

Leñador tipped his hat to the woman as he slung the sack stuffed with $190,000 over his shoulder.

She stayed at the table, not having the will to watch them drive away.

## LOG ENTRY 5

5:10 pm—abeam Pentwater
East winds to 19 knots.
Waves 0-1. Northbound at 9 knots

By 1937 all my type had started eyeing me different because I had become the 'Go Man' between my people and Señor Vanderdyke. I had many names: Jefe el hombre. Jefe el amigo. Boss man. Boss friend.

Señor bossed me what needed to be done.

I bossed them and it got done.

It got planted, farmed, harvested, ranched, hired and fired.

I even got married.

I coached. I pastored. I nursed. I doctored. I was judge and jury. I was hard and fair.

But I kept my people working. I kept them fed. I kept them alive.

By 1938 Señor and Señora Vanderdyke, took me again into the big house and they gave me a promotion. That was just before the Big War.

"You'll start handling more work in case I'm drafted to the war," he said.

Señora Vanderdyke cried.

"It'll be all right. Big farmers like me won't be drafted but if I'm called, I'll serve."

I looked at him.

He was brave. "It'll be okay because I have you to run the farm with the Missus if I leave."

I nodded. "I can run the fields. But who will pay the bills and manage the accounts?"

"My Missus will do that just fine. I'll start running things by her." Señor nodded to his wife.

The Señora didn't look very confident.

**E**ric followed Samantha out of class and down the hall and to her locker, where she dumped her books and went toward the auto shop.

It was a dead end so Eric hit the drinking fountain. When he looked back down the hall, she was gone. Between Auto Shop and himself was nothing but the Moes' Nest. He hesitated because it was Dwight and John territory. He turned away, knowing they hadn't dealt with him sailing away yet.

Throughout the school day, Eric went on learning about and studying Samantha. But he dogged her at a very safe distance.

Then she went into a realm where he could not follow. It was forbidden. No God-fearing, heterosexual male could be seen in the cosmetology wing of the high school. His mom said she would go there and get her hair cut if he ever came home from school with a C. Near to the impoverished hair salon was a handicap door entrance for townies.

Old ladies entered here for their free haircuts.

Eric slowed his pace.

He was in range of the perm smell.

Too close. He turned to leave.

Dwight and John braced him. Dwight was talking into his cell phone.

Ready to bolt out the doors, Eric paused.

The doors opened and Eric heard someone cussing. Swearing deep and harsh.

Eric faced Dwight and John.

"Erilic the derelict," Dwight said.

"Derelict the Erilic," John said. "Still sniffing your Central Snouze?"

"What are you talking about?" Eric stepped in quick and shoved Little John hard against the wall.

John slammed off it and stood still as if he got bounced off them for a living.

Bran and Evert rounded the corner.

A woman. A big one, crushing her tortured mobility cart, was trying to squeeze through the handicap door which kept closing on her because she was too slow. "Come on! Homer! Get me some up!" She yanked and sputtered as the electric whine of the cart struggled over a bump. With her cane stick, she kept smacking at the door opener and the rump of her scooter for some reason.

Eric turned and relaxed. A woman like that made up a whole crowd.

Dwight lunged and took Eric's head and bammed it into the locker then thumped it with his cast.

Eric went down on his haunches, back against the locker, staying as defensive as possible.

"Bran. Can you whip up something for Eric?" John asked.

"Come on," Bran said. "Evert's here."

"She don't mind," Dwight looked at her.

"Not as much as Eric," she said.

Bran walk up to where Eric sat and farted by his face. Bran grunted and farted again.

Eric kicked out and connected a foot to the back of Bran's thigh and dropped the boy in a heap.

"Hey!" Bran yelled, scurrying away on three limbs as Eric kicked again. "Watch it! It's not like I squirted out a juicy, wet one!" Bran crawled away and stood with John, Dwight and Evert.

"Evert was just going to class and she invited my mother to meet your missus," Dwight said to Eric. "My mom's been needing some work done on her hair for some time." He pointed to the woman in the cart who was giving the door another lashing with her cane.

The big woman had fetched up a sweat from the effort.

Greased hair was stuck to her sagging face.

John smiled. "Big Momma, do you think Erilic the Derelict could use a little trim?"

"Are you getting trimmed or are you getting trim!" she laughed out. "Come on, Homer!" She rolled forward a few feet and stopped.

Eric saw her humor as dangerous, lurking. Her green laugh was filled with motive he didn't understand.

"It's why you're here, right? Get a little trim for the tab!" Dwight kicked out at Eric, driving him to his feet.

All four took a step closer.

Homer wheeled toward the class.

What struck Eric as odd was how the big woman had boosted her cart as if to flank him also.

Beyond them was freedom. Before him was Cosmetology Class. Beyond the class was a brick wall and a drinking fountain. If he was a grizzly bear he could justify a charge.

Evert pulled out a pair of scissors. "It's Big Momma or you Eric. Who do you want Samantha to deal with?"

Eric put a hand to his scalp and it came away wet with blood.

"Come on, Eric," the big woman yelled and buzzed her scooter forward. They neared the salon door. "Let me have the Mex job! I hear she's real purty and can make a woman out of me!" She goosed Homer to get a clear shot at the door.

Eric saw beyond the cutsie bi-sexual photographs on the window. He looked beyond the spinning, adjustable chairs searching for a fire escape. Then his shoulders slumped and he walked into new territory.

A few girls of fashion anorexia stopped talking. They had clients. Their scissor hands starting shaking.

New to the room was Samantha. She was talking to the teacher who sat and took up every inch of the extra large chair at the desk. They both turned.

Eric heard the door frame shudder as the cart clipped it.

The teacher beamed a smile at the woman in the cart then furled a snarl at Evert and the boys. "You're late," she steamed at Evert.

"But I have clients!" Evert said.

The teacher smiled. "Well, nothing happens in fashion without compromise."

Eric was driven in by Homer nipping his heels.

Girls flexed their fingers in Restless Scissor Syndrome.

Dwight and John blocked the door and escape.

The place stunk. An old woman was getting stink in her hair.

"But it's my first day! I can't cut his hair," Samantha said to the teacher.

Inside Eric's head her voice broke into a thousand pieces like diamonds and bounced around in his ears. He crossed the floor to a corner chair, picked a magazine and swung it over his face.

"Honey! That's why we don't charge!" the teacher said and smiled assuringly to Eric.

"I'll do it," Evert said. "Burnt Barbie? You can cut Bran's."

Big Momma turned to the other two girls. "Which one of you'uns is gonna fix my filly?" Big Momma asked. "Just a touch mind you. I ain't going anywhere's and I've no one to please. Now Homer just gets all the pleasure!" she hummed Homer up them and they saw their future.

Samantha looked at Eric and saw the magazine advertisement in the mirror behind him. "Don't buy those kind." Samantha said. "They're *chafa*.*

"What?" Eric asked.

"They're no good."

*cheap, of bad quality.

"Sorry. What?"

"Don't buy dem."

"Why?" Eric had no choice but to stare at her because her silver dollar sized earrings were hypno.

"Do you really want me to answer that?" Her eyes were dead honest.

He looked at her and blinked.

She took that as a yes. "Tampax. It's because they…"

"What are you talking about?" Eric asked.

She nodded to his magazine.

He then looked at the two page ad for Tampax® with the mail-in rebate insert. He didn't want to look back at Samantha, but he didn't want to look at the ad either. He slammed the magazine shut, grimaced then opened his eyes at her.

"Eric the Derelict scoping the tampons!" Bran said to the class.

"Tampax," Evert said. "It's not the same thing."

"Really?" Bran asked. "What's the difference?"

Evert lifted the electric buzz and zapped on the power sheerer and leaned into Bran, cutting hair at the scalp.

"You're pretty fine looking for a Border Bunny," Bran said to Samantha after spinning his chair to face her. Fresh cut hair stuck to his nose.

Samantha pumped up Eric's chair to a good height, then leaned up next to him. "How do you want your hair cut? Like your skinhead friends, or something really *especial*?" she tied the cape around Eric's neck and yanked it tight an extra notch for good measure.

Eric coughed. "Doesn't matter. Whatever."

"Come on, Eric! Go for it!" Bran said above the buzz of electric sheers. "Hey, Eric? Tell her what you get when you cross a Mexican Spicle with a Michigan icicle!"

Eric lowered his head and watched his hair fall down and pile in his lap. He wanted to say that they weren't his friends. That he wasn't them. That he didn't like the crude woman. But he knew he had come in with them. He knew what she saw and he knew what she believed. He winced hard as her rotors ramped over the bleeding lump on his skull.

## LOG ENTRY 6

6:05 pm—abeam Ludington Reservoir
East winds to 19 knots.
Waves 0-1. Northbound at 9 knots

Two years after the Day of Infamy, Señor Vanderdyke left to fight the Germans. He was gone from 1943 to 1947.

Back home a local bank, which had been holding the notes on three neighboring farms since the Depression, sold us these assets for bond money. Some said they needed to show a G-Man that the area could increase farm yield and help a lean country.

I had learned of these notes from some tiny mice at the other farms and Senora Varnderdyke proved to be very shrewd with money.

So in 1947, when Señor Varnderdyke returned as a hero, I got another promotion. I got it because labor was shorter than ever with everyone in the factories, so I trucked up my entire village. Tunneled them up that is.

Matter of fact, we were so many that we had to keep to ourselves to avoid suspicion. Many never left the Michigan farm, which now had a ranching branch.

My Mexicans knew a good thing. They stayed low. Cool. Pruned while the snow fell. Fertilized when the fields were frozen and ranched and farmed when it was warm.

We built up our little cantina for the men and trade store for the women. We added a room for sick and injured people to the barn where the animal doctor checked over the livestock. He helped us for free.

∴

**S**amantha watched her mother primping in front of the mirror. "Whoa?"* she asked, checking a perfume sample in another language.

"I'm just going out."

"Just out?"

"Just out. *Cosas* never change.* Some *personas* never change.** *Pueblos* never change.*** " Ms. Lazzair said and stood up.

"With who?" Samantha asked.

"With one of your teachers. And you. If you'll come." The mother smiled at her daughter's youth, then frowned on her own reality.

"What teacher?"

"Just a person I was told to meet with."

"Told? Who? *¿Estás bromeando?***** "

"No. *Lo siento.**** There's more. She pushed an envelope to her daughter. It was withered and yellow. It had been sealed for a long time.

"*¿Es para mí?***** "

"*Sí. Sucedió esta noche, hace muchos años.****** You must promise me to open it in a very special, *muy peligroso******* place. And you must be very careful."

Samantha took the envelope and looked at her mother. The woman was scared. She was very scared.

From his chair inside Sebastian's, Eric saw Samantha walking across the spotty grass towards the docks. He turned and let his eyes follow her. Seeing her stop at the water's edge, he

---

*things
**people
***towns
***Are you joking?
****I'm sorry

*****Is it for me?
******Yes. It happened tonight, many years ago.
*******very dangerous

reached for his glass and missed it. Some water spilt into a small saucer that held butter.

"Relax, Eric," his father said. "She's a Mud Duck."

"Stop that," the mother said to her husband.

"Well, look at him. Getting his hair cut like this? No wonder he's swinging below the border belt."

"Keep your chin up, Eric," his mother said. "Aim high. Remember your friends," she said from a plastic face.

Eric looked back at them. Then at the others around Sebastian's. The place could carry two dozen more tables, but old man Sebastian kept them stored away so the joint didn't look so empty. He saw old man Thompson across the way with his biological. The Vanderdyke woman was in her corner talking to the waiter. She had her hand on his arm. And maybe two other families would come tonight. He had heard that the place used to be full. Docks crowded with yachts and sailboats. But that was before his time.

Noise was at the entrance and Little John's father entered and nodded to Eric's table and the others before he sat where he always did. At the bar.

Eric looked again at the people. The silver-haired, Vanderdyke woman in the corner used to be mayor. The hatchet-faced, narrow-eyed man was Sebastian. He owned the place and hung around his bar stool at the far end by the cash register. Evert's loser dad was there for his burger. He janitored with the Mexican Mo Matadork's at the school to piss off his ex-wife. Little John Henderson's father was at the bar.

It was the normal crowd.

Eric put a napkin to his water spill. *All of them are kind of disturbing people,* he thought. *Then of course, my parents are here in case I had any doubt.*

He looked back at Samantha at the docks but she was gone. *Smart girl,* he thought, *too smart to be here.* He looked around again. The place used to be private. It used to be a club with inground pools, fences, spas and security. Exclusive. And it used to be full. Now it was open to the public and empty. Present company excluded of course. *Of course,* Eric mumbled. But it still had the feel of danger for some reason, and he felt that Samantha shouldn't be on this side of Morguetown Lake.

"Holy Tamale!" Eric's mom hissed.

"I beg your pardon?" the father asked, then his fork slipped from his fingers. He tried to catch it, but missed and spun it in the air instead, making it land on his plate in a way that catapulted a glob of BBQ onto the his white shirt.

His wife looked at him and frowned.

No one else noticed the dropped fork. They all stared at the woman in the doorway.

Eric stared too. She may be fifty, but so was a woman named Farah Faucett, and his old man still bragged her up whenever he showed her pictures. Eric looked at the others.

Sebastian had his back to her, but his hand held the brass bar rail with a grip that could withstand a baseball bat attack. He faced the cash register, and Eric had a strange feeling that Sebastian was fixating on the gun inside it.

They were all frozen, as if the place never had a guest. *Never had a guest,* Eric mused in his mind. He turned back and watched the woman high-heel herself over to the bar and sit alone.

Henderson, usually good for a welcome of sorts, shrunk and went silent.

Her presence seemed to knock old man Henderson into his bottle.

"Who's that?" Eric asked.

"Shh," his mother said.

"I don't know," his father said.

Eric looked at the both of them. *Well, if you're not the most pathetic liars!* He ran his fingers through barren patches on his scalp. He felt where patches of hair had just been mowed and thought of how Samantha had taken some of her anger out on him. *Well, I deserve it.* He looked around the place. *We all deserve it.*

He looked back at the woman. Small town and a new face. A strong face. Then he knew. He knew everyone in the room knew her but him.

Then the door dinged and Mr. Puke entered. The teacher pulled the baseball hat tighter on his head, straightened his tie and looked around.

Eric moved his head in line behind his father's and watched Puke scan the room, then his eyes rested on the bar. He smiled and walked over to her.

Eric mumbled and excused himself, but doubted if his parents even heard him.

No one had noticed anything after the woman entered.

From across the clubhouse dining area, a big man leaned on his elbows to get a better view.

"Bring back memories, old man?" Evert asked.

Then Bran entered Sebastian's and Evert smiled. "He's here," she said to her father.

"Puke?" Thompson looked at his food. He had ordered early on, not bothering to wait for his daughter's friend. He looked at his burger, but it just looked back at him. It seemed to be too heavy and too far away to pick up.

Bran walked to Evert.

Evert nodded. "Bran, this is my father."

Mr. Thompson looked up at the teenager. "I'm not hungry. You want the rest of my burger?"

"Heck yes!" Bran said as he sat and pulled the plate over in front of him. "Can you pass me the salt?"

Evert wished again her mother was here. You can't make this up. She reached for her drink.

Evert's dad watched Sebastian, whose whitened face hadn't yet turned to look back at the woman down the bar. Stompson smiled and chuckled and looked at Bran. "Why does everybody call you Bran?"

"I've an asshole that talks a lot of shit," Bran said.

Evert choked on her drink.

"Nice to sit with an honest man!" Thompson took up his Pabst and tilted it at Bran.

Bran took a bite of the man's burger, nodded and chomped into it again.

The wind had clocked, bringing the chill of Lake Michigan inland as Samantha Lazzair entered Morguetown's bankrupt shipyard. At once she knew the all the vessels had been separated from their captains for a long time, and that the sailors were gone too. Sailed off to greener boats in deeper pastures.

"The year after your father drowned, the big lake dropped five feet and the boating around here died with him," an old, gaunt Mexican gaucho had said to Samantha yesterday as they walked the woods on the northshore of Morguetown Lake. It was an effort for the old cowboy to walk, because his legs were shaped like a horseshoe from a half century in the saddle. "We watch the lake go up and down every few decades, but she's been down for a long time."

"My father was a boater?"

"You're father was a sailor."

"And that is his sailboat!" she pointed to the glowing vessel on the lone mooring in the stillness of the lake.

"No. The vessel you seek is *muerto en el astillero.** He

*dead in the shipyard

pointed across the lake. "It's over there."

"What happened? She had to squint across the lake as sun made diamonds on the ripples as she followed his finger and saw the shipyard from afar. It was between the bankrupt coffin factory and the old breakwalls that dammed up sand dunes so they wouldn't choke the little harbor entrance.

He hitched his pants and they sat on a log. He rolled a smoke, struck a match with his thumb and inhaled. "That fence came around those boats like a net. Someone trapped a passel of sailboats thinking he could sell them. But then they got vandalized and there they sit. They sit there rotting. Rotting like the entire town."

"It's still there?" she had asked.

"It's there. It's name is *Southern Cross*. Why don't you know that?"

Samantha now faced west and felt the chill of night. She took in the haunting, dark blue, after-sunset sky. As she lingered for her bearings, color left and she found herself in shadow. Only then did she exhale deep and relax. Night was the only thing Michigan and Mexico had in common. A shiver came and she shook it off. Cold wind over Morguetown Lake rolled in some fog which cat-walked between and under the boats around her.

She dragged her fingertips along the hulls of graffiti-tagged sailboats as she searched. Above her, stars were snuffed by fog. Moisture seemed to be the only sign of life among decay, mold, chemical and stagnation of the shipyard.

Her green deck shoes swirled mist from warm, black puddles as she worked her way deeper into the shipyard. Now among bigger and older sailboats, she started to circle them. Some rested among oak saplings with hulls buffed by branches. Crispy brown leaves created dark shadows under the hulls like tunnels in a cave.

Then she saw the old sheet of plywood covering a gaping hole of one of the larger sailboats and she stopped.

She let her eyes circle the area, taking in every shadow and rustle of branch against hull. Eyes accustomed to the night, she walked to the stern and read the name, SOUTHERN CROSS, in the faint light.

Her chin dropped and all was still. She had found her father's sailboat.

The metal jackstands supporting the hull had sunk into the flaking asphalt and made indentations into the hull. The thick keel had knifed into the earth. Although the monster could fall and crush her, it also drew her closer.

She stood a wooden pallet against the twisted jackstand, but the wood had rotted and it didn't reach high enough. She looked at the mangled rudder, but it was too far beneath the hull. Something gleamed in the weeds and shadow of the neighboring boat. She pulled an aluminum ladder out from under a rusty chain.

She leaned the ladder against *Southern Cross*, climbed to the top, and stepped up onto a rub rail of rotted teak running along the hull below the deck. Reaching, she hooked her fingers on the gunwhale and hoisted herself on deck. High above on the transom, her bare legs felt free. She slipped off her muddy shoes and moved barefoot into the cockpit of the fifty-foot derelict. Stepping over a twisted aluminum mast, Samantha avoided a tangle of wires that once stayed spars to the wind. Cold dew was on the topsides and she moved slowly, wary of a long overboard fall. On the foredeck she folded her cold legs under an old sweatshirt and waited.

To the east, the moon rose over Morguetown Lake and glowed through an area of fog. Several boats away, a lone mast framed itself in the lunar beam like a crucifix. The ground fog, made blue in the moonlight, created the illusion that the boats were actually afloat. The area gradually brightened, and soon a series of sirens sounded in the distance as the lunatics awoke.

Samantha pulled strands of black hair from her face. Some were anchored in place, cemented to her cheeks with dried tears. She saw where trees and sand dunes had breached the shipyard's fence and drifted around the line of boats on the west wall.

Her swollen eyes saw weaving and dancing leaves around the boats. Branches stirred like waves on water as a night wind spilled more fog.

A small smile came as she thought about how the hot winds of home moved the prickly pear and mesquite to dance. But it was a sad smile, like those that link people after terrible wars.

She drew out the envelope and broke the seal. Inside was the newspaper clipping. In moonlight she read:

> *September 21, 1981. Allister Bendolly, 26, delivering the Bill Thompson sailboat, Southern Cross was claimed by Lake Michigan after the Coast Guard cancelled their three-day search. A rogue September storm drove the sailboat onto the Grays Reef Shoals at the abandoned light house about 28 miles west of Mackinaw Bridge. Allister is survived by his wife, Nicole, 18, his father, Señor Bendolly, 60 and Señora Bendolly, 41.*

Tears fell. Written lines blurred. "Thank you mother for telling me." The soft wind swept the words from her mouth.

Then her eyes lifted and she looked west. From over the dunes she could hear them now, waves roaring on the sand, taunting her.

The old obituary felt heavy as the wind folded it over, trying to tug it from her grasp. She wanted to say it so bad; she had planned it. She looked at the old boats around her, balancing on deep keels and gradually being swallowed up by sand, trees and mud. Above her came ghost patches of star sky, which brought a darker spell to her world.

Moments ago she seemed a bastard child of a white Latino woman who had somehow gained respect in her poor Mexican village. Her name had been only Lazziar.

Until now. Now it was also Bendolly. And her grandfather was a powerful man. A man of means who owned the largest farm in Michigan. A farm that supported hundreds of families! A farm that took thousands of people to run.

She shook her legs out of the sweatshirt and stood into the wind. A hint of rain and the pleasing scent of open water was in the air, but she mainly smelled dead boats. She was a Bendolly!

She looked again at the defeated and broken ships below her. They ached for rest, for a burial at sea.

Her eyes went hard. They dried in the wind as they looked over *Southern Cross* and she shook her head.

Boats around her seemed to slink into the darkness, fearing her damnation. Samantha edged forward, onto the huge bowsprit, with nothing below her but darkness. The hull shifted and then went still and she knew the sailboat hated her back.

She looked toward Sebastian's and saw the small restaurant beyond a few sagging houses with cluttered yards. She now knew why her mother could walk with confidence.

She suddenly felt cold, and a little squeamish. She knew that the time was near when she would meet the one called Kapin Kirk. She would soon meet her grandfather.

*As for my father? I guess this is as close as I can get.*

❀

Eric stood panting under the buzzing light in front of Sebastian's and reviewed the search circle he had just run between Coffin Light and Morguetown. *Samantha sails and I know she lives on Vanderdyke land.* He turned and walked toward the bankrupt shipyard. It was a long shot, but so was she.

John saw Dwight twitch his cheek for the third time as they waited behind the trees in front of Sebastian's. John smiled. "He blocked your last punch, you know," he said. "Don't forget that he's the little weasel for chasing the fox. But if he can't sniff her out, we won't be able to."

"Sebastian said there's never two misses without a third," Dwight said. "But I ain't gonna miss!"

Wind stirred and more mist was driven inland from the big lake.

Eric passed.

They waited, then followed. They stayed to the shadows, still hoping they could get her too. John had been doing some thinking about her. He wasn't one-armed like Dwight. He wasn't going to go for just a pinch.

Eric paused at the fence near an ancient dumpster and peered at the first wave of trashed boats inside the shipyard. He squinted, knowing she was near and mumbled something against the darkness. Deep in the yard he thought he had heard movement and leaned closer against the chain link fence and looked between two vessels.

Dwight swung his fiberglass arm in a chop, expecting Eric to duck.

Eric stared into the dark for Samantha.

The cast struck Eric, splitting the skin to the skull. Down he went.

Eric didn't even twitch.

Dwight looked at John and then at the blood against his cast.

John nudged the body with a foot. "Sweet dreams, pup cake!"

"Sebastian'll dig that!" Dwight said.

They ran off, keeping to the alleys.

From the deck of the old sailboat, Samantha's skin chickened up as she watched the three boys come together at the fence. She watched two run off and waited a few minutes, peering at the one laying on the sidewalk.

No cars drove by.

No one stopped to help.

Wary of an ambush, she crept out of the darkness from behind the fence and saw the haircut. Frowning, she looked up and down the street. "Eric," she whispered, and went to him through a cut in the fence. When she saw the blood, she took a knee and stopped the bleeding with pressure.

Then she dragged the body into the shadows and leveraged the boy onto her back, using his arm. The force groaned the ladder but it held the double weight as she climbed. Atop the old sailboat, she dropped him into the cockpit. When his head thudded the fiberglass flooring, he moaned.

She took off her fleece and laid it over him. After elevating his feet, she climbed down and walked two blocks to a store and bought some stuff. Back in the abandoned shipyard with Eric, she laid out the medicine. Under moonlight, she chose some saline eye water.

Then she leaned in and looked at the wound for the first time in the blue light of her cell phone. Seeing some fatty white skin under the blood soaked matt of hair, she wiped off the blood. A smooth red thing in the middle of the long gash looked hard and she wondered if it was his skull.

She pulled the wound open and flushed it by blasting it with the eye water. She washed out the entire scalp area with the liquid.

Eric winced in pain and moaned.

"Relax," she whispered and dried it with gauze. Then she opened a tube of Krazy Glue® and kneeled over his head.

"What...?" Eric stammered and took everything in. He sat up, but fell back down because someone spun the sky.

She caught him. "Good. You're awake. You're not going to puke are you?"

"What are you doing?"

"Stitches."

"Stitches," he said and looked at the glue. "With glue?"

"Mexican stitches."

"What?"

"What?"

"Does it work?"

"*Sí!*"

He looked up at the night sky. "Knock yourself out."

"*¿Qué?*"*

He was wondering what had happened when he blacked out again.

Samantha pinched the long gash on his scalp together, squishing out more excess blood. She wiped it clean and drew the wound closed by stringing some of his hair across gash as she blew the glue dry. She glued the rest of the gash shut the same way. After blowing dry a few more layers, she stood—then sat down quickly.

She closed her eyes and listened. Nothing could be heard after the soft disturbance, but she held still and waited.

---

*What?*

Soon the night sounds of the area bugs droned up and she wondered if they had stopped grinding on their own or if someone was out there.

After a few minutes of listening, she became scared. When the bugs started, she went to the ladder and lifted it up and rested it softly out of sight on the deck of the boat.

Mrs. Nelson paced and held her phone with both hands, but she never called the police. She knew her son was gone but that he wasn't exactly missing. "You're involved in this?" she asked her husband.

"We're all involved in it."

"Well, I don't like it."

"None of us do, but it's not going away. If anything, it's coming back," he said

"Well, I don't like it. I never did."

"I'll look for him," and Mr. Nelson left. He drove down to the Henderson place, one of the few remaining houses on Morguetown Lake between Sebastian's and the channel. Killing the car lights, he went up the steps. Before he knocked, the door opened and Little John stepped out.

"Where's Eric?"

Little John raised his palms.

"You git 'im?"

Little John nodded. "You were right. He was tailing the Bean Ball like you said. He was a Buck-in-Rut. Never even saw us."

"What'd you do?"

"Slash whacked him."

"Out cold?"

"Pretty much."

"I can't find him. Show me."

"Okay." Little John got in the car and stopped and pointed at the trees across from the fenced in boats. "Right there."

Mr. Nelson turned off the engine, got out and walked over. He did a full circle and then settled his sights on the abandoned shipyard.

"This bad?" John asked.

"Dunno. You leave him laying right here?"

"Uh huh."

"And you ran her off?"

"We never saw her. Figured she high-tailed herself back to Gringoville. Was her mom really in Sebastian's?"

"Yup."

"My dad's home drunk. Dead drunk. What's going on?"

"Nothing."

"Yeah, right. Like I'm going to believe that. What's going on?"

Nelson looked around. "Your old man will get over it. He wanted a nip of her biscuit a long time ago but she went jalapeño instead and he never got her salsa!"

"Well, he ain't over it yet," Little John said. "He ain't near over it."

Samantha was asleep and then she was awake. Her eyes flashed but she dared not moved. It was late. Very late and the stars had made good progress across the sky. Sound had stopped from a patch of land where the bugs had gone still.

The boat gave another shudder and the eyes of Samantha flared. She then felt the footsteps in the mud far below.

The footfalls were moving quiet.

Stealth.

Wrong.

She knew it wasn't someone taking a walk. Nor was it a

search party. The hull next to hers glowed under the beam of a flashlight and then light spilled on the hull of SOUTHERN CROSS and shot up into the sky. She looked to Eric and saw him breathing smooth and soft. Only her eyes moved as she checked the old ladder, still hidden from view on the deck. She prayed that Eric would not stir but did so without moving her lips or breathing.

Then the footfalls moved away, gaining speed.

*Why did they slow around Southern Cross?* The ground was gravel and chipped asphalt and she felt that she had left no tracks. Yet the person had paused. She didn't think it was a teenager either. The footfalls had been around too long. They were those of a man; a man with a light in the dead of night who knew that *Southern Cross* warranted a visit.

Her mother was right.

Morguetown was not safe.

# LOG ENTRY 7

6:35 pm—abeam Ludington Lighthouse
East winds to 19 knots.
Waves 0-1. Northbound at 9 knots

In 1948 and 1950, Señora Vanderdyke gave birth to Mighty Mike and Texas Tex. A boy and a girl. It was a decade of peace and joy.

Señor took the boy to the tractor when he was old enough to sit.

Señora doted on her baby girl something primal. She adorned her girl in the pink and snowwhite outfits that the women of Mexico North had made for her.

With all those beautiful dresses, every day was like First Communion for little Texas Tex.

For Mighty Mike? He had his choice of tractors to ride! He was in heaven!

ric woke up warm, tucked into a couple of fleece blankets. He saw a jug of water by his face and felt a raging thirst. He tried to sit up, but splitting head pain held him still. It didn't hurt when he blinked. Then he saw her face next to his and blinked some more.

Her face was shrouded in fine black hair and she was asleep.

Seeing her, scared him upright onto his good elbow.

Thirst invaded and he chugged the drink. It felt like someone was twisting a canoe paddle under his scalp and he had a kink in his neck. He lowered his head back to a dew-covered, musty cushion and stared at her.

"Hey, Eric," Samantha said half asleep.

"What happened?"

"I fixed your head. Then you got the shivers *muy mal** so I stayed with you to keep you warm." She was going back to sleep.

"What happened?"

"They got you. *Hombres malos ¿Oyes eso?***"

"What?"

"You hear that?"

"No."

"Listen."

Faraway, halyards rang against a hollow mast.

He turned back to her but she was asleep.

Hours later, dawn found them together and cold under dew-soaked fleece. The sun broke the skyline but warmth was an hour away.

"Why were you at Sebastian's?" she asked.

"We've been eating there since, well... since before I was born anyway. It's a family thing."

---

*really bad
**Bad guys. Do you hear that?

"I'll bet," she said and went alongside him. "But you've never sailed?"

"No. How did you learn?"

"Mo."

"Why come here? Why Morguetown?"

"Work. Maybe I'm still trying to figure it out. Maybe someday I'll sail Lake Michigan north to Canada above Lake Huron."

"Why?"

"*No hay nadie.*\* Maybe up there, there are no people. Maybe there is no ugly. *Sin ningún odio.*\*\*"

"What's that?"

"No hate."

"Why can't you just say it?"

"I did. Why can't *you* just understand?"

He wanted to say something, but only slander came to his mind. So he sweet-potato-pied and he shut his mouth and pondered.

"What? she asked.

"What?"

"You said, 'Song of the South!'"

"I did?"

She nodded.

He felt her breath and turned to see her eyes. They swelled before him as she looked at the sky. Tears streaked down her temples and he felt useless.

She was crying and he could not help her so he watched the lines of tears glisten down her temples and run into her hair.

After a while, he traced the trail of tears with his finger.

"Have you ever seen the Abandoned Lighthouse?" she

---

\*No one's there
\*Without hate

asked, her eyes were deep, big and scared.

"Most of them now are abandoned."

"What's 'The Abandoned Lighthouse'?"

"I don't know. I've never really been on the water."

Looking away, hair pulled over her ear, she nodded north.
"They say there is a giant abandoned lighthouse by Mackinaw."

"What's wrong?"

"No one has ever told you about it?" she rolled on her side
and faced him with huge eyes and blinking tears.

"Told me what? Why are you crying, Samantha?" he asked,
liking the sound of her name. He could have been covered in
a few inches of snow and her eyes would have melted it. They
pushed him back to the sail he had with her. He heard the
waves boil along the hull. He felt the darkness and tasted the
fog.

"I heard the water at the top of the lake is called the
Straights of Mackinaw. And up north there are many grave-
yards. Many shipwrecks. Where the waterways narrow.
Where many have died." She bit her lip.

He saw her teeth release her white lip.

"I heard that up in Mackinaw many lighthouses don't
shine anymore. That they haven't for many decades."

"They don't need to, I guess," he said.

She looked down at him and spoke.

*El Arrecife de Gray hierve blanco.*
*Gemidos metálicos se oxidan por la luz de la mañana.*
*Los dientes del fantasma de Derecho vendrán esta noche.*
*¡El lago Michigan abandonará sus muertos!*

"What?" Eric looked up.

"Have you never heard this?" she asked. It goes something like this in your language.

*Grays Reef boils white,*
*Metal groans rust in the morning light;*
*Ghost teeth of the Derecho will come tonight.*
*Lake Michigan will give up her dead.*

"You seem to know it well. You say it as if it were a song. When were you there?" he asked.

"I've never been there."

Eric was quiet. He had never been there either. It didn't really sound like a destination spot. "I think I saw your mother last night."

"It's my father I'm looking for."

"He run off?"

"Do Mexican men run off?"

"It's not what I meant."

*"Entonces di lo que quieres decir!"**

"What?"

"Then say what you mean!"

He thought for a moment. Saying the right thing about her father seemed very important for the future of their conversation. "Where is your father?"

"He drowned at the Abandoned Lighthouse."

All went quiet. Eric somehow got his arm down flat and she found her way onto his shoulder. "I'm sorry," he said after a while.

She exhaled emptiness.

He looked at her. "You can have my dad if you want him."

"Did you know that the name of this boat is *Southern Cross*?"

Eric felt his arm tingle as blood-flow got squeezed by her head. But he knew the same blood was being pressed through his memories too. Both went numb. But he knew he would

---

**Then say what you want to say!*

forever remember waking up to this beautiful girl.

"The last time my father sailed was on this vessel. He drowned and was lost at sea." Samantha said and turned and faced him. "Sail with me to the Abandoned Lighthouse."

"Okay," he said.

"Why does Morguetown call their lighthouse 'Coffin Light'?"

"Why does Samatha Lazziar have so many questions?"

She smiled at him so he would tell her no lie.

"Because of the Coffin Factory. The one that wrecked our town and then left," Eric said and smiled.

"But the factory came later. Years after Coffin Light. Right?"

"Maybe so."

"So?"

"So what?"

"So why was a coffin lid on the lighthouse door years before the factory came?" She lifted her head and stared at him.

He lowered his eyes.

"Tell me."

"No."

"Why not?"

"Okay, I will. But what happened, happened long before I came along."

"¿Qué?"*

"On New Years Eve, they gather. They meet at Sebastian's and lock the door. My parents and their friends." He watched her interest rise. "I don't know. It's weird. But when I was young, I remember them getting drunk. When they were drunk they always talked of Coffin Light."

"Who?"

"You saw them," he thumbed towards the water. "The los-

---

*What?*

ers of Sebastian's. The one's gawking at your ma last night."

"Your dad is one of them?"

"Heck yes! They're all the same."

"What do they say?"

"Nothing good, Samantha. They never say anything good."

She rolled to her back and looked at the color filling the sky. She liked this Eric. She gave him a probing look. "Are you good?"

He shrugged. "Me and the others always remember playing pool and games on that holiday! You know, staying up late and being together. We're like family except with more dysfunction."

"What's that?"

Just problems.

"So you're not related?"

"No."

"So?"

"So?"

"So?" she prodded.

"So the town hates the ranch and the Mexican bandit who stole it from Vanderdyke. That's all, Samantha. Don't make it anything more than it is."

"That's all? Then why has there been a coffin lid on the lighthouse since…?" she stopped before saying a date.

"Let's put it this way." Eric tried to measure her curiosity. "Cap'n Kike is the owner of the Mexican Farm. Right?"

She shrugged. "I just moved here."

"Right. Really? Anyways, there's this old hombre named Kapin Kike, or whatever his name is, and he owns the ranch you live on. Or he used to. Nobody has seen him in Morguetown for a long time. I've never seen him. Only a few seem to even know him. My dad. Henderson. Sebastian, and Texas. Bull Stompson, who is Evert's dad, maybe does. They all know him and they haven't seen him for the better part of a decade."

"Really?"

"Yeah." Eric felt his confidence rise.

"Are they looking for him?"

"Why?" he asked.

She shrugged.

Eric smiled. He never had a girl like *this* hang on his words. "Doesn't matter. But his son once had a boat at Sebastian's and was the first Mexican member of the yacht club."

"What's wrong with that?"

"Between you and me? Nothing. But let me just say that when he drowned at sea or whatever happened up there at the Abandoned Lighthouse, nobody around Sebastian's was too upset about it. Matter of fact," Eric nodded to her, flexing his know-how, "after he was drowned is when they put the coffin lid up and, well, we've been calling it Coffin Light ever since."

She turned away and hid her tears.

He touched his scalp, fingering the glue.

When her tears cleared she spoke without facing him. "And do you think he drowned?"

"Me? What do I know?" he put a hand in her hair and combed out some tangles with his fingers. "Here's what I think. If it was an accident and he drowned it would have all been forgotten. So it probably wasn't because they still talk about it when they're drunk." He withdrew his hand, not wanting to spoil a good thing.

She held her breath.

"Nope, Samantha. I think they all had some part in helping that Mexican Mermado disappear. I think they did something awful to him because he was the rich dirt farmer's kid. And I think they pinned the coffin lid on the lighthouse to rub the stink of the mischief into that old farmer's nose. But I never really thought about it 'til now for some reason. You know what? It doesn't sound too good, does it? Good thing I'm probably wrong. I'm just a poor kid talking to a pretty girl!"

*¿Así que tu padre fue uno de los hombres que asesinaron a mi padre?"\**

"What? Come on! Speak Englisho."

"Kapin Kike's kid probably drowned by accident," she said.

"I like your innocence, Samantha. You should ask your people. They might know better than me. But when they are drunk at Sebastian's, they gloat. Blood is on their hands." Eric nodded to himself at saying this. It was the first time he had ever put it together and it felt good. He could be wrong, but what did it matter? It had happened before his time. He combed some of her hair again and she stayed still. "Are you okay?" he asked.

She stayed still.

He felt the line of glue on his scalp and wondered why his moron friends cared so much about him chasing this Dust Devil.

The council convened for a ten o'clock black coffee at Sebastian's and the last one in closed the door, flipped the OPEN sign to CLOSED and locked the dead bolt.

"She looks good," Sebastian said.

"Shut up!" Thompson said.

The woman nodded.

"Well, she does look good," Henderson said, leaning back and spraying eye drops in his eyes.

---

*\*So your dad was one of the men who killed my dad?*

Ms. Vanderdyke looked at Nelson, then turned to the janitor. "Bull?" she asked.

Bull nodded.

"What do you think about Nelson's kid being all lathered at the mouth over her kid?" she asked.

Nelson looked up from the floor. "They don't call them 'greasy' for nothing. It'll be over soon."

"Your boy tell you that?" Thompson asked.

"He'll come around. It ain't like ya'll never whiffed some spice before," Nelson said.

"How much do you think the woman knows?" Sebastian asked. "I mean, she waltzed right in here with the limper. Maybe…"

Texas leaned forward and drew the men up in their chairs. "She's the Bean Dean's daughter-in-law! She knows it all. And if *she* knows, her *kid* knows. And if *her* kid knows, then *your* kid knows! I'm a Vanderdyke. I see the picture. I had it framed on my plate with vegetables on the side!" She said this to Nelson and winked at him, knowing he liked her best when she used her maiden name.

"She doesn't know. She wouldn't let her kid trounce around *here* if she did. It'd be too dangerous. Too reckless. You don't gamble with a kid's innocence." Thompson said, taking another gulp of hot coffee. "But she looks good. Gooder than I imagined. He looked at Henderson and Sebastian, "No wonder you two wanted to ride her wet back in her glory days!"

"She doesn't know," Henderson said. "Hell, how could the old man know?"

They all turned and gave him the stupid look. Then all the men turned and looked at Vanderdyke.

Ms. Vanderdyke looked back at them. She knew they'd never change and that is why she liked them so much. Like herself, they were way beyond change.

Samantha sat her mother at the kitchen table and dropped the news clipping of the obituary between them. Since they had arrived, the woman had been softening and looking more at her daughter.

Her mother touched the obituary as if it were a frog. "I'm not going to talk of this now," she said and walked away.

Samantha raced after her. "What else am I going to find out? Morguetown knows more about my dad than me! It's a discrimination I can't fight!"

"Morguetown is more than a few old men at a dead yacht club."

"Old men? Is that what we call *asesinos** up here?"

"What did you just say to me?" The woman didn't like it and she didn't like the question. She swung the door to shut her daughter out but Samantha blocked it with her foot.

The door came open.

The mother just stood in front of her daughter and withered ten years in ten seconds. "What do you want to know?" The mother's eyes narrowed. "I don't owe you. Look at this place! I don't even owe Kapin Kirk! He's a strange old man and so was his son." Her tone had a final ring to it. She went to the window, opened it and looked down the dunes to the lake. A cold wind blew into the house. It brought a chill. "Pack your bags," the woman said.

Samantha came to her, dropped to her knees and took her mothers' hands. "Would you just tell me? Tell me what happened?"

Mrs. Lazzair struggled to lift her heavy eyes and faced the open water. She was trapped.

---

**assassins*

"If my father was so strange, why did you marry him? Who was he? What did he do that was so awful that it made you leave Michigan? Or maybe you weren't married to begin with? Maybe…"

"I was married. We were married, Samantha. You were born out of a marriage. You were born in love." Mrs. Lazzair looked at her daughter and saw what she herself used to be: Fire and ice. She put fingers to Samantha's hair. A slow, forced smile cracked. Smoothness spread over the wrinkles and the daughter saw a rare thing. The mother reached and took hold of her daughter's hand and lifted her. But she kept looking out the widow's window.

"He was a fine man. I met him in October after apple harvest. We married *rápidamente*.* Didn't have too. You know how to count. We just wanted to," Ms. Lazzair said. Her eyes hazed over. "Your father just loved me, Samantha. I laughed more when I was with him than I ever have before…and after.We didn't have anything. Didn't need anything. Didn't want anything but each other. He called our love '*tres velas al viento*.'** Senora Vanderdyke let us winter in this same, thin-walled summer cottage," she pointed out the window. "It's the same lake. Same bedroom. Same sheets. The kitchen and bathroom towels are the same. It's the same smell, but we saw it as a mansion. He had a small boat and took me far out on the water every evening."

Lake winds, open water air and screaming seagulls filled Samantha's mind. Waves boiled over the carpet. Windblown sand stung her legs.

"The nights were so dark, the water so restless but soothing, the stars so close back then. We could burn our fingers by touching them," she was down to whisper.

---

*right away
**three sheets to the wind

"Winter was so cold. I had never seen snow, or heard its haunting silence. He installed that cast iron woodstove, and we'd drag our mattress from the bedroom every night to be next to it. Outside was frigid. In November everything was orange and red. Then frost blurred the inside of our windows. By December snow came off the lake and drifted us in. In January, the lake builds massive ice shelves like those from glaciers.

"In February moonlight we'd traverse miles into the jagged icebergs to where the water was breathing and rumbling. It is the *ártico** in February. He dragged me out there. He had to hear the waves," she smiled. "By March he was still tying a rope around me because I would fall so much on the ice. Spring came and every day he threw me in the ice water, Samantha. He just threw me in to hear me scream. Every night it was a battle that lasted hours. But he always won. He always threw me in the cold water and I always screamed at him," the woman laughed to herself. "Then we'd run back to our beach fire, blankets and each other. We celebrated your pregnancy on that beach. Always together, always alone. Always smiling."

Samantha's mind was with her mother's spirit for the first time. She felt the sun and the wind. The burn of the cold water and the sting of frost in the snow. She felt Michigan. She had come home.

"But spring tricked us, Samantha." A small puff came from her nose. "Your father was asked to help deliver a big sailboat from Mackinaw for someone at Sebastian's," her voice faded.

The silence brought Samantha back to the room and she knew now that some truth is unbearable. She saw her mother staring, not seeing anything that was before her. Her mind had gone home. But the years and tears had stayed away. She

*Arctic

was now beyond rescue. The weight was crushing.

"He never came back to us, Samantha," she cried from the deep shadow of her soul. "He never came back to us, Samantha." The tired, aged woman raised her dark, sunken eyes to her daughter as she spoke. They cracked large wrinkles and then the woman fell to the floor and clutched Samantha's foot and all she could do was wail. "I couldn't keep his name. It just hurts so bad. I loved too much." She weakened and looked up. "I'm old, Samantha. I have been old ever since. But I brought you here that you might see that I once was young. That I once was alive. That I was once good."

"So my name is not Lazzair?" Samantha asked.

"It is. My maiden name is Lazzair. You are Lazzair."

"But my father was Bendolly?"

"Yes. And you are Bendolly too. *No te había contado de él antes. Pero te lo cuento ahora.*"*

Bill Thompson sat alone in the elevated Commodore Chair of the sunken yacht club. His daughter had just left. "You sure it was that boat?" he had asked her.

Evert nodded.

He didn't answer or hear her return question. Slowly, painstakingly-patient slow, he had quieted all ripples from the past. He inhaled his Swisher Sweet™ and watched the small boats bounce on the waves as they tugged the mooring lines in their slips. It was as if they were laughing at him. His world was again in motion and making him seasick.

"What's so special about that piece of crap big boat?" Evert asked.

"Good question. You always ask good questions. Do you remember the name?"

---

*I hadn't told you about him before. But I'll tell you now.

"Ya. *SOUTHERN CROSS.*"

He looked at her. "It's your mother's boat, Evert. It may someday be your boat."

# LOG ENTRY 8

7:30 pm—abeam Big Sable Lighthouse
East winds to 18 knots. Gray sunset.
Waves 0-1. Northbound at 9-10 knots

In 1960 death fell upon the farm. Señor
Vanderdyke left us and Señora gave me
another promotion: Train Mighty Mike to farm
and ranch.

I did.

Mighty Mike named me Capin Kirk after his
TV space hero.

During the next six years, I grew Mighty
Mike's work force to over one thousand in peak
harvest. But better than that, I kept them in
line in the west property, which was the shanty
town that Bay View Valley had been calling
Mexico North. It was a confusing time for many
back then. Maybe that was why Mighty Mike
built us a church and moved in a priest to help
us.

When they entered the school cafeteria, they saw Eric sitting with the Señorita Sam. They saw her tasseled, teasing black hair. Their eyes gave way and they stared over her thin white blouse. They changed course because of her.

Eric looked at them as they walked up.

Samantha exhaled as they circled.

"What's up with you? You eating in Bean Town now?" John asked Eric.

Many of the dark haired, Hispanic students looked at them, turned and kept eating from their paper sacks.

"You want an apology?" Eric asked. "Here's one. Get over it."

"When they stop getting over the fence, I'll stop getting over them!" Little John said. "And now you're over the fence too."

"Shut up!" Eric said and turned away.

"How about you?" Dwight nodded to Samantha. "Did you mud dog the Rio Grande just so you can get over my fence?"

Samantha took a drink and looked away.

"Quiet huh? No habla Engla? Well maybe you'll talk if I cross your fence!"

"How's your arm?" Samantha asked.

He lifted the cast as if to club them.

Eric stood quickly, bumping the table as he did so. "Dwight, I never thanked you. Because of your club, I spent the night with her. Kinda weird how things worked out, ain't it?"

"Too bad you never woke up to take advantage of it!" Dwight said.

Shultz, the lunchroom bouncer, one of the largest and most unemployable men in town, came rushing over. He had gotten hired with settlement funds after the food-fight of

1994 when Lizzy Lu, a potential Prom Queen according to her parents, got her cheek cut to the bone by a flying tray.

Big Shultz snuggled in between the two parties. His loose flesh bulging the 5X shirt. His stomach touched Dwight and John and backed them up. He did nothing forceful to induce labor or a power struggle; just a controlled gesture.

But everyone knew Shultz wasn't right in the head. He protected his double-wide trailer with razor wire. And it isn't a simple feat to run electric current through razor wire, but he did that too.

"Erilic the Derelict," Dwight nudged little John and retreated their posse.

"See you going down," Little John said to Eric, then turned to the girl. "Maybe I'll see you going up. Taco Bella! Taco Bella! Toco Bella! You wanna meet my fella?" He sang out as Shultz maneuvered them back to the white-washed section of the cafeteria.

Eric looked into Samantha's eyes then lowered his.

"They're *loco!*"* She said. "They're sick. Maybe you should stop dogging me," she said.

"Okay," he looked to leave.

"Wanna go sailing with me?"

"Sailing?"

"*Sí,*" she said. "No fog tonight. Let's go an hour before sunset."

"Okay."

"You sure? You're not going to *tener demasiado frío?* Be too cold?"

"I'll be fine," he smiled. "Good things always happen to me when I'm with you!" he touched the gap matting on his head.

"One more thing?" she asked.

---

*crazy
*be too cold?

"What?"

"I'll have to take you on Vanderdyke land. You know, to get to Mo's boat."

"So?"

"So, you're white. Not too many white eyes on Mexico North."

"I don't have a problem with that. I don't have a problem with you. I only have problems with them. Them and their parents."

"What about your parents?"

"I got problems with them too."

"They know you went sailing from Coffin Light?"

"Ya."

"The haircut? I mean, well, look at you?"

"They know."

"The beating you took. The night you followed me? How I glued it? How we stayed together?"

"They know."

"And...?"

"And what?"

"Well, isn't it all because of me? I bet they hate me now."

"Now?" Eric looked around. Then he glanced up at the ceiling to see if the A/C just slammed down the temperature. He faced her. "Samantha, they hated you long before *you* arrived. They hated you before you were *born*."

"*Sí.*"

"Hey! I'm Eric. And you're Samantha. And all this? All this ugly? Don't buy it. The town does. But that doesn't mean I do."

"Your parents were there."

"Where?"

"Sebastian's."

"So? So was I," Eric confessed.

"Señora Vanderdyke was there."

"So?"

"So we may have to buy it. She makes everyone around her pay."

"She hasn't made Cap'n Kirk pay yet."

"You sure about that?"

"Maybe she's still trying!" Eric said in triumph.

Samantha looked at Eric. She looked at him long and hard, as if she were interested in something behind his eyes. As she stared at him, he had to look away.

Then he turned to face her again.

She turned her body away from him. "*¿De verdad no sabes, Chico de Espárrago?** she asked as he took a bite from his burrito.

"What?"

"I don't trust your friends."

"Never do."

Dwight followed Samantha into the quiet custodial wing of the school. As if it were a prison with dangerous areas, he let her roam deeper away from the flow of the students until she knocked on Mexico Mo's office door.

No one answered and she looked up and down the hallways. She missed seeing Dwight somehow and entered the Mo's door.

Dwight turned. When he saw no one, he sprinted to the janitor's door and framed himself in the doorway behind her. He stepped in and the door closed.

Samantha turned, met the cold eyes of Dwight, scanned his dirty fiberglass cast and felt the cold patch on her heart expand.

---

*Do you really not know, Asparagus Boy?

The last time she had gotten upset by him, Leñador had been contacted. Now she felt the full understanding of the scare that faced her.

Dwight had two gifts: He was dangerous and disturbed.

"Where's Mexico Mo when you need him?" Samantha's voice was quiet. "I have to leave him a message."

Dwight's eyes danced on her body. "I'm thinking about leaving you a message."

"Really?" she asked. *"¿Después de tu último mensaje*\* I didn't think your last message worked out for you?" She allowed her eyes to sweep the room. "This is the only dirty place in the school."

"Maybe he's like me. Maybe he likes it dirty!" Dwight took a cigarette from his pocket and waved it towards the room. "He's an old man," a laugh slid through his lips. "What do you care? You giving Mo a hair cut job?" He lit the smoke.

Samantha watched his cigarette hang on his lower lip as if it were stitched in place.

He stared along her, savoring the taste. He was in no rush. He knew where he was and what he wanted.

She took a step away from the door and felt the cold cement wall against her back.

"What's he to you? He packing you for pesos?"

"Mexico Mo is a friend."

"What?"

"A friend. *¡Él ha usado tu odio para destruir tu pueblo!¡Pero si me tocas él te dará una paliza!*" "Hey!" Dwight snapped his fingers. "Wrong country, Parle English or nut'n around here!"

She gave him a striking look. "He's the only blood father I have, thanks to this town. You and your cowards hated my

---

\**After your last message?*
\*\**He used your hate to destroy your town! But if you touch me  he will break you bad!*

father. Killed a Bendolly, you did! So what if I only have Mo. He's Mexican! Passion. A Grandfather! *¡Y usted debe considerar el poder de su amor con gravedad!*\*

Something dinged inside Dwight's head and he heard. His mother had been barking and muttering the name Bendolly every time she was able to scalp foodstamps for tequilla. He searched back into the deep caverns of his mind but found nothing. But it stopped him nevertheless.

Samantha watched him and she knew that he had heard her.

Dwight dragged deep, held the smoke in his lungs then blew it out through his nose. His eyes went empty. "I know what you're thinking!" He nodded to her.

*¿Que usted necesita ayuda psicológica verdadera y profesional?*\*\*

He held up his hand and pinched the air. "Dora, Dora, Dora! I want to explore you!" He walked toward her but stopped at arms length and stared.

Her back was near the wall and she was a fine looking figure of a girl. Her hair was sprawled over and in front of her shoulders in a mess of curls and danced over the front of her blouse.

He reached out with his good arm and tugged a little on a renegade strand of hair.

She closed her eyes, hating his closeness.

"If you scream I'll club your teeth out," he said.

She went against the wall except for the hollow of her back.

Dwight let go of her hair and stepped back fast. Too fast.

She opened her hands to the flat of the wall, ready to push herself off it. Something was wrong with him now.

---

\**And you should mortally consider the power of his love!*
\**That you need serious, professional, psychological help?*

"You're a Bendolly who?" he asked and stepped farther back. He looked at the closed door in fear. He was going to say something, but didn't. The name took the blood from his face as if it were sucked out by a straw. He lunged out the door and she heard him running away.

The sailboat rested on a lone mooring on the north shore of Morguetown Lake. Virgin Vanderdyke forest crowded the lake for a mile in each direction. Samantha and Eric left the two-track trail for a well-worn path inside the shelter of the forest. They walked along the water for a good bit before they came to a small boat. They boarded and shoved off the dingy and she took up the oars.

He looked at her dark hands coming out from under a yellow sailing coat. "You sure it's okay with Mo? I mean, it's a nice sailboat."

"He's worried about the shallow channel, but beyond that it is just open sailing."

Eric pulled the strings on his gray MORGUETOWN P.E. hoody. "It'll be cold on the lake."

"Good. No crowds. How's your head?"

"Itchy." Eric spoke over the sound of creaking oarlocks. He tried not to shiver in the stern.

"¿Estás bien? You good?"

"Dunno if I can much help. Sailing's confusing."

"You'll be fine. It's sand everywhere. Even if we crash we can't hurt anything."

"Well, I about froze last time."

She stroked the dingy to the sailboat as if she had eyes on the backside of her skull. "The wind has changed. Warmer water."

"How do you do that?"

"What?"

"Drive the boat without looking ahead?"

"Drive the boat? Nice *náutica!*"*

He found himself at the back of the sailboat and read the name, *EASTERN SKY*, across the transom. He reached from the dingy to the stern ladder and she shifted her weight. He saw how she leveraged the dingy's aft gunnel under the ladder for stability. Then he took hold of the ladder and heaved himself up with his strong arm. On deck, he looked down at her in the small boat.

She smiled up to him. "Relax, Eric, I'm just taking you sailing."Then she brought the dingy to the bow, released one of two mooring lines and tied it to the dingy. She stood, balanced herself in the small boat, then lifted a leg to the sailboat's gunnel. She took a hard grip on the bow pulpit and chinned herself aboard.

She smiled, undressed the mainsail cover and freed the halyard from a slide on the toe rail. She took the line from the rail, swung it around the spreaders and attached it to the top of the mainsail.

Eric followed her to midship.

She handed him the halyard line coming off a mast winch. "Tail this halyard," she said and she cranked the sail into the sky.

He kept the line tight. "What's a halyard?"

"The line that hoists the sail."

"Why don't you just call it a rope? What's hoist mean?"

"*Tonto,*"** she smiled. With the vessel moored into the wind, the sail rode the runners to the top of the mast without stress and she cleated and coiled the halyard line.

Then they walked to the cockpit and she kicked the main-

---

*seamanship

**Idiot

sheet out of the teeth to keep the boat from sailing. "Watch out for the boom," she smacked the long aluminum spar that held the bottom of the mainsail. It rose and fell in the wind as the sail lapped in the breeze.

"Why's it called that?"

"*Un estampido de velero!*"** She said, signaling that it was explosive.

"What?"

"Be careful here," she ducked under the boom and pushed back the companionway hatch and led him inside. The interior hardwood was bright and he could stand tall. The many portholes let in the light and the skylights were very bright.

"Cool!" he said. "Deeper than I thought."

She opened a hanging locker and pulled out a thick wool sweater for herself and gave him the same yellow windbreaker he had used after his swim. "This one fits." Then she went to the V-berth and pushed a headsail up through the hatch out onto the bow.

He followed her up onto the deck and watched her hank the sail to the forestay. Staring at her white shorts and dark legs, he concluded that she was very touchable. He watched her feeding the heads'l sheets though the amidship blocks, loop the ends around the big cockpit winches and then she pointed at a winch as she whizzed it with the sheet.

"Don't get your fingers sucked under the sheet lines with these."

"What's a sheet?" he asked, admiring how much stuff she knew.

"The line around the metal cookie jar shaped things." She tapped the winch and it gave off a metallic hum.

He nodded. "Why's it called a sheet?"

"It controls a sail. That big white thing that we fly on the

***A sailboat explosion!*

mast is a sail." She walked him up to the foredeck. "Ready to go sailing?"

He nodded. "I know what a sail is."

She smiled and her whole face was just two big eyes and white teeth. "Lift that line from the bow cleat and set us free!" She said.

"You mean take the rope off that pointy metal thing?"

"You got it." She left him there, listening for the thick mooring line to splash in the water by the dingy, as she walked back to the helm.

The vessel drifted south as she hard ruddered to port and brought the port bow under the wind. She sheeted the main and the big sail tightened and caught the soft north wind and the boat dipped five degrees to starboard and slid off to the east away from the main channel.

Eric dropped to all fours on the deck and catwalked back to the cockpit as they glided over some shallows.

"How come we're not getting stuck? I thought sailboats were deep."

"Mexico Mo had some of the keel clipped on this one," she said from the helm. "Thats' why it's a little *achispado tipsy*," she flopped her hand around. "It goes pretty shallow, but it heels quicker."

He came to the wheel and she slid in behind him at helm. He pulled his hands from his pockets and put them on the wheel.

Pulling some leather gloves with no fingertips out from under a teak hatch, she slid them onto her hands as they ghosted between dead factories towards Sebastian's. Soon they were in the deeper water where the river current cleared out the swamp silt and carried into Lake Michigan.

"Eric, you're sailing!" She left him at the helm, stepped to the mast and raised the headsail with a dozen good pulls. It filled the sky and she looped the halyard on a mast winch and tightened the sail to the top. Then she tied it off and coiled the halyard. Eluding the whipping sheets, she came back to Eric and stood behind him again. *"¿Te va bien?"**

"I think so," he said, nervous about agreeing to what he didn't understand.

She tightened the genoa sheet with the starboard winch, which tamed the luffing headsail. The boat heeled another ten degrees, increased speed and bore down on Sebastian's. The place was a small patch of yellow-green grass between a steaming paper mill and the empty coffin factory. Water gurgled along the hull and she swung the wheel counterclockwise, spinning the sailboat north and into the wind.

The sails luffed again, then the genoa backwinded. "This is a tack," she said, popping off the tension from the starboard winch and letting the genoa sheet release to sweep the foredeck, flounder against the mast and whip the port stays. Then she used the port winch to grind tight the headsail, powering Eastern Sky to re-track and jump with speed. The mainsail tacked itself and the sailboat dove for the channel on a starboard tack, leaving a large swirl off the transom between them and Morguetown.

"So a tack is a turn?" Eric asked.

*"Buena navegación, Eric!"***

"This is so cool!" But then he looked ahead at the breakwater narrows and frowned at Coffin Light rising before them. He turned to Samantha and liked how the wind blew her hair over and exposed her windward ear, upper jaw and the right side of her neck.

"We have to stay on the north side of the channel," she said. "Turn up."

---

*You doing okay?*
*Nice navigation, Eric!*

"Because of Coffin Light?"

"What? No. Always sail high on the wind in tight spots as well as some TSS stuff," she took the helm from him as they entered the long parallel piers. "Look, the gringos catch fish early today."

"Mexican fishermen are gringos?"

"Close enough."

He waved to the dark haired dandies, fishing from the north pier which was landlocked because of the big farm. Eric grunted at their bamboo jigging cane poles, but lifted a hand a few more times nevertheless. He looked at the girl sailing and said nothing.

A few of the old men waved back. But most just stared at him.

She kept her eyes straight ahead.

"Is this your first time sailing Mexico Mo's boat alone?"

"I'm not alone."

"I don't think I count."

"You ready to steer?"

"No. We'd crash for sure," he spoke over the freshening breeze as he looked at another group of Mexicans who were waving at them. They sailed by. "Do you know all of them?" he asked.

"Some." She then nodded to the south break wall where some Morguetown men sat with their butt-cheeks drooping over the sides of their five gallon fishing buckets. She nodded to the south and smiled. "It's like were sailing out of the Rio Grande."

Eric nodded to some south townies as he sailed on by then he stared on ahead.

One of the Morgue-men was bareback and lassoed his wife beater to the girl as the others laughed.

Samantha turned away.

To the starboard, fishing from the pierhead, were the oldest of the migrant workers, who seemed to have seniority to fish the better spots. None waved back. They were as still as the lighthouse across from them and as weathered as the rocks.

Coffin Light came abeam to port. Another trash can was by it. Toppled over, garbage had been dumped out along the base of the lighthouse.

Eric looked at the huge rust stains on Coffin Light. The brown streaks were coming out from under the dark red paint. Only the coffin lid seemed to be in good shape. He looked north and saw a much different marker on the pier head. It was painted a sharp, smart green. "Why the different colors?"

"Red. Right. Return," she said.

He looked to the open water, wondering what that meant.

# LOG ENTRY 9

9:20 pm—abeam Manistee Lighthouse
East winds to 18 knots.
Waves 0-1. Northbound at 8-9 knots

1961, the year after Mighty Mike lost his father, was a year of unrest. But Mighty Mike always found peace in how we stayed to ourselves on the west line. He snuggled more housing into the worthless sand dunes and we survived on beans, beef and corn tortillas, and whatever other fixin's that Señora let us glean off the land or find in the Trade Store.

"You're Dawn to Darkers, Kapin Kirk! And your hordes are saving the day! Wet Back Heart Attacks! We've the best farm of Bay View Valley! And you don't even tingle in Tequila Town on pay-day!" Mighty Mike bragged of us, complimenting the policy we set up during the war years that kept our people to our people.

We worked the ranch and stayed on the ranch.

Truth be told, the Vanderdyke's town, Bay View Valley, always seemed to uninvite us immigrants. On occasion we had to go to town. And doing so always brought trouble. Trouble for us meant trouble for Mighty Mike, so we put an end to going into Bay View Valley for the most part. Those with the habit of leaving the farm and finding mischief found themselves booted from the ranch.

And back then the town had its own problems. Martin Luther King had held a rally down in Benton Harbor and the blacks were all riled.

But we didn't cause trouble for the town or Mighty Mike.

In return, he gave us more area. We sang our songs, cleaned and cooked our food, raised our children and buried our dead.

Us and our shanties. Like we cared. We had food, water and medicine for the taking. We stayed alive. Kept our families under strong roofs and even saved some money to send back home!

r. Henderson nodded to his son, grunted at the two teenagers with him and closed his phone. "Hungry?" He pushed a half eaten plate of chips and cheese toward the boys. They couldn't see anything beneath the layers of diced jalapeño peppers.

"Nice!" Bran said, scooping some. "Double Enders!"

"What do you think, Dad?" John asked. "It's Dwight's idea sort of. Because of his inspiration."

"She's a Bendolly, huh, Dwight? Well, the name doesn't ring a bell. But keep it mum and I'll ask around."

"So you think it's a good idea?" Little John asked.

"Of course. It's good to hassle the passel once in a while," he said. "But hit the waves hard to get the scum off the water line." He nodded to his Bayliner resting in the water beyond Sebastian's patch of crab grass, then he turned to the boy he didn't know. "You're the one who was here the other night? With Bull and his girl?" Henderson nodded to Bran.

"Yes."

"What's your name?"

"Bran."

"Good. I guess. I mean good." He turned to Dwight and gave an approving look at the hair cut down to his scalp, then he eyed the cast on his arm. "It true the Peanut M-n-M's candied your arm?"

Dwight nodded.

"How'd your mom take it?"

"She knows I'll geet 'em."

"Maybe now's your chance. Flush 'em out," he turned and nodded to his son. "Run the gas almost to empty. I don't want old gas in her over the winter. It fouls the carbs. And don't throttle her up in the shallows. I just got the trims fixed from last time."

"Sure," John said as he put on his go-fast sunglasses with

lenses slightly bigger than his eyeballs. He led his friends out the club doors to the docks on Morguetown Lake.

The sailboat rolled, dipped and diced along the gentle waves in a steady north breeze. Its bow dropped a foot or so into each valley and surf bubbled along its waterline. They sailed west into a clouded horizon. The sun had been blotted and Samantha steered towards a patch of bright, hoping to see color break out from beyond the gray.

A few miles into Lake Michigan, Samantha and Eric were glancing back east toward the harbor as it sunk into the water.

"How fast are we going?" Eric asked.

"Five knots or so."

"What's a knot?"

"It's complicated."

"How'd you learn to sail?"

"I'm still learning."

He shook his head. "Where are you from?"

She looked at him and thought about saying Vanderdyke's but hesitated. "Mexico."

"And your mom?"

"What of her?"

"Was she the woman at Sebastian's?"

"Yes."

"But she's…"

"I know. But my father was Mexican."

"Where's he?"

"I don't want to talk about him."

"So your mom and dad used to live around here?"

"Yes. But I've been away for most of my life."

"Why'd you leave?"

"Leave what? Bay View Valley? Morguetown? It's just a spot

of mud in a patch of dirt, Eric. It's not much of a *comunidad.*"*

"I know. But to go below the border?" he saw her hand tighten on the wheel. "I mean it's like where our factories go when they're on the cheap. It's not where people go."

"It's just a sail, Eric. We're just going sailing. Why do you care if my mother likes living one place over another? Why do you care if I do? Have you ever seen the *montañas de la Sierra Madre* after a dusting of snow? You ever visit your town's orphanage just to play with the *niños?*"

At this he took notes. He knew one more stupid question could land him overboard.

Her dark eyes grew bright as the western sky lit them, but they sparkled a chill from behind a sea of black hair that ran free in the wind.

"I just never met the people who had the courage to leave, that's all. Except you."

"Well, I never met any that had the courage to stay in a dying town that let a coffin factory rename its history. Except you, that is," and she smiled and the sun came out and turned the gray water to blue. Off their stern the light painted the trees of autumn and the sand dunes to fire. The sails went white and the chrome and teak sparkled. Diamonds appeared on the water as if a giant hand was rolled crystal dice across blue carpet.

He wished for sunglasses. As the sun stabbed his eyes, he turned to shore to let them rest. *How did she know Bay View Valley changed its name because of that stupid factory?*

"Hey," she said, snapping her fingers in front of his face. He turned.

"You sailing, Eric," she said.

He smiled back.

---

*community

The old man fishing the north pier wall held his cane pole and exhaled thick curls of white-blue smoke. The smoke lingered along his dark lips and sunken facial pores until the wind took it away. He pressed out the stub embers with calloused fingers and flicked it into the muddy channel.

Turning east he watched a lone boat with three boys plow through the narrows towards the big lake. Even his eyes, long accustomed to sun and weather, had to squint at the sparkles on Morguetown Lake until his gaze reached the south end of the lake. Nestled between his stink-smoking paper mill and his decommissioned coffin factory, he saw the docks of Sebastian's Yacht Club.

Two boats had been moored there, but one of them was now nearing. He had been watching the boat come his way with some concern.

He now looked at the powerboat that had crossed the harbor and assessed the three teenagers, each of whom had been extending their middle fingers towards him and the other Mexicans who were fishing the north pier.

Old Kapin Kirk then looked west and lowered his wrinkled, furry eyebrows because the sun had come. He welcomed the slight sting it made on his dark coat as he located the patch of white canvas of the sailboat on the horizon. Beyond the sailboat, he stared deep into the western sky.

Little John passed Coffin Light, finished saluting the Color Guard and goosed the Bayliner's throttles, letting the vessel squat its stern down for a deep gulp of good drink. The propeller grabbed and the boat shot on plane. Adjusting the trim tabs with his right hand, he lifted the stern until the craft bounced evenly as it took on the waves.

He carved at them for a few minutes until no people could

be seen on the breakwalls. He looked back at Coffin Light and when it was the size of a pencil lead at arms length, he throttled down lowering the boat off plane.

"Break out the hardware?" Dwight asked, nervous about giving a command near the captain.

Little John nodded.

Liter size CO2 canisters were screwed into paintball guns and hoppers were snapped into place. The hoppers were filled and they chucked the empty ball buckets overboard.

John scooped some special ammo from his pocket and rolled it into *his* hopper.

"Lock and load, ladies! We're doing a few fly-bys before we go weapons hot!" John yelled, as if he commanded a SEAL team.

"So we're like pirates?" Bran yelled over the wind and engine roar.

"Yea!" Dwight yelled back.

"Is this a felony?" Bran asked.

"Naw. Barely a misdemeanor! But there ain't no way Nelson will press charges!"

"Only a Mr. Meaner?" Bran asked, knowing his resume was lacking.

John stared forward from behind the wheel, facial skin rippling as he peeked his head above the wind screen. His teeth were dry because he had been smiling so long.

Little John aimed the Bayliner at the target until the last moment then he banked hard to the right and sprayed wake mist across the sailboat. As he sizzled by on an upwind track, his exhaust fogged across the sloop's deck. Back in open water, he rounded the powerboat hard to port and roared back at the sailboat going head to head.

❀

Eric swung his face back towards Samantha. "It's them!" he said like a relocated witness caught by the mafia.

"They're going to hit us, aren't they?" she asked.

"Morons," Eric said as the vessel charged close and braked hard, forcing its own surf to broach its stern. The Bayliner's inboard outboard propeller cavitated, searching for a bite of good water among the bubbles. More exhaust choked the sailboaters. Nothing could be heard as the engine screamed.

Eric and Samantha squinted in the smoke. The sound hurt their ears. They took hold of what was at hand.

When the Bayliner was stern to, John tilted up the engine shaft until its propeller whizzed in the air like a fan, then the captain sunk it into the water and sprayed hundreds pounds of wash into the sails, tearing the light air, genoa headsail from its deck clasp and sliding it up the forestay.

Soaked in prop wash, Eric saw into the enemy cockpit as three boys raised paintball guns and cut down on him and Samantha, firing at will. Hundreds of splats pounded the hull, decks and sails.

Dozens of balls stung Eric and Samantha as he yanked her from the exposed helm to shelter below the cockpit gunnels. He heard and felt the paintballs impacting her as his head smashed the floor and cracked open the glue over his scalp wound. Breathless, the sailors winced under the bullet-buzzing sky as paintballs slapped sail, fiberglass and aluminum.

"Let go!" she yelled to Eric in pain and rage. In a lull between volleys, she stood and stared at the attackers. It was one thing paintballing up a hull and sails. Quite another aiming at a person. She saw their barrels lower and she stared them down.

"Get down!" Eric hushed up at her as if they were in a graveyard at night fighting man-eating bats.

"Nice Bean Boat!" Bran yelled and Dwight lifted his gun above his head with his good arm in victory.

Samantha looked at her ripped headsail and the mainsail pummeled in paint. She saw her topsides and all the smears. Then she focused on Eric, cowering at her feet, blood oozing down his face and covering one eye. She reached down and took hold of his shirt and pulled him up until and stood him alongside her.

"Erilic the Derelic!" Dwight yelled above the drone of the Bayliner's engine.

Little John palmed the wheel and brought his idling boat abeam.

"Why you doing this?" Samantha yelled as her eyes opened larger.

Dwight's gun barrel rested on his shoulder, stock down and the dangerous end up.

Bran aimed his at his feet.

The boat finished its last turn and Little John's barrel went white with smoke as it rested along the windshield.

The open black eye of the barrel stared at its target.

Eric took the front of the stream along his chest but the paintball trail ran up and over his body as he staggered back and fell. His head was down by the cushion when he felt Samantha crash down beside him.

Her head cracked hard off the edge of the white cockpit cushion and held still.

Before him, her eyes dolled back to white as if drawn by lead weights and then he saw her nose. It lay crooked and bent distinct, a fleck of open, white cartilage changed color before him and blood started spewing forth.

Blood sprayed down her cheek and pooled red on the white cushion.

❈

The old man, fishing deep among the rocks on the open-water side of the north breakwall, watched his feet getting wet with surf spray.

The old Mexican, with his back to pier rock, ignored the fish tugging his line. It had long since swallowed the hook. Along the left side of his head ran a lone wire into an ear piece. From inside his jacket, he adjusted the squelch on his VHF marine radio. He listened to static and he waited.

# LOG ENTRY 10

10:10 pm—abeam Portage Lighthouse
East winds to 17 knots.
Waves 0-1. NNE at 9 knots

By 1963 our neighbors were now getting landlocked by Mighty Mike's range and they didn't like us none at all. They were so unhappy about Mike's spread that they charged Señora Vanderdyke double the price of their properties when they sold them to her.

We had no neighbors to the west of us now and the Vanderdyke Land spread all the way to Lake Michigan. Those few decrepit cottages that were caving away on the dunes became the new base of Mexico North.

With control of our own area, trouble for the Vanderdykes all but went away. On the rare times one of us had to go into Bay View Valley, we never caused a stir because none of us lingered.

But then John F. Kennedy got himself assassinated by going against big business or something and fear got into the country. Trouble got worse in the east. The Far East. And we learned new names like Vietnam and Saigon.

I'm just a poor migrant dirt farmer so don't take this to market, but it seemed we went deeper into war to heal from losing JFK. As if that ain't the pig farmer calling the town a stinkpot!

Sometimes a good walk can clear the head. Sometimes a talk. But the three men did neither. Henderson, Nelson and Thompson got into Nelson's truck, and drove the one mile to the beach and parked. From their seats, each lifted his own pair of binoculars and scanned the horizon through the windshield.

"Got them! Due west." Henderson said.

Nelson and Thompson focused and saw two boats so close together they looked as one. Nelson turned his glasses north at the line of Mexicans fishing. "Pick Polers," he said. "Lots of them."

"Think they're biting?" Thompson asked. "Perch dinner would be good about now."

"He's there. He's in that Spanish sprinkle somewhere." Nelson opened the door. "Let's go see."

They crossed the sand-covered sidewalks onto the cracked pier and walked to Coffin Light.

"This sure has a bee in her bonnet," Henderson said.

"That's one lucky bee," Thompson said.

They stopped and looked down at a fisherman on his bucket. "Anything happening?" Nelson asked.

The man turned. "Nuttun."

"What about the Bambo Crew?" Nelson nodded to Mexico North.

"Nuttun either. It's Chimmi Chungo night for them too."

"Are there always this many?"

"Seems a little high."

The three walked on and stopped below Coffin Light.

"What's your take on this Bran kid?" Nelson asked Thompson.

"He's a kid. Besides taking the Browns to the Super Bowl, I don't think he cares about much else."

"He's not like your boy," Henderson said.

"Hey, if it wasn't for Eric, we wouldn't have known about Lazzair until last night!" Nelson said. "My boy's the only one who Paul Revere the whole thing! Granted, he did it with his wrong head, but he did it nevertheless. Because of us you had a week to prepare yourself. And she still drunk you good by the sounds of it."

"If ya gotta get drunk over a woman, might as well get drunk over Bendolly's woman," Henderson added.

Thompson looked across the way. "So what's he look like?"

"Dunno," Nelson said.

"Well you seen him last!" Henderson said.

"Ya, but that was six, maybe eight years ago."

"Then how does Texas know he's in the Mex?" Henderson nodded to the gringos. "When's the last time she seen him?"

They looked at each other.

"It's his granddaughter sailing with my kid," Nelson said. "He's over there. He's learned his lesson."

"You sure we're staying ahead?" Thompson asked.

Henderson turned with Thompson and faced Nelson.

Nelson nodded. "Staying ahead is the game of the dame. Captain Kirk will be watching the boats. He knows better than to take his eyes off the boats. Maybe now we'll settle it."

Henderson nodded to the west. "She's luffing now. Our pirates are doing their painting!"

Eric reached out and took Samantha's cheeks, soaking his fingers and palms in her blood. He saw the white of the bone of her nose against her dark skin.

As blood poured into her eyes, they blinked back alive. She held still. "Eric!" she called out, gurgling blood out of her throat.

"Stay down!" he hissed as he held her.

"*¡Consigue el fusil! ¡Usa el fusil!*\* Scare 'em! Eric scare 'em away!" Blood glazed her white teeth to red as she spoke out.

Eric stared and held her. She was alive! Ducking as paintballs stung and shattered against the boom above him, he heard the sail above dance wild as if it too were reeling in pain.

The tinkle of glass was heard and what looked to be pieces of glass spun over the deck like drops of water in hot grease.

"*¡Abajo la mesa! ¡Úsalo!*"\*\*

"What?" he asked in a scared, impossible tone.

"Under the table! You scare 'em away!" she stammered and pointed down the companionway hatch as a blood drool hung from her chin like a long, red leech.

Eric reared to all fours, then dove for the cabin door as something stung the back of his thigh with incredible force. The impact steamed him forward and he tumbled headlong down the steps and found himself on the floor on his back. He looked at the square of light above the steps and saw her face looking down at him. He saw blood coming off her chin.

She was pointing at the table, stabbing the air with her finger. "*¡Consigue tu rifle! ¡Toma tu rifle!*"\*\*\* She yelled above the violence of the sails above her, which boomed and luffed, tortured by the wind and wave.

His head was a ringing bell as he tried to understand her bleeding lips. All went slow. All went sideways. His leg hurt bad.

He looked under the table. The weapon was strapped to its underbelly with Velcro. Reaching, he took hold and ripped it loose and rose to his knees. Palming the pistol grip of the heavy-barreled rifle, his left hand, greased in her blood,

---

\**Get the rifle! Use the rifle!*
\*\**Under the table! Use it!*
\*\*\**Get your rifle! Take it!*

reached up to the yellow, aged wooden stock. The long banana clip brushed against his left forearm. The old Russian rifle felt heavy, awkward and lethal.

"¡Ayúdame por el amor de Dios! Ericko!"* She was hiding again, driven down by pain.

Hearing her scream, the drone of the engine through the hull and the taunts of Little John, Dwight and Bran changed something inside Eric. Something that would never be changed back. He stood up and looked up the companion-way ladder. He took hold of the round pin on the right side of the barrel and pulled it back toward the pistol grip. A long, evil looking brass bullet was visible for a moment, then he released the slide, letting the force of the recoil shift the bullet into the firing chamber.

Then Samantha dove down the stairs and landed in a pile at his feet. She withered like a burning snake and she was screaming. *¡Ellos me dispararon, Eric! ¡Gravamente me dolieron!*** She was holding her back.

He stared at her sprawl for a moment.

No girl is supposed to lay in her own blood.

He put a foot on the step and lifted his body out into the light.

Samantha dove and pulled off the VHF radio mic and depressed the button with her thumb. The white radio mic slipped in her hand and went red. "*¡Servicio de Guardacostas de los Estados Unidos!*"***

Unexploded paintballs and a few marbles pounded into the open companion way in continuous roar, dislodging pictures and items from the bulkheads. Then wood splintered and the porthole shattered, sending glass into Eric's face. He

---

*Help me, for the love of God! Ericko!*
**They shot me, Eric! They hurt me bad!*
***United States Coast Guard Service*

whipped a frightened stare down to Samantha. "Say U.S. Coast Guard! We don't speak Tabasco Joe!"

"U.S. Coastguard! U.S. Coastguard! Sailboat *Eastern Sky* needs your help! Come in *Guardacostas!*" In a panic she repeated the message then the squelch chirped.

Eric took another step and turned back to the opening and heard the radio.

"This is the U.S. Coast Guard, Muskegon Harbor Branch can you confirm?"

"Help! They're shooting at us! They're firing at us!"

"U.S. Coastguard Muskegon Harbor Branch, Say again! Are you 'on fire' or are you 'under fire'?" The power of government transmission boomed.

"Sailboat, *Eastern Sky*, is. . . Eric!" Samantha's screamed and looked up the companionway opening, dazed.

But he was gone.

"Eric! Eric *ven acá!*"* She yelled a nasally pitch. Her nose bent off to one side. Red drops beaded on and ran down her yellow jacket.

*Eastern Sky* lurched in the wakes of the attackers and its sails slammed about, twisted and knotted by the wind.

Samantha screamed in pain. "Sailboat *Eastern Sky* is being shot at off Coffin Light! *Los hombres malos nos están disparando!*"** Another starboard porthole shattered and she screamed horror into the mic as glass clinked across the navigation table.

"U.S. Coastguard, Muskegon Harbor Branch confirm, *Eastern Sky* are you ON fire or TAKING fire?"

"Help! *Eastern Sky* is *bajo ataque! Bajo ataque!*"*** We are under attack! Mayday! Send help!" Samantha was still

---

*come here!
**The bad guys are shooting us
***under attack

screaming and shaking, but the bullets slowed and started getting selective, pinning her inside. Huddled down by the Nav Station, she couldn't stop her bleeding and squeezed the VHF radio, blood spraying off her upper lip as she huddled next to the Nav Station.

Dozens of voices came across the radio channel 16.

More blood sparkled on her sweater and the floor was slippery with it.

Eric looked down to her one last time from where he huddled in the cockpit. He gripped the assault rifle with both of his bloodied hands and lifted himself to his knees.

The three men of Coffin Light ignored the confusion of the sailboat at sea and focused their lenses on the Rio Rats canepoling for carp.

"I got nothing," Henderson said. He turned back toward the cover of Coffin Light and looked for his boat.

"Whatta ya got?" Nelson asked Thompson.

"Nothing. Not even Mexico Mo and it's his boat!"

"We're not after a janitor. We want Chris Gringo. The Candy Man!"

"All I got is a line of Border Babel with one of them taking a piss off the north end."

"Well they're dancing now," Henderson said, looking west.

"Just find the Beef Thief," Nelson said and took out his camera and snapped on a heavy, long lens. "I'm going to shoot every one of them. They're all as old as time."

"I'm empty!" Bran yelled over the drone of the motor.

"Jet wash her down and let's bolt!" Dwight yelled.

Little John nodded to this.

Good advice. Short. Easy to remember.

John backed the Bayliner's stern toward the middle of the sailboat and again raised the prop up until it sizzled the water's surface. Guiding the throttle forward, he unleashed a thunderous, tornadic vortex spinout at the sailboat.

They all watched the prop.

Eric peeked up and lifted the heavy weapon and squeezed the trigger.

Nothing.

He looked near the finger guard and flipped the long safety switch down and re-aimed. Now, tight on the stock, his left hand clenched the barrel grip and froze the weapon. As fast as he could, he fingered the trigger and thudded 7.62 mm rounds into the engine cover of the prop-spraying Bayliner. In seconds he rampaged a dozen shots. As the stern cover chipped apart, sparks in the breeched engine room ignited fire.

The three powerboaters thought they heard the engine backfire, but then pieces of teak and fiberglass began to shear off and levitate around the stern like bees driven from a hive. They lifted their eyes to the sailboat and saw continual fire-flame coming from the disturbing black barrel of an assault rifle.

As the blasts concussioned off the weapon's discharge, the air around the paintballers went electric and everything from their teeth fillings to ear hair cried danger and shock.

Little John awoke first and, like the captain he was, goosed the boat full throttle ahead but he forgot to lower the prop drive back into the water. The propeller chinked along the hull of the sailboat, dulling the soft aluminum prop on the thick fiberglass.

Bran farted without even trying. "That's not a paintball gun!" He yelled and pointed. "Or Airsoft™ either!"

Captain John corrected the collision, submerged the lower

unit and jammed throttles forward again. He jumped the Bayliner a boat length away from the sailboat.

The move pressed more gas and fume into the compromised engine compartment and the area blew apart, detonating blast fire and shrapnel into Dwight, blowing him clean through the windshield and up onto the small bow.

The explosion catapulted John into the shoebox-sized forward hold under the steering console. His shoulder separated at the socket as it punched through a bulkhead.

Bran got in a little jump, enough to clear the side of the boat. If he had been wearing jeans or any other cotton pants (and especially underwear) he might have been injury free.

But the flash of orange, fire air nipped him, superheated his fleece pants, and fused the molten fabric into the back of his legs, buttocks and whatever else it could find hanging. Heat searing acrylic burned into his skin. It took a few moments for the cold water of Lake Michigan to douse the inferno of his pants, which had branded a good sizzle on his bells, scrotum and sphincter.

The explosion swung the attacking craft's bow toward the sailboat. Fire spread from the aft of the Bayliner to it's midship.

Dwight dove off the wounded vessel and onto the bow of the sailboat.

Little John, torched by his proximity to the chemical fire, dove out of the dead end storage locker, dragging his arm, and fell into Lake Michigan like a punch drunk sailor.

Dwight stood on the sailboat bow and looked at Eric in the stern.

Eric raised the weapon, bringing the barrel online with the stowaway.

Samantha had come topside like a flooded out mole. With her head out the companion way hatch, she saw the way Eric was looking down the barrel at Dwight. "Eric! No!" She yelled out, then ducked below and away.

Eric looked at her and the motion tightened his finger and depressed a cartridge. Firing the weapon without being ready, it knocked him a step back.

Dwight didn't feel a thing.

The round punched through the aluminum mast, waffling the lead as it did so and slowing the projectile to a thousand feet per second. The right side of Dwight's head went numb as his ear disintegrated into red vapor. His good hand clasped the gash, his broken arm lifted its bent cast above his head in surrender to make sure no one doubted. Then he collapsed.

Eric turned the weapon back to the water and emptied the remainder of the clip into the side of the boat at the stern, delaminating the waterline area, splintering the hulls integrity.

Water flooded into the Bayliner.

Orange flame and black smoke billowed out.

Eric didn't want to cripple the boat. He wanted to sink it. He dragged on the trigger until the weapon clicked empty.

Samantha came back up and stood next to him, still holding a red cloth to her face and a hand over her ear.

Dwight was on the deck screaming, feeling for his ear and looking around for it.

"Get off my boat!" Samantha yelled forward.

Dwight lifted both arms above his head. Ear blood glowed his hand like red neon.

Eric turned the smoking gun barrel back to Dwight, who dove overboard.

Samantha looked at Eric and they nodded to each other. They both looked at the rifle, understanding for the first time the universal language of an assault weapon.

# LOG ENTRY 11

12:30 midnight—abeam Frankfort Lighthouse
East winds to 17 knots.
Waves 0-1. NNE at 9 knots

Maybe J.F.K. getting shot had hurt the country more than most thought. I know it hurt Señora Vanderdyke.

She didn't speak much about it for a year or two. Eventually she seemed to get her smile back.

Maybe it was the world we live in, but she and many others seemed to learn it wasn't such a great world.

We learned it was a world of killers. Of violence. A world of death.

The leaders who came after J.F.K. seemed convinced of this. They started looking for enemies until they found some hiding in faraway places like Asia.

Thompson heard the echo of rifle shots and turned his binocs to the open water. Henderson stared west too, the skin over his knuckles ready to give birth to bone. *If my stupid kid...*

"Hey, Boss," Thompson called to Nelson.

Nelson kept photographing Mexico North. "We gotta find him over here, boys." He spoke cold fact. "If she's kin, he'll be there!"

"I think you better look to sea," Henderson said.

As Nelson turned to the west all three took a step forward at the same time.

The crew of *Eastern Sky* ignored their discombobulated boat and left the sail floundering in the waves and wind. Instead, they watched the powerboat's bow point upward and belch black smoke. Samantha was forced to take hold of the mainsail sheet to still the raging boom. She now stood, but movement in the stern caught her eye.

Little John had boarded.

He stood like a rat. One arm hung limp, its sunken shoulder even with his sternum as if he had come from the depths.

"Eric!" Samantha yelled.

"Erilic the Derelict," Little John said and took a step forward and placed an orange container between his legs and unscrewed it with his good hand. From the emergency flare kit, he pulled out a 12 gauge flare gun, flipped it open and stuffed it under his arm pit that hung lower than normal.

Little John smiled. "You're empty!" he said and pulled out a thick red shotgun shell from the case and held it up for them to inspect.

Samantha watched the main sheet blocks on the deck groan in pressure as she held the mainsail against the wind.

*Eastern Sky* started to turn strait downwind as it obeyed physics and she released her grip. The boom swung; the metal spar shot at John.

John ducked.

The boom swung past him and rattled, loose in the wind as it pointed at the sinking Bayliner downwind.

"This ain't the cartoons, Weedy Gonzales!" Little John smiled. Despite the injury, cold and shock, John thumbed the 12 gauge cartridge into the firing chamber of the flare gun and flipped the barrel closed with one hand.

Off the starboard, a lone hiss of what looked like steam, bubbled at the surface, then it flashed blue with flame. Coming from a submerged propane tank that had broken a seal, the fire hissed underwater, igniting the solid string of gas bubbles like a fuse. A few feet down, the propane tank exploded with one-third the heat of an atomic bomb and turned a good volume of water into vapor and steam. Heat energy smashed up and into the mainsail, ripping the boom back across the cockpit like a like blunt scythe.

The sail caught the hot gust and transferred the energy into a full jibe.

Sailors call the spar a boom for a reason.

The reef winch made first contact.

The hardest part of Little John's skull, his forehead, took the brunt. His good arm had come up on impulse to block the spar but collapsed under the pressure. The hand, still holding the gun, sandwiched itself between the boom and the skull, saving his life in splintering sacrifice and firing the metallic fueled shell off into the sky.

The boom never slowed as it airborned the pirate into a complete flip.

John landed on a stainless steel lifeline stanchion. The lifeline popped off a rivet, allowing the steel post to impale him through the right side of his lower back. The metal post punched out of his stomach. A massive blood-slick pooled down the port side deck, then swirled down the port scupper and painted the side of the hull.

Screeching, John tried with both damaged hands to take hold of the stanchion coming out of his stomach, his voice wailing death over the open water.

Dwight and Bran then franticked away from the ladder of *Eastern Sky*. Unignited fuel and oil glazed their faces and hair as they treaded water.

Little John tilted his head up off the deck and looked at his wound. He screamed and screamed.

Eric went to Samantha, took her blood-soaked towel and put it to her nose. He turned her away from Little John. The SKS in his hands was still smoking as it pointed down to the cockpit grates. He dropped it.

Pieces of burning sail were falling off and sizzling into the water downwind. Vapor formed back into water and ran down the mainsail and dripped off the boom onto Eric and Samantha.

He fingered the wet hair off her face. "You alright?" Eric asked.

Little John screamed.

She nodded, knowing she hadn't convinced him. "Sheet the main," she pointed.

Eric pulled a line and in a few moments the boat stabilized and slid away from the fire on the water.

From the helm, she looked ahead and saw the foredeck ablaze in Dwight's blood.

Eric looked at Little John but could only blink.

Little John screamed, driving his voice out to sea because his head, which had exhausted his neck strength, now hung upside down over the boat.

Samantha dropped her towel over her shoulder, looked to the foredeck and saw the jibsail busted at the luff. Above her the mainsail held shape and they were making way, but it was melting and the holes were burning wider.

The flames on the water were now behind them. Black smoke poured forth like in a Chinese smokestack.

The sailors watched the bow of the Bayliner rise vertical, exhale the last of its vapor in a hissy-fit, and sink.

Swimming away from the fire, Dwight and Bran floundered in the debris field, searching for something to float on.

Despite their tattered, smoldering sails, water gurgled alongside *Eastern Sky*.

Samantha rose and faced the wind. When she saw the bloodbath on the bow she slumped back down behind the wheel. She handed Eric a dock line. "Can you go forward, pull down the sail and tie off the bottom of it to something?"

Little John screamed.

Eric found muscle again in his legs and did so.

She watched him slip and slide in Dwight's blood.

A hundred yards later, they had enough speed and she swung the wheel, turning the sailboat into the wind and tacked the boat back toward the crime scene.

Little John screamed.

Eric stared at his bloody foot prints on the deck and saw that they followed him back to the teak cockpit grate by the rifle.

She snapped her fingers in front of his eyes and pointed.

Eric uncleated the high line from the port winch and he retightened the headsail on the starboard.

She focused ahead, bearing down on the debris field and the two floaters. The black smoke in the sky signaled a disaster for the Coast Guard and landlubbers.

Flashing rescue lights grew bright as a white boat with an

orange stripe sprayed white water as it powered in from the south.

Eric heard the voices on the radio blasting for the first time. But he didn't hear the information.

John screamed.

"Check him out," Samantha pointed to John.

"How?"

She shrugged, looking at the impaled teenager hanging over the boat, dripping blood. "Maybe push his feet back and get his head aboard."

"What?"

"Spin him a little and get his head on the deck."

Sending John's right leg overboard, Eric spun the torso around the stanchion, took hold of the mass of bloody scalp and lifted the heavy head onto the deck.

Little John screamed and reached his good arm to clamp his hand on Eric's shirt. But John's fingers felt like hot dogs. He cursed and screamed.

Eric didn't envy him. Didn't envy him none at all. He walked back to Samantha. "What about them? Let them drown?" he pointed forward.

Her eyes flared at him above her bent nose. Blood had darkened her face and was now drying across the front of her coat. Much of her hair was stuck in the coagulate below her nose and chin. Skin around her eyes had turned black with bruising.

Little John screamed.

The radio squawked profusely from below.

Ash of burnt mainsail spun off downwind.

"What?" Eric asked.

She shook her head. "Drag 'em," she ordered and pulled another dock line from the slide in the cockpit backrest. She looped a bowline. "Loop this end back there on that," she pointed to the stern cleat. "Throw this end to them. Tie a knot at the end first." She gave him a look that he thought was probably like the one Mo had given her a few days ago when they threw him a line.

Eric obeyed as she sailed into the debris field, bouncing smoldering pieces along the hull.

John screamed.

Eric wondered how John's shoulder had gotten sunk next to his ribcage. He threw the rope to Bran and Dwight and watched them grab hold.

The hair on the back of Bran's head was long gone and the scalp was peeled and blackened by oil, grime and burn.

With no ear and a heavy cast, Dwight's eyes flared like a weighted down, sinking cat.

"What about him?" Eric stood next to Samantha as she tightened the headsail sheet to get more speed. He nodded back to Little John.

"Stand clear," she pointed up. "The sail and topping lift are failing. The boom will drop when they burn."

Eric stood upwind and watched Little John get somersaulted all over again in his mind. He saw the many different colors of paint on the boom from the bullets.

"But what about him?"

"Never been on a farm?"

He shook his head.

"He's been *empalado*."

"What?"

"Impaled."

"I know that!"

"So if you lift him off, he'll bleed out and die."

Eric wanted to say "so" or "good riddance" or "ain't that the point." He wanted to say it so bad he wished he knew a language she didn't so he could utter it. He pouted a glance at her but was afraid of her look. He saw that her cheek was bruised black and her lower lip had swollen where it had filled with blood.

And then the forty-one foot Coast Guard Cutter with its bright white hull with its orange stripe circled *Eastern Sky* at full speed at a hundred yards out. Soldiers with stainless steel shotguns lined the deck. Another with an orange life vest over thick black Kevlar, manned a 50-caliber machine gun mounted to the foredeck chain plates.

Eric realized that the armed vessel was the last thing some people ever saw.

It was a ship of death.

# LOG ENTRY 12

1:10 am
—approaching Frankfort Point Lighthouse
East winds to 17 knots.
Waves 0–1. NNE at 9 knots

In 1964, a few years after power had been transferred to Mighty Mike and electric had been strung out to Mexico North, Señora Vanderdyke had us a school built alongside our church. She also had plans for heating the long line of cabins with wood stoves.

Mighty Mike worked the produce, while his mother gave focus to the physical and mental health of his work force. He was now running the largest farm in West Michigan.

I remember the first time she came into the school to teach the niños. Back then our chicos y chicas were her only grandchildren.

She divided the children in three groups of twenty and taught each class for una hora a day. When word got out that she taught ingles, two evening classes were added for nosotros los tontos. us, the stupid ones

I once stopped by and saw her with seven children on her knees and others scampering about. I didn't know how to say it then, but it seemed that they were teaching her.

Señora Vanderdyke looked at me with an expression of joy and purpose. "Capin Kike?" her face then frowned. "Did you know my daughter says children are not for her?"

"These niños bother you?" I asked.

"If she doesn't want life, what else is there?"

"How is she doing?" I asked, remembering the Texas Tex girl who wanted to show me what was under her skirt just last year.

"Trash. She runs with trash with no father to rein her in."

"'¡La bella y las bestias!' is what we say in Mexico."

"Beauty and the beasts, huh? Well if half of what I hear is true, it's more like Beauty and her Breasts!"

"Señora, that's why I'm hoping for a boy," I say, and this explodes Señora Vanderdyke.

"Your wife is?"

"Yes!" I say with a blush, for my wife is young. She is much younger than I.

"Captain Kirk, this is wonderful news!"

I smile.

**S**ebastian turned up the VHF radio and watched the faces of Stompson, Henderson and Nelson. The four were alone at the bar with their imaginations. They didn't have to imagine too much; voices of pain and violence filled in the gaps.

Thompson seemed the best to weather the wear and he rounded the bar and suds-up fresh glasses from the tap. As he slid the Pabst down the bar to the stunned group, he couldn't help but smile. "Sorry about your boat," he said to Henderson.

"It's insured for twice its value."

Nelson stood, turned and rested his back to the bar. The rest did likewise and they all faced Texas Tex, who was fingering through the digital pics.

She put the camera down. "Did you see him?"

"If I would have seen him, I would have taken his picture!" Nelson was disturbed. "He's crafty. I know that. He's planning something, sending Lazzair our way."

"Well we sure sent them something too!" Henderson said, and nodded to the VHF. They all turned and huddled around the news coming off the open radio.

Kapin Kike faced north over the open water, keeping the pier rocks behind him and Coffin Light. He nodded to a trusted amigo and the man approached. "I heard gunfire on the radio," Kapin Kike said low.

"*Sí*," the old man nodded.

"*¿Cuántos disparos?**

The man shrugged his shoulders. "*Veinte***" rifle shots. Maybe more."

---

*How many shots?
**How many shots?

"*¿Ruso? ¿Siete punto sesenta y dos?*\*
"*Sí. Lo siento.*\*

Kapin Kike frowned then looked at the man. "Are the three amigos gone?"

"*Sí, Señor.*"

Captain Kirk nodded and let the man ease back into the migrant crowd around the green light on the north pier. He pondered the damage a full magazine of 7.62 bullets could wreak on a power boat.

The Coast Guard wake lurched the sailboat so hard it almost slung Little John clean off the stanchion. The impaled one elevated his pitch to torturic levels.

"This is the U.S. Coast Guard, Muskegon Region," the power of their signal blasted. "All marine vessels in the Morguetown Region stand clear of Hailing Channel 16. *Eastern Sky. Eastern Sky.* This is Captain Veltman of the Rescue 41 Cutter, St. Knott. Stop forward progress, heave too, and prepare to be boarded. Keep away from your weapons. Halt forward progress and prepare to be boarded!"

Because of the chop in the waves, Samantha held course and kept her sails tight. The flames spread to the headsail.

Eric and Samantha watched Captain Veltman, who was waving fiercely from the command helm. The same message blasted over the megaphone.

John wailed and withered. Red foam sprayed from his mouth.

Samantha looked at Eric. "Set them free." She nodded to Dwight and Bran.

Eric flipped the line off the cleat and set them adrift. He

---

*\*Russian? Seven point six two?*
*\*\*Yes. I'm sorry*

saw a crewman holding a video camera from behind the gunner who was aiming a mounted machine gun at them.

Then a hard-hulled Coast Guard inflatable entered the scene, brandishing its guns. It surfed in for a closer look.

Samantha's face, chin and neck were streaks of dried blood with fresh blood oozing over, and Eric knew he didn't look too good either.

His hand went to his scalp, and he remembered how it had looked before the attack. His fingers came away wet, and he knew that blood was oozing onto his neck.

The Coast Guard boats entered the floating debris field of smoking cushions, lifejackets and flotsam and scooped up the two wounded swimmers. Medics with red crosses on their blue uniforms rushed them across the deck on stretchers.

"This is Captain Veltman of the rescue cutter, St. Knott. Stop forward progress, heave too, and prepare to be boarded! Keep away from your weapons, halt forward progress and prepare to be boarded!"

Eric looked at Samantha. The command came in stereo, both from a megaphone loudspeaker and from the radio on *Eastern Sky.*

Little John screamed something that sounded like "Help!"

The Coast Guard ship then roared abeam. The soldiers behind their captain readied their shotguns. The two filming, gawked as they held out their small cameras.

"*Eastern Sky.* Your vessel is afire. Injured are displayed. An assault weapon is visible and you are in violation of federal law for withholding and denying access to a felony in the jurisdiction of the Executive Arm of the United States of America. Your alleged enemies are secure. Heave to and stop forward progress or we will commandeer your vessel using all power at our disposal!"

The ship jumped on plane for a few seconds and came

ahead of them. The smaller vessel fell back as to avoid a cross-fire.

"What's that mean?" Samantha was at Eric's side and saw the Captain point. Two soldiers with M-16s had Dwight and Bran.

Samantha watched the gunner yank back a lever on the 50 caliber machine cannon and swing it ahead of the bow. The air went electric with a raw stream of fire and sound as dozens of 50 caliber rounds boiled the water ahead of them for a second or two.

Point taken.

Samantha swung the bow north and backwinded the headsail. She pitched the wheel back to the starboard, forcing the headsail to hold the pressure of the backwind. She hove to.

"Heave confirmed, *Eastern Sky*. U.S. Coast Guard rescue cutter, St. Knott preparing to board." A huge blast of white $CO_2$ from a military grade fire extinguisher doused the sails and rained powder.

Uniformed men boarded and trained their barrels on Eric, because the rifle was at his feet. "Halt!" they yelled as they charged, not in the mood to see the SKS come alive. A rough hand in a biohazard glove pushed Eric back.

Little John was still screaming like a cat getting its stomach flossed by barbwire.

Samantha was separated from Eric.

Two soldiers jumped onto the bow, one slipping to his knees on Dwight's blood. They lowered the sail and sprayed chemical flame retardant on it again. "Foredeck secure!" They repeated this twice before it was confirmed by command.

"Cabin secure!"

"Stern secure!" yelled others after one shoved the assault weapon into a plastic bag. Another gloved hand put the orange flare gun into a bag.

Three medics boarded and ran to the midship to help Little John.

On the cutter, a soldier rolled film. Another took pictures. Eric looked at Captain Veltman. "What about her?" he pointed to the girl. "They all attacked her! Why aren't the doctors helping her?"

"What?" the captain asked over the horn, drowning out the engine roar.

A gloved soldier stood next to the captain holding the bagged weapon, barrel up.

"Hot Weapon One coming aboard!" The SKS was moved like Nitro Glycerin as the message repeated down the line. The same soldier carried it across, never letting it change hands for safety. "Hot Weapon Two coming aboard." Another took away the flare gun.

"*Eastern Sky* secured!"

Two soldiers boarded the sailboat, rushing a stretcher to the Little John.

"You okay ma'am?" a soldier asked Samantha, shouldering his M-16.

"Are they locked up?"

"You're safe."

"Captain aboard!" a Coast Guard crewman called out.

"Are you the captain?" Captain Veltman asked Eric.

Eric shook his head, then nodded to Samantha.

"Are you the captain of *Eastern Sky*?"

"*Sí*," she said.

"What happened?"

"You heard it."

"You're for real?"

"They attacked us!" she said, as a medic with plastic gloves started examining her face.

"Where's their boat?"

"I sunk it!" Eric said.

Tools were handed down to *Eastern Sky* and carried back to where John was screaming. An IV had already been fed into his arm. A soldier took a drill and started backing out the four long bolts that held the stanchion to the deck, talking via soldier radio to the crewman below deck who was securing the nuts. Blood sprayed as the drill spun out the screws.

Helicopter rotors were heard thumping in the background.

A soldier started to examine Eric. When he made Eric stand, he saw the hole in the back of his jeans and touched the area with a gloved hand.

"Hey!" Eric called out, and the pain made him sit.

"Where are the enemy weapons?"

Samantha shrugged, then pointed down into the lake.

Eric twisted his torso to look at the back of his aching thigh.

The soldier took out scissors and cut away his jeans and Eric stammered.

"Samantha!" he yelled out.

She looked at him and he pointed. Wedged under his skin of his thigh was a huge knot and a slow trickle of blood.

"What is it?" Captain Veltman asked.

"A marble," Eric said, his face going white. "They shot us with marbles from paintball guns."

"Photograph everything!" Captain waved a man onboard.

"They shot her," Eric said.

Water splashed in between the vessels as waves tried to break the rafted boats apart.

"Are the shooters handcuffed?" she asked.

"Looks like you did your fair share of shooting back." Captain Veltman said.

"Hey, I didn't shoot them. I just sunk their boat," Eric said.

"With an SKS?"

"What's that?"

"The type of Russian assault weapon we recovered at your feet. One boy seems to have a bullet burned head with no ear."

Eric looked down. *Oh, that weapon.*

Two sheriff vessels arrived on scene and more civilian vessels were coming. From the sky, rotors of a white and red Coast Guard Huey Gunship out of Grand Haven circled and down blasts of wind were rippling the water and blowing about.

Soldiers secured the sails again.

Eric's right pantleg was cut off mid thigh and another military paramedic handled triage over the marble sunk under his skin.

"I say we leave it until they get to the hospital," the medic looked at Eric.

"Whatever," Eric said as the leg started shaking a throb for some reason.

"So you're the captain of *Eastern Sky*?" the Coast Guard Captain asked Samantha.

"*Sí.* Yes sir."

"You're name?"

"Samantha Lazzair."

A medic had thumbs on both sides of Samantha's nose and opened the wound, checking for shrapnel. She kept saying "Ouch."

"Is he your only passenger?"

"Yes."

"What happened on the bow?"

She looked at Eric.

He shrugged. "They attacked and then came aboard sir."

"So you shot off the ear of the one on the bow?"

"Actually that was an accident," Eric said.

John had now stopped screaming because the medicine in the IV had moved him into a comatose happy place.

In the relative quiet Samantha leaned over and looked to the cluster of men around John.

"And what of him?" Captain Veltmen asked as men lifted John onto a stretcher with the stainless steel stanchion still protruding through him. The port life lines had been severed and were laying limp along the gunnels

"He boarded too. In the back sir, and he came at us with a flare gun," Eric said.

"How then did he get impaled?"

"Their boat blew up and jibbed the main and then he…" Samantha twirled her finger in front of her in a circle.

The captain bent down and with a plastic bag, lifted two marbles the size of paintballs from the cockpit. "Is this what they shot you with?"

"Are you serious? One of those is in my leg?" Eric asked.

The Captain bent down and picked up a few marbles rolling around in a pool of blood and shook out another evidence bag. One of them was a paintball that he tried to break it. "Frozen," he said, and a man took some close-ups.

Another soldier scratched findings onto a report pad.

Another photographed the soldier next to him and filmed everywhere the captain pointed.

The Coast Guard Captain nodded to the sky at the two news helicopters that circled around the Huey. He was yelling now.

A basket was being lowered from a rescue helicopter.

"This'll be high profile. We're towing you back. We will escort *Eastern Sky* to Morguetown. He nodded to a smaller

Coast Guard Zodiac style vessel where several men were donning thermal suits and dive gear.

Another powerboat was securing a tow line to the bow. A police vessel was picking up and tagging debris.

"Step aboard the St. Knott," Captain Veldt pointed to Eric and Samantha.

"Can we stay on Mo's boat?" Samantha asked.

The Captain hesitated and nodded to a crewman. Two reflector taped life jackets were handed down. Captain helped Samantha into hers and a gloved soldier helped Eric stick his bum arm through. Blankets were handed down and the armed soldier helped wrap Samantha.

The rescue basket hovered above the deck of St. Knott as a soldier with a wired stick grounded it.

Little John was passed from the sailboat to the Coast Guard vessel and into the basket and was lifted into the sky.

Little John's mouth was open and he was spraying snot and blood as he screamed from being moved from his happy place. No one could hear him over the down-blast.

The helicopter left. The news helicopters had been pushed back.

"Stern clear," someone yelled, handing a line that was pulled in and coiled.

"Stern clear," St. Knott repeated.

"Bow clear."

"Are they dragging us home?" Eric asked Samantha. He looked at the soldier at the helm who seemed able enough.

She relaxed, leaned back and all but collapsed against Eric.

He felt his leg and the girl next to him. He sensed her jerking every once and a while as the medic touched her face with medicine.

"You okay?" Eric asked her.

She nodded. "*Sí. ¿Y tú?*\*

He nodded.

"Are they going to be all right?" she asked Eric.

"Who cares?" Eric said.

"I think so," the medic said.

Samantha stared at Eric for a second, shook her head, and turned from him. She sat up and slid away.

Texas Tex reached over and turned the radio down and looked at the faces. Over the years she had earned their support. Her team was ready; her henchmen were willing.

But now they were again nervous and looking to her.

She nodded. *Nervous was good. Nervous would work.* "You know they're all coming here," Texas said.

They looked at each other and nodded in the gray light. Sebastian. Henderson. Nelson. Thompson.

"We will get him into court with this. It'll get him in the open. Then we'll at least know who we're dealing with," Sebastian said.

It was too good to be true.

"What did your boy do?" Henderson muttered to Nelson, making others around them back up.

"We can all pretty much agree that my boy can't do much of anything except sniff Tan Land and take a beating," Nelson said.

Henderson smiled.

Texas looked at Bull Stompson, Nelson and Sebastian.

"Whatever happened out there, it had to be done," Henderson said. "Latino Bandito can't hide on the fruit farm forever, picking and choosing how he dangles us for Coffin Light!"

---

\**Yeah. And you?*

The others looked at each other and nodded.

"We should have done it long ago!" Nelson said.

They agreed to this too, except for Thompson.

"It's Mexican Mo's boat," Bull said. "It might not be enough to bring him out. I mean, Mo's just another mop."

"It's not the boat we're after," Henderson said. "It's the Alamo."

They grunted.

Morguetown Lake was coming alive with strobes. The sounds of mob footfalls were on the road.

Sebastian opened the side door and let the others out into the night. Then he turned and flipped on all the lights. He dinged the cash register open and checked the till.

Customers were coming!

# LOG ENTRY 13

1:30 am—abeam Frankfort Point Lighthouse
East winds to 17 knots.
Waves 0–1. NNE at 9 knots

In 1968 Mighty Mike died in Vietnam and Señora Vanderdyke caved and let her daughter, Texas Tex, return to the estancia with her second husband.

He glared at me from across the table for a few weeks, pouting about how the farm could be doing better. One night he gave his speech. "We got to sell for higher margins!" he said again. "And get more cash crops. More asparagus!"

Señora laughed.

"What's so funny?"

"We have a sandy base to our soil," I said.

"So? We can triple our money if we grow asparagus!"

Señora looked at me and smiled again.

I guess no man likes to be laughed at.

"Just because you can't grow it in Mexico, doesn't mean we can't here! I know how to do it. My people can, but I got to control the farm. The pepper poppers have to do what I say or they can mush their mules back to where they came from!"

I looked at Señora.

"Grow asparagus in sand you say? What's Spanish for asparagus, Captain Kirk?" she asked.

"Espárrago," I said.

"Sounds like they have it in Mexico after all," Señora said.

He stormed away the next day. As they drove away, Texas Tex rolled down her window and yelled, "It's all your fault, Farmer Brown!"

They shacked up somewhere in town.

I warned all my gringos.

After Texas Tex was gone, I went to Washington, the apple state of the Pacific Coast, during the slow months and learned about Hydrogen storage. It's pretty interesting stuff. We changed over our barns to insulate this Hydrogen and started selling fresh fruit year-around in 1970.

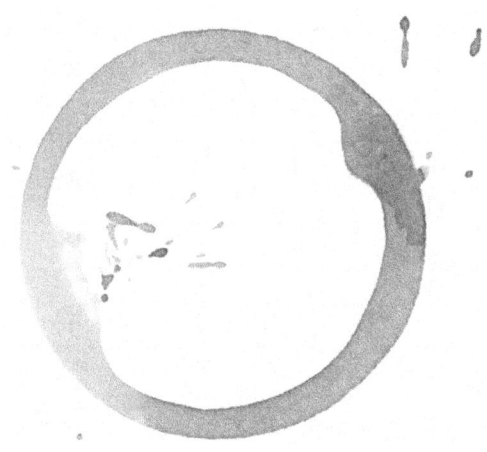

Gapers, drawn to helicopters like wiseman to stars, crowded Coffin Light. More arrived every minute. They gasped at every sweep of a spotlight over the carbon-charred sailboat. They cringed when the light revealed blood pools on the decks and the slicks along the hull.

The three men were rubberneckers in the sea of faces.

Henderson hounded up some courage and turned to Nelson. "Where's *my* boat?"

Nelson shrugged, frowning at the girl leaning against his son in the stern of Mexican Mo's sailboat.

"Where's my *son*?" Henderson asked next.

Nelson turned from Eric and his Spicker Licker. He ignored the question as the Coast Guardsman stood above the couple with his right index finger over the trigger of an M-16.

The parade passed.

On one sheriff skiff stood a pile of folded blankets and a heap of burned and stained boating gear.

"My boat?" Henderson asked.

Mr. Puke sat in the rocks with his binoculars and watched the gathering of Mexicans across the channel. He ignored the hundreds of Morguetowners behind him who moved up and down the breakwall like carp too dumb to climb a fish ladder. He didn't have a clipboard or a laptop. He didn't even have a camera because he saw himself as the last of the breed. He wanted a story.

Around him the mobbies talked like the tonka twins in a tornado-trashed trailer park. They blinked to the rhythm of the sheriff strobe light flashing the frazzled sailboat as it got towed in under a dark sky.

Puke was a purest. Not only a teacher of journalism, but a journalist at heart; always prowling for the right story.

"Move it! Move outta the way ya lards! That's my boy out there," a fat woman screamed from her mobility cart. She swayed from port to starboard as her vehicle took on the potholes of the pier.

Pukeson didn't care if his story would sell more papers or make someone rich; boost ratings or get him a promotion. He had been there, done that, and tasted nothing because of it.

He wanted a story that would get him fired. Get him run out of town. Get a brick through his front window. Maybe a screwdriver in the front tire of his car. Sugar in his gas tank. Something! Anything that would show signs of life in this apathetic town.

Behind him land-based piranha news crews scrambled to send along their digital film feeds of sea cops towing in a crippled sailboat that was still afloat after a shoot-out on the high seas. Let them feed their machines. Let them infuse.

Pukeson's fingers combed his beard as he watched the Mexicans from afar, shielding their eyes from the occasional blast of a spotlight. Around him, the crowd left with the passing of the police parade. They followed it down into town toward Sebastian's place. The only dock in town that was still floating became the ground zero for the investigation.

Puke had seen the blankets around two of his students. He knew one had been airlifted away. He understood the pirate angle after he heard that Dwighto and Bran had been taken by the big boat. He was, after all, from Morguetown.

Maybe those of Mexico North had no TV to watch it on. Maybe. He saw their faces glow in the flashing red and green lights of the pier heads. Hundreds of them were still there.

Coffin Light was empty but the northside was full. *Huh?* he thought. He waited. Minutes passed. It was just him on the south side now. Hundreds of Mexicans on the north.

When he looked around, he found himself confused. He

lifted his binoculars and trained them on the Mexicans, then footfalls behind him made him lower the glasses and hold still. Someone behind him had a determined walk. A march. The walk of a person who knew what had happened.

He turned but saw only news trucks and their satellite antennas poking skyward from the beach parking lot. He shook his head. Since the VHF radio calls were public, recordings of the screaming girl boosted ratings. Fire. Blood. *If it bleeds it leads!* Guns and guts made the stuff of headlines in this culture. TV: the Coliseum of the Country!

He knew tomorrow they would be off chasing another story and he spit. He discharged a vile, back-of-the-throat glob of waxing phlegm. When it splashed into the channel, he wished it would have splatted against faces of the sugar daddy newsboys.

*They wouldn't know real news if it bear-trapped their ankles. Where's the ethic? The responsibility of serving your fellow man?*

He thought about the footsteps that had passed behind him and disappeared.

Mr. Puke didn't chase stories and he certainly didn't make them up. He brewed his stories. He aged them. He was a high school senior in 1981. He didn't have to make up news. He lived in Bay View Valley before it sunk to Morguetown in the shadow of Coffin Light.

He looked to Coffin Light now. It stood alone against a dark sky. Its six-second red strobe was the only color. Then he spotted the glow of a cigarette at the lighthouse.

Puke remembered when coffin door had come to be. It came after a storm had killed Kapin Kike's kid from Mexico North. He had drowned in a sailing accident. He started to think deeper; darker and with more imagination. *Maybe the coffin lid was there as a cruel reminder.* His fingers combed his beard. *Did it come about the same time as the coffin factory? No.*

*It came before.*

The boat parade had passed and the lights of the whirly-birds beamed down on Sebastian's. Puke lingered, admiring. He admired how the Mexicans across the way gathered around their lanterns. He liked how they lived in a time when they didn't seem to have anywhere to go. Being on the lake fishing was good enough. Being was good enough. *They're from a different time, a different age. Another culture and a different page.*

"Come Homer, don't fail me now!" A heavy voice came from behind him. He turned slowly, knowing he was shadowed in the rocks.

A woman, a real big hunk of a female, got off her groaning electric cart. "Homer! Homer! Homer!" she scolded, cursed and kicked the cart. She pulled a hammer out of the cart's front basket, rattling a few glass bottles. Then she stomped off towards the lighthouse, favoring one leg and forcing the last of the gapers to stand aside.

"Capin Kike! Capin Kike of Coffin Light!" the woman horsed out her bellow. "You ready for some more?" She held up her hand and shook the hammer at those across the channel. Then she swung the hammer at the coffin lid, booming an eerie, haunting, deathy sound.

*A calling out from inside a coffin?* Puke hunched forward to get a better look.

The lighthouse strobe above the big woman kept flashing as if to reiterate her words. "Capin Kike! Coffin Light!" she bellowed into the night.

Across the channel, most of the Mexicans were watching the pounding on Coffin Light.

Puke sank lower into the cracks of the breakwall but he didn't know why. Maybe it was his imagination. Or his undying hope that a big story was somehow buried in the roots of his pathetic town. *Why had so many Mexicans voted to keep the town's name?*

*None of them had stood when the pirated sailboat was towed by! Why stand now?*

The steady pound of the hammer kept echoing off the coffin lid.

*Was it summoning the Mexicans?*

*Was it warning them?*

*Was it reminding them?*

Puke didn't know.

Sebastian hung up the phone, opened the door to Officer Belt and waved him inside. He walked to the breaker box and snapped on the dock lights.

Officer Belt followed across the empty room and out the French doors to the docks. Belt spoke into his shoulder microphone, guiding the party to the docks like an airport controller.

Sebastian nodded. He had agreed with most of the questions and demands of the Sheriff and Coast Guard throughout the night. He held down his hat to keep it steady when the news reporters brought their birds in low for that special shot. Two birds landed in the grass-lined cracks of the empty parking lot of the factory.

People poured into Sebastian's place and ordered three dollar beers. Life was good.

He liked the line of tape across his roadside property line, keeping everyone away from the docks and inside his joint.

Chaos on the docks out back. Crowds of onlookers inside. The cash register dinging open again and again. Sebastian grinned.

It was like old times.

In the cold of pre-dawn dew, Evert felt Sebastian's grass itch her bare ankles. In the shadow she watched for movement in the patrol car around the corner. Content that the occupant was asleep, she slipped through the fence where it leaned toward the empty coffin factory and walked to the docks.

All was dark and still. The Vanderdyke land beyond the inland lake was but a darker shade of black.

Evert stopped and inhaled deep. She liked Morguetown. She liked how she had just returned from the hospital where she had nursed Bran, who moaned on morphine as he slept on his stomach. She recalled how she had layered his burned back and buttocks with medicine.

She liked how she got TXT messages in the dead of night. She liked the feel of the candle in her left hand and the heavy bolt cutters in her right.

The woman shivered under a heavy blanket in a deck chair. She jumped when her front door opened after a knock. She felt the footsteps cross her house and watched her door vibrate as knuckles rapped on it.

The deck light turned on and she swung from the brightness, upsetting the wooden deck table at her feet. She knocked off the VHF radio, which spilled its batteries as it struck the floor.

A very old man stepped out of the house and came onto the deck. He closed the door behind him and looked at the woman.

She turned away, letting the wind blow dry her eyes.

"Nicole," he said.

She faced him. "Samantha's hurt. Young men are hurt. Allister calls me from his grave and Cap'n Kike stands before me on the Widow's Walk. Is this how you wanted it? Is this the working of some little plan?"

"I have no such plan."

Breath burst out her nose.

"*¿Está bien Samantha?*"* he asked.

"*Ella está gemiendo de dolor, pero también está durmiendo.*\*\*

"*Bueno.*"

"It is why I'm out here. It is quiet. I'm safe with Leñador out front. You know him? *Él es un chico bueno. Músculos muy fuertes.*\*\*\*

"I know him. He now guards Samantha."

"Do we need to be guarded with his axe?"

"*Leñador es un chico bueno.*" The old man took a step closer.

"You look smaller," she said.

"I feel smaller."

At this Nicole smiled. "It's good to see you, Señor Alfredo Bendolly."

"*Gracias por volver.*\*\*\*\*

She turned back to the lake. The flashing lights were finally gone. If she leaned out, she could see the lighthouse and its lonely red flicker. The western sky was dark purple, void of hope. She turned back and watched him walk up to her. "*¿Quién golpeaba la Luz de Ataúd? ¿Oyó usted?*

"*Sí. Una mujer mala.*\*\*\*\*\*\* Bad times."

---

*Is Samantha okay?
\*\*She's groaning in pain, but she's also sleeping.
\*\*\*He's a good guy. Strong muscles.
\*\*\*\*Thanks for coming back
\*\*\*\*\*Who was hitting Coffin Light? Did you hear?
\*\*\*\*\*\*Yes. A bad woman

"Are we in danger?"

"*Sí.*"

"*¿De veras?*"*

"*Sí.*"

She stood in a rush and went to the railing. He jumped beside her and both looked due south, down towards the flashing Coffin Light.

The sharp crack of metal against wood drifted up to them from the channel. Hearing his name being screamed out from far away, he looked at the woman and decided to tell her the truth.

Inside the sailboat, Evert lifted the bolt cutters to the copper line behind the galley. She clipped it above the solenoid, smelled the propane and listened to it hiss out of the line. She turned once again to the soft flicker of a candle, shining from inside the stainless steel sink in the galley.

It was time to go.

Feeling blood stick under her shoe, she climbed the companionway steps, closed the doors on the sailboat and hopped onto the floating docks.

She wiped off her feet on the wet grass and walked across the lawn toward the factory.

At point blank, the brilliant beam of a cop flashlight squinted her eyes and made her look away, blinded.

"What are you doing here, Evert! Hasn't there been enough for one night?"

"Hey, Officer Belt," Evert said and then the night sky behind her split in an inferno. The blast blew her hair forward and knocked Belt a step back.

As a mushroom cloud zenithed, she saw every detail of the

---

*Really?

uniformed cop. Then the area darkened except the reflective windows of the building before her, which glowed orange in the blazing sailboat fire. Bits of shrapnel landed around them.

Officer Belt stepped up to her and straightened his back. If she was brave enough not to flinch, so was he! "What have you done?" He pulled out his handcuffs and took a step towards her.

"I don't know what you're talking about."

He clamped the bracelets on her and started talking about her legal rights.

Evert had always wondered what it would feel like to say, *I don't know what you're talking about,* to a cop who had her dead to rights.

Now she knew.

It felt pretty cool.

But the feeling didn't last. As he led her in front of his police cruiser he stopped and yanked down on her handcuffs.

With her hands behind her back, she stood defenseless and the officer fondled her body.

"Finding any weapons?" she asked as he groped in the faint light of the streetlight.

"No," he said. "but I'm still searching."

When his search was complete, he opened the back door and put a hand on her head so she didn't rap it on the metal of the car frame as she took her seat.

The hospital shift supervisor was called to the scene and concurred with the nurses. Behind their huddle was a hulk of a woman balancing on a mobility cart.

"Carts can't leave the main lobby," the supervisor said.

"Don't talk to me about Maine's lobbyist! You think I care about some lobsters?" The huge woman lunged her machine at the man.

Dwight turned away from the door and put his head under his pillow.

"I can't hear the TV with your mom out there hollerin'," Bran said. "Pass me the remote."

Dwight slung it. "Better than her being in here!" He heard her cane slap the wall.

"The desk junkie said Homer could come up!" the big woman roared in the hallway.

"It's against policy."

"Policy this!" she whapped Homer's rump with the can as if it were a donkey.

"We have wheel chairs in the main lobby."

"Oh! Like I have time for one of my son's cuties to lug me around and embarrass him? He's embarrassed enough. He just got himself Mexed Up again! He's the one on the news, you know."

"I'm afraid your cart, or Homer, will have to be moved off this floor. This is an ER extension floor."

"Well, I'll tell you what you can extend!" the mother fumed fierce. "My boy gets Mexed Up and now this? Look at him in there!" she nodded to the super. "And where am I going to sit for my visit?"

"We have wheel chairs for you."

"What do you mean, wheel chairs? Hey! Dwighto! You hear that. They're saying I need two chairs!"

The supervisor, assisted by rent-a-cops, helped turn the irate lady back to the elevator.

Dwight listened. He knew she was upset and under duress, but that was her life.

She could red-line during an infomercial.

Back on the main level, the supervisor got the woman into a wheel chair and had an orderly move her toward her son's room. Then he activated all the security cameras monitoring the hallways.

This hefty woman was a ticking lawsuit.

LOG ENTRY 14
2:00am—abeam the shallows off Sleeping
Bear—South Manitou Lighthouse to port
East winds to 17 knots.
Waves at 2-3. NNE at 9 knots. Reefed Main

The decade of the seventies was spent
fighting the Weed Wars. And though a big part
of Señora Vanderdyke died alongside Mighty
Mike, another part came alive in hatred
against her daughter.

"Texas Tex has misplaced her underwear,
bras and brains somewhere inside this sexual
revolution!" Señora Vanderdyke was keen on
saying. With a vengeance, she came with me as
we continually purged the farm of Texas Tex's
marijuana plants.

Tex's third husband had a taste for the ju ju
and they were always lacing our farm's massive
produce with lines of grass.

"It won't last," Señora Vanderdyke said to me as she watched my young son play on the floor next to the big table. It was just her and me and my son inside her big house.

"She'll grow up soon," I said.

"High times are changing. With that Nixon thing the president doesn't have much power this decade, but things will change back."

"What's it mean?"

"I banned my daughter from the farm."

"She's your blood. Think about it."

"Her and her hippies aren't my blood! I'm shamed away from Bay View Valley."

I watched the old woman smile at my son.

She turned to me. "They say a leader is coming out of California. This Reagan feller. Not afraid to make Libia a pancake. Cook 'em all at ten thousand degrees in a millionth of a second! My kind of feller! Among other things, he wants to appoint a Drug Tsar. If he gets into office and my daughter keeps scamming our land, we'll lose the farm to the Feds. Change is in the wind."

"So our Peanut Farmer is going to lose?"

"It's likely. He's too nice. Texas will lose too!"

"She'll change. She'll come around."

"I've filed papers," she slides them across the table to me. "I'm old and ornery, but I'm sane. She comes around again, you kick her off your farm!"

Fcap rom across the inland lake, along the south border of the big farm, they gathered and watched the boat burning. They stayed inside the shelter of the trees, where there was a fire pit and benches. Though the air had an autumn chill, no fire was lit.

The blaze across the way was enough for the moment.

Alfred Bendolly sat and stared over the water.

Santasa, Carlos and Terro sat quiet off to his left. To his right sat the foremen of the farm, ranch, trucking, and sales departments. In front of him sat Leñador, who by nature of his work in providing wood to the homes had his pulse on all the families of the *estancia*.

To Alfred's immediate right sat Ms. Lazzair and her daughter, Samantha, with some white bandages on her face.

To a man, their eyes had narrowed and hardened at seeing the girl's bruising. Sixteen stitches had closed the wound. It would leave a scar on her nose. Maybe disfigurement.

It is not good to leave a mark on the face of a Mexican girl.

Next to Leñador rested his double-edged axe.

"So you *do* have a plan." Ms. Lazzair said. Her voice was low and even, filled with depth and gravity.

"*Sí*," Alfred said. "I have a very old, very simple plan."

"And it's true," Samantha said, looking at Mexican Mo, the janitor. "*Usted es Bendolly el padre y Mo Mexicano.*"*

"*Sí. It's true.*"

Samantha then looked around at the men. They nodded. They were the most aged, calm and leathery group of hombres that she had ever laid eyes on. She met their look and awareness came to her, for they peered at her with the same respect and gratitude that they had from day one.

She was Samantha Bendolly, sole heir of Alfred Bendolly. She looked at the leaves at her feet and said nothing. Every-

---

*You are Bendolly Sr. and Mexican Mo.

thing around her as far as she could see was in her name. Her heritage. Except the dumpy town. But who would want that?

On the hip of one of the men a phone glowed, and he opened it and read the text. He looked at Alfred and nodded low, confirming something discussed earlier.

"Your sailboat," Samantha said.

"Señor Stompson knew who I was," her grandfather said. "But soon all of Morguetown will know. They want me into their courts."

The girl looked at Señor Bendolly, the very person who had lowered himself to be a Mexican Mo at her school. Tears came.

He held out his arm, and drew her next to his shoulder and held her. His touch felt as true as when she had helped him out of the back of Leñador's old truck in front of the school.

She lifted her scared, scarred face to him. "I'm so sorry. I didn't know it would come to this."

Ms. Lazzair looked at her father-in-law. Then she took a careful look at all the men in the circle.

It was true. Alfred Bendolly had woven them all into his plan. The entire fabric of the plantation was leveraged.

She looked at Leñador and his axe. She then saw pistols in the waistbands of some of the other men. Maybe Bendolly did steal the farm. From her vantage, they did appear more like banditos in the low light than farmers, ranchers and tradesmen.

A sad smile came to her then. If she had seen one of the men thumbing the blade of a machete, it would have truly warped her into another era.

❁

Bull Stompson hard-heeled himself down to the water's edge like any other bug of the night being drawn to flashing cop lights. He nodded at the array of law enforcement departments represented and smiled at the OPEN sign on the door of Sebastian's.

Old Sebastian. Making a killing on the gapers buying each other another round of drinks!

Bull looked at his watch. It was four a.m. He had to be at work in one hour. Like that was going to happen. He entered the yacht club with no yachts and was waved over by Sebastian, who finished giving a fireman change for a ten. They waited for the fireman to sit back at his table with a view.

"Big night for you," Stompson said.

"And you. How you doing?"

"You tell me. Evert's in the joint and her mother's coming. Line me up some beers."

"You like this, don't you?"

"I'd like to be a fly on the slammer wall is what I would like. The old hag will lose her beans!"

"When?"

"She's coming at eight." Bull looked at his watch.

"And her lawyer friend?"

Bull nodded. "You better be right on this," he threatened.

"It's better than right. It's picture perfect." Sebastian said and topped off another beer for his friend. "On the house!" he turned back and joined the firemen, who decided it was safest to let the boat burn down to its waterline.

Safety first.

Bull didn't feel like consorting after he got the evil eye for keeping the Fire Department up all night, so he left. But he wasn't up to going to an empty trailer, beer or no beer. And with his Ex enroute to Morguetown, he didn't really feel like much of anything.

So, in a burst of irritation, he decided to clear his head with a stroll.

He walked the mile or so out towards Coffin Light, keeping Morguetown Lake to his right. The road used to go along the water's edge for a bit, but since low water times, the brackish, lowlands had become overgrown with willow and shrubs and blocked sight of the water.

Maybe it was his kid facing prison that made him sit on the pier until sunrise. Maybe it was the happenings of long ago. Either way, when he got up to move he was cold to the bone.

He soon put Lake Michigan behind him, then swore at the closed sign at Sebastian's because he needed a shot to spark some blood flow. He found himself along the string of deserted factories and rotted buildings to his left. They clung to the waterfront of Morguetown Lake like fungus and were posted with signs and fencing and blocked all water access.

The first sign of life came on the right hand side of the road. It was between a boarded up hair salon and one-man insurance type buildings. It was Rexter's. A corner-like store had a small produce section and an aisle of canned food. Pop, beer and chips filled most of the store. It was about as decent of grocery store as the area could expect.

Beyond Rexter's was the housing area that branched off the main drag with limb-covered roads. The houses were steep-roofed dwellings, all built in the style of the fifties when industry ruled the town.

Bull mused. *It's not a bad town except for those infernal, crapped out buildings along the water and the rotten paper mill!* Then he noticed all the real estate signs crowding every street corner to his right. Most boasted incentives like, 'Reduced' or 'Must Sell'. *Aye! It's a crapped out town alright!*

After he choked his way past American Paper, frowning at

the steaming mounds of pulp wood and the billowing stacks of stink, he rounded a street corner and found himself in the business district of Morguetown.

The sky was turning gray in the east.

He passed the one room library, the courtroom and the fire post. At the next corner he came to the Police Station, with their one room holding cell. A patrol car was parked outside, and the Chief's old truck was sitting next to it. Bull entered and nodded to a retired fireman who volunteered nights at the desk to avoid the boredom of his TV.

"Chief's that way," the old man nodded.

Bull never broke stride.

The old man held still, knowing it was never good when Chief was out of bed.

Evert was in the conference room with one hand cuffed to a wooden chair. Chief was there with Officer Belt. Another man was present with a woman he had never seen before.

Officer Belt had the look of a beaten dog. One that was beaten bad.

"Hey dad," Evert said.

"Hey Mushroom," Bull said.

"Sorry, dad," she said. "Does this mean mom's coming?"

"We still love you."

The man next to the Chief looked at his watch.

Then the woman said a few pleasantries and started the meeting.

Chief squirmed.

The man handed Chief a sheet of paper and Chief passed him the video tape from Officer Belt's cruiser. The woman played the tape of Belt fondling Evert.

Bull started swearing.

"This confirms Sebastian's security camera," the woman said.

Chief turned red.

Officer Belt stammered something.

The woman took notes and lifted the recorder to make sure it was rolling tape.

"May I have your tape now, Mr. Thompson?"

Thompson looked around the room. "Sebastian's tape?"

"Of course."

Bull slid it over and the woman played the same scene from a different angle of surveillance.

Chief started swearing. *They weren't bluffing.*

Evert looked at the handcuff.

Belt turned green.

The woman sat and looked at the police. "Our client is in Wisconsin and doesn't wish to come here. She knows your Department is dirty, but this is shameful."

A form was slid to the Chief. "Our client wants her daughter released or we will file suit in federal court today."

"Go to hell!" Chief stammered. "We got her dead to rights on Felony Arson, Destruction of Property and Criminal Trespass!"

"Do you?" the woman said. "The whole town was around there that night. And Sebastian himself said that the boat is registered to none other than Señor Bendolly himself, and that the Mexicans were on the water before it happened."

"That's a damned lie!" Officer Belt said.

Chief pushed his lips with his tongue. "What do you want? Do we need to lawyer up?"

"Who's talking lawyers?" the woman lawyer asked.

The man nodded agreement. *Who mentioned lawyers?*

Bull Stompson felt he was at a tennis match.

The woman pointed at Officer Belt. "We want him done. Gone. Around children no more."

"Publicly disgraced? No problem!"

"Not necessarily."

Chief stood, walked to Officer Belt and held out his hand. "Your gun and your badge, short-eyes."

Officer Belt swore and gave the girl a questionable look.

Then the two lawyers representing Evert on behalf of the girl's mother stood up and watched Chief unhook Evert.

"What now?" Evert asked. "I'm free?"

"No. The woman said. "You're in our custody. You're going home."

"Wisconsin? I don't want to!"

All the adults looked at her.

"Prison here. Freedom there. Your choice," the lawyer said.

Evert stood and left with them.

Chief muttered something about policy and paperwork and followed them out.

Bull looked at his watch and then at Officer Belt. "You okay, Belt?"

Belt nodded. "It didn't look that bad did it? It didn't really look like I took advantage of the situation, did it?"

"She'll get over it," Bull said. "Everyone has to take one for the team sooner or later."

Belt smiled. His career just took a blow. He could relate.

Mr. Puke looked over his class. All were there. Bandaged and broken-winged and dinged, they were there. They sat like one big dysfunctional social experiment!

After two weeks, four assemblies and the crises counseling team summoned for the third day in a row, Morguetown High School was getting back to normal. The administration had held teachers meetings last night and had given a scolding about how to be respectful of the crime victims as well as the bailed out perps back from the hospital.

But since the tom-foolery didn't happen on school grounds, no suspensions could be levied.

Puke smiled to his class, nodding to Bran, Eric, Dwight and Samantha.

"Gunfights at sea. Boat burnings. Misguided teenagers. Only in Morguetown, town of opportunity!" Puke started class. "Eric and Samantha, welcome!" He turned. "Dwight and Bran, welcome."

The class went quiet. It was being talked about.

"Too bad for Evert. And if John were here, we could all play bridge!" Puke was starting class. "So, Bran. Tell us what happened. Let's just lay it out on the table."

"I don't know if I should talk about it, Mr. Puke," Bran said as he stood with crutches as instructed by his pain level. "I mean, I can barely fart without bleeding. And Little John is still fogged, you know, milking his meds as best he can."

"Dwight, can you tell us some news?" Puke asked.

"Sure, I guess. If you want to," Dwight said.

So much for privacy, but such was the benefit of a teacher who rode the probation fence.

Dwight pointed to Samantha. "Her grandfather is a Mexican Mo and also Señor Bendolly. That's the trouble with the whole thing. Maybe he's a janitor like Evert's dad because he's the barrel bottomer, but I think he's mustering us with some sort of Mexican Mo Jo. But what do I know?"

Samantha looked at Eric for help.

"Eric?" Puke asked. "Summerize!"

"They attacked her boat, ya know, so I sunk theirs." Eric said.

Puke looked at Bran. "That true?"

Bran nodded. "And we all got more trouble coming. We're all going to get jacked in jumpsuits because of this."

"Are you two comfortable with our discussion?" Puke

asked. "I think we're healing. And since we're not making it up, we're on Bumpo Time now!"

"What?" any one of the thirty could have asked.

Puke step in front of them like Moses. "Natty Bumpo. Poster Child of the American Hero."

"Bumpo?" someone asked.

"Yes. Bumpo, the redneck who first defined America," Puke said and he faced the window. "And we haven't changed much. Your book shows us maturing to Huck Finn, but it took a hundred years!

"Adventures! Fighting. Rescues! All driven by hate and fear!" Puke said as he turned to the class.

Thirty students stared at him.

He looked back out the window at the falling leaves. His hand went to the glass and his skin shivered. He looked at the graded D- papers piled high on his desk filled with his bad news corrections. He stepped away.

Something touched him deep inside.

He looked at Samantha Lazzair and saw her scarred pride.

He looked at the entire class, the entire generation lost in space. "And Evert sent flames into the night to light the sacrificial light!"

Students stared at Puke. Some were nervous. Others were waking up.

"Helter Skelter," Puke said.

The class grew still as students usually do when they are in the presence of insanity.

Puke pointed to the clock. "Maybe I should have listened to the administration and not talked about this. Not a word should be spoken!" He opened his arms like wings. "The church bells all were broken!"

Puke put one of his hands on the partition and leaned his face against it. From against the wall, he looked at the class.

Feeling the cold cement along his cheeks, he watched his finger trace the groves in the concrete. He closed his eyes. "All and all, I'm just another brick in the wall."

Puke turned and looked at the sack lunch on his desk. He went to it and lifted it to the class as if were Show and Tell time. "How can I have any pudding if I don't eat my meat?" he asked them.

They looked back at him. They didn't have any answers to these kinds of questions.

These kinds of questions don't get asked on the Standardized English Test.

# LOG ENTRY 15

2:50 am Crossed Good Harbor Bay
Abeam Leland
East winds to 21 knots and building.
Waves back to below one foot. ENE at 6 knots.
Hdsl reached well.

In 1980, Señora Vanderdyke died and left me the sole inheritor of the farm empire.

"Bendolly is the only one who knows how to run it." The letter told the probate as it was read by the team of lawyers that Señora had hired to insure my inheritance.

Texas Tex fumed at the judge.

He threatened to have her removed from the meeting.

I felt for her. And if Señora Vanderdyke wasn't so adamant about her being kept away, I'd have worked with her. But seeing her in court, and seeing how she and her own looked at me, I knew I was in for a war. I didn't blame her none at all. The decade before the Vanderdyke Farm Empire reached peak harvest and had became the largest produce supplier in the Midwest.

But the jewel of the Vanderdyke land was the two miles of Lake Michigan Coast and the two miles of commercial land along the entire north end of the town's deep harbor lake.

We had a bumper crop that year because a volcano on the west coast created enough snow to insure summer saturation. The water level had come up five feet in Lake Michigan and we could irrigate 90% of the farm.

The town of Bay View Valley had built a municipal marina and one of Texas' friends developed a Yacht Club on the South end of the Bay View Harbor Lake.

I now managed over three hundred families. Over a thousand souls. Over two thousands hands. Fruit from our trees never touched the ground. We ran 2,145 acres of apple trees. We harvested 570 acres of blueberries, 690 of strawberries. We planted 3400 acres of corn, carrots, potatoes and other roots. We ran 15,000 cattle on a mere 4120 acres of pasture for beef and fertilizer.

We had 37 outbarns.

Mexico North rebuilt the church and the school, and now 128 homes gave people shelter. We kept over 1400 acres for lowland drainage and welling and 1320 acres of forest for heating the cabins with wood.

**E**ric watched the water pool in the bottom of his glass as ice melted. He adjusted himself in one of Sebastian's chairs. Now that everyone around him had finished complimenting him and slapping his back, he settled into studying the situation as food was served to the guests around the large table.

He wasn't fooled. Just because they sat him at the head of the table, didn't make him a leader.

Then the food came and steaks of beef or salmon were placed in front of people as their orders came.

His uneasiness increased as the Vanderdyke woman kept smiling at him. His parents, too.

Moments ago, Dwight had helped his mother up to the table, where she had goosed Homer one too many times, making the table rattle and the glasses spill as the mobility cart got parked.

But no one seemed to mind. Smiles abounded.

Dwight took off his coat, exposing his new T-shirt, 'Call Me Earless'. Then Dwight turned and all at the table laughed. The back of the shirt read: 'I'm the victim of a violent crime!' He faced the table, tipped a salute to Eric and sat.

Eric had a chance to see everyone relax as they laughed at Dwight. It was a reconciliation dinner, but the ice hadn't yet broke. Around the table were the Thompsons.

Officer Belt, who had been suspended for some reason, sat next to Bull.

Hendersons were there. Little John, out of the hospital just yesterday, was in a wheelchair next to Homer. He had a bowl of soup in front of him.

Bran and a man who looked to be his father sat with him.

Matter of fact, Eric settled into seeing that it was the normal crowd at Sebastian's—except they were all seated together.

Dinner was pleasant and uneventful.

But with dessert came two strangers everyone seemed to know except Eric. Seated at the head of the table now, Eric grew uneasy as the men sat, opened legal pads and drew out pens as if they were swords.

The taller one nodded to Sebastian. "Mr. Sebastian, we thank you for involving us in this terrible injustice."

"You're welcome. You're always welcome here," Sebastian said. "Would you like something from the bar?"

They shook their heads, and that seemed to disappoint the owner.

Eric wondered who was booting the bill.

"Mr. Henderson," the lawyer looked at the man's son, "John," he paused out of gravity. "After viewing the film footage, we are truly stunned by your courage, fortitude and will to live. You're a triumph. A triumph of life!"

All clapped.

The Hendersons nodded. Little John nodded again to Dwight for good measure.

"Ms. Stem? Dwight?" the man said. "We admire all courage in using humor to deal with this horrible trauma."

Big Ms. Stem beamed at her boy. Her own boy surviving a gunshot wound. It was her proudest moment. She had even washed her hair.

A small man sat next to Bran. He was new. He looked around with some nervousness at first, but said nothing. His son, Bran, sat next to Bull's daughter, who had been allowed a visit for the occasion. Bran sat still and uneasy.

"Brian Foote? Or should we call you Bran?" the man asked.

People smiled.

"Bran it is."

Bran smiled and lifted a hand to his voters. He knew who he was.

"Burned on over 40% of you skin and still going to school without missing a beat! A testimony to us all on diligence and procedure and pain management."

Bran waved again.

"And those of you ambushed by the Mexican Mafia, the same Clan who burned Bendolly's sailboat," he looked at Sebastian, Evert and then his eyes stayed on Mr. Belt. "We look forward to re-instating you back to your rightful positions of influence and protection."

By this time Eric saw the spindrift on the water, so to speak, and watched his parents fidget as the compliments started clocking his way.

Bran's father stared at Eric and Eric stared back. The man did not nod at him.

It was the first negative Eric saw that night.

"Mr. and Mrs. Nelson!" the man said. "It's a horrible thing indeed when assault weapons are illegally placed in the hands of youngsters and the firm of Lamanski and Drummond cannot thank you enough for instilling gun safety to your child who, in moments of extreme crises and duress, handled a weapon of destruction without taking any human life! Well done! We applaud you!"

Everyone clapped. A chair slid backwards and one person stood and led the applause.

Mrs. Nelson cried. All those times she yelled, *'Don't shoot your eye out!'* when he had taken up his Red Ryder to shoot birds at the feeder had paid off.

Mr. Nelson raised his hand as if to say that the men were pushing too hard.

"And finally, tonight, we come to Mr. Eric Nelson," the lawyer took one step back from the table, hinting at a blast. "After decades of power moves, ambushed elections, industrial sabotage, illegal immigrant labor that stole jobs from the neighborhood work force, environmental hazards and direct undercutting of school taxes, you alone fell victim of the power and utter disrespect for the law by Señor Bendolly. And you survived!"

Chairs shot back as many around the table stood up and clapped.

Eric reached for his glass and tried to look at them all. He withdrew his arm so nobody would see it shake.

The men sat.

A few of the women, Big Momma in particular, kept clapping.

The tall lawyer raised an arm. All went silent. He stepped up to the table and rested both his hands on it. "And you, Eric Nelson, through fate and the power of the laws of the United States of America, you have been given the authority to put a rope of justice around the biggest bully in the territory and drag him out of his den and bring him to justice!"

Two chairs tipped over as Bull and Sebastian stood too quick and started clapping. This time, everyone stood. Except Big Momma, of course.

Then Eric saw Bull Stompson step towards Sebastian, exposing Bran's dad, who was still seated as he coolly reached for his glass of beer and emptied it.

Since everybody was standing anyway, Sebastian raised his hand and motioned all to the bar. "Drinks are on the house!"

Everyone cheered.

The greatness of the moment was now final.

Eric waited until everyone was too drunk to follow him before he snuck out. Wary of every shadow, he entered the shipyard and made his way to *Southern Cross*. He climbed aboard, saw Samantha, and pulled up the long ladder and rested it on the deck. He went and sat next to her, content with the safety of high elevation.

They were again on the boat that failed to keep Samantha's father alive during that fateful storm so long ago.

"Can this boat really help us?" she asked.

"It looks like a good sailboat, Samantha."

"Is there such a thing?"

Another long silence came. They were getting harder.

He didn't know how they were ever going to get out of the maelstrom. "I keep seeing his blood spray red mist across the water, Samantha."

"You don't have to talk about it."

"Do you want to hear me?"

"If you want to."

"I want to," he said.

"Did we have to shoot?"

"I don't want to talk about that," Eric said.

"Talk about something else then."

Eric leaned back against the companionway door and picked the leaves off the floor one by one and began flicking them at her feet. Humidity from the lake was high and it was cold and damp in the yard. "Dwight was on the boat after proving harm."

"And after they shot me," she said.

"When I saw your blood I would have killed the whole town. Why is that?"

"My mother said this town is dangerous. She also said the town is already dead."

"We shouldn't have gone sailing."

"Sailing is good."

"Being in the open is bad."

"I don't want to argue."

"I should've shot them all, Samantha."

"You only shot one."

"Do you sleep at night?"

"Not yet. You?"

"No. I'm afraid. I'm afraid and real angry. I should have killed them all and I wouldn't be so afraid."

"Then it'd be worse."

"No it wouldn't. I wouldn't have to watch my back."

"With the pictures of the bloodied dead inside your head, death would be in your eyes."

"So?"

"So you wouldn't be among the living."

"Dwight's trouble."

"I know."

"I think they will still hurt us. I mean really. And maybe next time they will leave more than a scar," he nodded at her and touched her nose.

She smiled.

"Would they have really killed us?" he asked.

"They hurt me bad, Eric. The prosecutor may move to premeditation if I testify."

"What's that mean?"

"Prison."

"This is my fault."

"You saved me, Eric. I know that much." She stood up and looked around at the boats. It was the kind of weather where the sky went from white to gray to black with no warmth or color. One had to dress for all seasons as the sun crossed the sky. The weather seemed lost between autumn and winter.

Lights were flickering on around town.

Eric and Samantha turned their collars to the cold and damp. Winter was coming.

"We gotta start dressing warmer, Sam."

"It won't do any good."

Eric thunked his head back against the cabin. "What's inside this ratty old boat?"

"My father's boat is not ratty."

"Actually, it's the shipyard's boat."

"Don't call it ratty." She looked away from him, crying.

He sat there, not knowing why, and it drove him to speak. "What's wrong?"

"It's all I've got of him, Eric. Don't be cruel. I can get that anywhere."

"Do you know what we should do?"

"What?"

"We should fix this old boat and sell the movie rights to Disney."

"They only want good stories."

Eric stood, went to the edge of the boat and lowered the ladder. He climbed down to the ground and listened. A faraway tattered tarp stirred in the wind. All else was still and natural.

Samantha came down.

"How bad off is this boat?"

"I don't know?"

"Whose boat is it?"

"I don't know."

"Well if your father was sailing it down for somebody, then it belongs to somebody. I bet at one time it was expensive."

"Should we bring it up? I mean ask?"

"I don't know. That's your history." Eric went up to a large sheet of plywood that had been screwed over the hull above the keel and tilted his head to look at it. Some big holes were above the waterline, but the big Band-Aid was a sheet of plywood below the waterline. It had been there for seventeen years and its edges were rotten and flaky. He took hold of a corner and pulled a screw loose. "Do you know what happened here?"

"Yes."

"What?"

"She'd been shoaled, Eric."

"Is that bad?"

"Yes. She's been sunk."

"That's bad."

"Salvagers screwed plywood over holes, bought a bunch of bilge pumps and limped her back to port. The water pressure, epoxy and screws hold the patches to the boat."

"How does a drill work underwater?"

"These are bolts. You brace the hole underwater and get the pumps going. Then pressure holds the wood in place and you hand drill from the inside. Then you screw the nut on from the inside. One person can do it, but it's easier with two." She ran her finger along the plywood over the flat ends of bolts.

"They're symmetrical," Eric pointed out.

"What's that mean?"

"I don't know. Why would a salvager take the time to be artistic when doing a temporary knock up job that only needs to hold a few days or hours?" he pointed. "Stainless steel. Why spend the time and money?" He yanked on the wood and popped it over a screw. He reached for a better grip to rip off the entire sheet but she grabbed his arm.

"Don't!"

"Why? I think you just found a door into your father's past."

She stepped between the boat and the boy. "I can't go inside this boat."

## LOG ENTRY 16

5:10 am—abeam Cathead Point
Nervous by the west!
Starting to gray in the east
East winds to 22 knots and building.
Waves 0-1 because we are hugging the coast.
Course NE at 10 knots. Reefed mains'l.

In 1981 they invited me, a little old Mexican, to be on the Board of Trustees of Bay View Valley Chamber of Commerce.

I made a mistake. I accepted.

Maybe that's why, years later, my son made his mistake. He became a member of Sebastian's Yacht Club.

After his death, I kept some secrets. Only I knew about Bull Stompson and his Miami Vice Scarab conducting a Search and Rescue at the Abandoned Lighthouse before the Coast Guard had even received the call!

Or that Nelson, Sebastian and Henderson were aboard the Scarab near the shipwreck site and were helping with the search.

And I kept a secret about Texas Tex.

But these things and many others became unimportant because my son was now gone.

The next year I never left the farm. All I did was start buying off the county roads that cut through my farm. And maybe a farm or two when they wanted to sell.

If I wasn't going to leave, no one was going to enter.

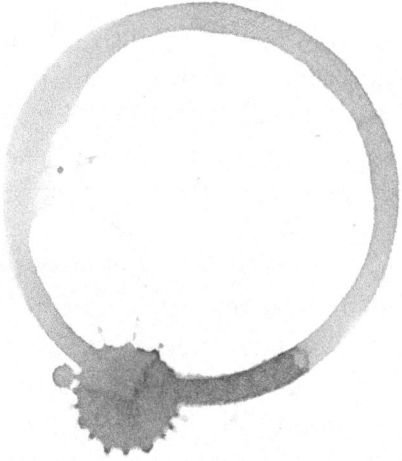

**E**mployment changes came to Morguetown High School. Mr. Puke received an indefinite suspension for violating school rules. He used the classroom to invade the privacy of the victims involved in a crime, and he encouraged students to debate sensitive events not yet judged by a court of law.

A Mexican Mo resigned from the Sanitation Department, giving credibility to the rumor that one of the old janitors was in fact the owner of the largest farm empire in the state of Michigan.

Officer Belt's police beat had been replaced by Shultz, who had somehow gained rent-a-cop status.

Shultz shaved his head to look more official. Someone said the buzz made him look like a Boot Camp recruit. Thus he became Officer Boot to the students.

The change that stirred the kettle, however, was the four new community service workers; the four alleged delinquents who were ordered by Judge Rhinheart to work off 400 community service hours around the school. He even supplied them with orange jumpsuits from County Lockup.

"If you can make messes on the water, then you can clean up a town!"

Eric, Dwight, John and Bran heard the hammer.

Bill Thompson didn't like this ruling. To him it was unfair, because he was assigned the oversight. And he had to catalog their hours and accomplishments. He now had a responsibility. That wasn't good. He didn't like the bottom of the barrel being too far away.

"Get over it," Rhinheart had said when he protested.

Bull hoisted his legs up onto the worn dip in his desk, banked hard in a swivel-wheeled chair and looked at the four young men in his room. He lifted the paper from the court to his eyes, noting the four young men before him who had pled magic at their hearing. He grunted, liking slippery systems.

Rhinheart almost had his hands on the Lazzair girl, but Cap'n Kirk's lawyers got wind of the stink and snuck in the sniffers. They took the fine.

Bull pointed to the name on his chest. "I'm Bill around here. Eric, you sit over there."

"You proud of being our boss, Bull?" Little John asked as he slumped on his crutches.

"You proud of taking on an SKS with a limpdick paintball gun?" Bull turned to the three. "You proud, Earless? How about you, Fartless?" he nodded to Bran.

"We did okay," John muttered.

"That's below the belt," Bran said.

Bill coughed. "You three are alive because Eric and Cactus Cutie showed you mercy. "Right, Eric? They're okay because you didn't kill them, not because they were good. You three gave PW Eric power over your lives. Now the judge gave me power over your lives. Violate me and you violate the judge. Violate him and you boys will learn the lasting and final meaning to the word 'violation' at County Lock Up! You understand?"

Eric nodded.

"I understand it, Bill Thompson, sir!" Bran said.

"Why the 'sir' crap? I'm a janitor. One of the other Mexican Moes. You boys allergic to any stuff? Got any issues?"

"I got issues," Bran said. "ADHD, SAD, OCD and RLS."

"That's beautiful, Bran. But if you go AWOL, you go to prison. You got that?"

Dwight, John and Bran nodded.

"You four just chill and do some work and then you chill and do your time. Got it?"

"Got it," Dwight said.

"Okay," John said.

Bill looked at Bran.

"What?" Bran asked.

"Welcome to your world of 400 community service hours. Welcome to my world!"

Eric looked at the others.

They looked at him. "Nice to have you with us again," John said to Eric.

"Why didn't you lawyer up with the Taco Bella?" Bull asked Eric.

Eric shrugged.

Bull handed him a five gallon bucket. "The Mexican Moes knew about Bendolly flying his Magic Carpet around here, so now none of them are doing squat!" He nodded to the bucket and a stack of putty knives. Bull faced them. "Gum," he said. "When that bucket is half full you're done for the day. And I know the difference between fresh gum and under-the-desk-hard-gum, so I welcome you to my war!"

For dinner, the parents all went to Sebastian's. They added an extra casual night together per week. Started to sit closer too.

Dwight, John and Bran sat down hard at the table in Sebastian's. John arched his back as he did so then held his stomach. The three of them looked at their hands. After thousands of gum removals, they weren't hungry. Or maybe having Dwight's mom nearby affected them.

"Quite your moping, Little John! Homer ain't that heavy."

"It's my guts," John said. They had just lugged Homer up the three steps into Sebastian's because the place didn't have a handicap ramp.

"Sebastian's! Twice in as many weeks!" Big Momma said.

"My type don't the op to come high side very much. Ain't that righto, Dwighto?"

Dwight looked at his water. One hand went to his ear, which was now just a nuppy of scab.

Mr. Henderson entered, looked around the place then crossed the floor to the bar.

"My old man's here," Little John said.

"He's not *that* old," Big Momma said.

"Evening gents," Henderson said and nodded. "Ma'am. Good to see you. Can I buy you a drink?"

The woman smiled at him from under a plaster of hair. "You need to do better than that if you want me to whistle Dixie," she said.

The man smiled for some reason and nodded for her to roll herself up the bar.

When it was dark and safe, Eric left the joint and met Samantha in the shipyard. It only took about an hour of drinking at Sebastian's before he became invisible.

Together they stared at the plywood patch over the hole in the hull of the big sailboat. Above them the night sky dropped cold dew and a shift in wind swirled the last of autumn's oak leaves. Cars motored along the street lined with closed-down factories. The stink and drone of the paper mill a couple blocks away fell over the sinking shipyard.

"I'm going inside," she said.

"Inside that boat is the rot and water of the years," Eric said, pointing to a brown line that oozed from the bottom of the hole.

"I'm going in," Samantha said. "You coming?"

Eric just looked at her dark eyes, hidden by hair.

"What if she's filled with water?"

"How? She's been leaking there since forever," Samantha pointed a low spot in the hull.

Flexing his sore muscles from scraping gum, Eric agreed. He looked up and down the hull, beginning to wonder if any good was here. He looked at the plywood screwed into the hull, took out a crowbar, shimmied it between the hull and wood and looked at her. "Ready?"

"We're going up through the bilge, Eric. It ain't gonna smell too good."

He nodded, levered the soft wood off the hole and stepped back so the black water wouldn't soak him when it poured out.

Nothing.

They leaned in and inspected the repair over the hole.

The four men were seated at the bar. Mrs. Nelson was back at her table with the Texas Vanderdyke. The big woman had just wheeled herself over to them. Behind them they heard pool balls cracking on the table as the boys shot around.

"Your kid slip out for dessert?" Sebastian asked. "How dare he not buy it here!"

Mr. Nelson looked to the door.

"I like your kid," Henderson said. "I haven't got my insurance check yet because they say it was involved in a felony, but I like your kid."

"Why's that?" Nelson ventured.

"Because he's gone again. He's as predictable as white on rice."

"That so?"

Henderson nodded. "Some white on rice sounds good about now!"

To this they lifted their Pabsts in agreement.

Samantha and Eric climbed up into *Southern Cross* then lifted and rested the ladder on her deck under general security principles. They settled in the big cockpit.

"So someone patched the hull but left the wood to hide the work. Why?" He looked at her and sat the crowbar down without a sound. "We got any business poking our nose into this?"

"Yes."

"Whose boat is this?"

"Who cares?"

"I do."

"Like you, I've been here twice."

Eric looked around. The masts of many sailboats stood silent around him in the dark. Just lines of color against the night. Many of the spars were tilted as their boat settled into the mud like leaning Alaskan trees in melting permafrost.

"Why do you want to go inside?" Eric asked.

"You really don't know, do you?"

He looked at her.

"After all these years with all your family's New Year's Eve drunk teachings, you still don't know." Her face, shadowed to dark gray, leaned forward so he could see her eyes. "My father was murdered on this boat."

Eric took her hand and pulled. "We shouldn't be here, then. It's not safe."

Her face went to defiant sarcasm. "You think?" She made no effort to move.

"How do you know he didn't just drown? You know, drowned at Coffin Light?" He pointed across Morguetown Lake. "The up north Coffin Light."

"So why is it not safe to be here? Why do we pull the ladder up. Why are we watched?"

"What do you want, Samantha?"

"I want to go in the sailboat."

He held still. It was why he had come, but now it seemed to be moving too fast. Too many questions and some way-wrong answers.

Sound came and they turned to the roadway. Beyond the fence a truck had stopped and was idling. Even in the darkness it looked to be a very old, very crippled truck, whose engine had worn out countless mufflers.

The dented truck door creaked, then popped open as it violated a twisted metal hinge.

Samantha's head whipped up and around. She stood quick and took up the ladder.

By the time Eric was near her the ladder had been lowered overboard.

She started descending. "I gotta go," she said and darted off into the night.

Leñador looked at Samantha sitting rigid across his seat against his truck door, then he turned back and looked over his steering wheel. He had driven her home as told. His engine had been turned off, and he had been waiting for her to stir. Now he saw the whiteness of her knuckles as she held her hands.

He looked up at her home on the sand bluff. A soft light was on, but so far Samantha had made no effort to leave his wood truck.

Then she lifted her eyes from the cold sandy road beyond where a floor used to be and looked at him. "*Leñador, tómame a la playa. Quita el frío. Construyamos un fuego para luchar la oscuridad.*\*

---

*\*Lumberjack, take me to the beach. Scrape the cold. Build us a fire to fight the darkness*

*"Puedo hacer eso."*\*

They left the truck and trekked dunes to the beach. A north wind was moving and Leñador used his body to shield the match flame until fire jumped to the dried leaves. Breeze fanned the flame to the wood and warmth came. The trees behind them were black and the sky was gray on this late autumn night.

A half click south was Coffin Light, blinking its red eye every few seconds against a sky with no stars. The soft stillness of Lake Michigan was heard as it patted the sand with small surges.

Soon the flames lit their faces. An old blanket kept off the wind. Feet to the fire, butts on a plank, they stayed warm.

"Winter is near," she said. "What are we going to do?"

"Fix your boat."

"You don't have to."

"It's not about me. It's just about. About you and your mother. About broken hearts. Us all being free from the town."

"You still think it will work?"

"Sometimes," he reached across her, pulled her face upward and kissed the side of her nose, his lips feeling her scar. He didn't want to ask about her healing, but knew it was slow. He knew girls take facial scars the hard way.

"What about you?" she asked.

"What about me?"

"You won't be able to protect me."

"Yes and no. I trust the Captain. We all do. He has never failed us. He has an army here if he needs it!"

"Do you think he should come?" she asked.

"Go to Coffin Light? No one can keep him away. That's where it happened, Samantha. It's where they murdered your

---

\**I can do that*

father. Think of it this way. Your grandfather isn't returning to Coffin Light. Your grandfather has never left. *Quizá esto lo liberará.*"*

Evert looked at Bran during the red flashes of Coffin Light as she leaned back against the polished coffin lid over the lighthouse door. This allowed her to look north over Mexiland and contemplate the fire on the beach. She hung up her phone then watched Bran try to get comfortable.

"I can't sit on my butt," Bran whined.

She smiled at him.

"Imagine a world where you can't sit on your butt," he said as he rolled to his stomach and rested flat on the bird poop among the trash. "That's better," he said and pulled an elbow under his chin. "I can't even sit on the can, man. Why are we here again?"

Dwight, John and Eric Nelson walked the pier and joined them.

She handed Eric the binoculars. "It's true, man. It's them."

Eric focused the lenses and peered into the darkness of the north. It was dark as river mud but he raised the beach fire a hundred yards beyond the green beacon. Only one girl in the area had her hair. He lowered the binocs.

Evert took back the glasses. "She's using you, man. That's all they do is use us!"

"Who's she with?" Dwight asked. "Him?"

"Him," John said.

"Hopefully they're a thing!" Dwight said. "When I get 'im, it'll break her heart. A twofur!"

Eric shrugged.

Dwight snatched the glasses from Evert and found the

---

*Maybe this will set him free

fire. He lowered them slow.

"It's him?" Little John asked. "The big one? The arm bender?"

Dwight nodded. "Looks like it."

"It's him," Evert said. "He's the one who picked her up from the boat, right Eric?"

Eric nodded. "I guess so. Not too many trucks in the world can still drive in that condition."

"Our country is two-ply toilet paper to those people," Evert said. "They use one of our plys to wipe their nasty. They use the other to wrap their dubbies." She turned to Eric. "Why'd you two pick my mom's boat to hang out at?"

Eric stared at the fire beyond the channel. His eyes blurred.

Dwight rubbed the ache from inside his cast. Cold air shot into his head on the side with no ear.

John took a step toward land, using his cane in one hand and holding his stomach with the other.

Bran rolled himself to his knees and pushed himself up. "Don't worry about her, man. That's why their called jalapeño pop-hers, man. They liked to get popped! Get it? It's like corn in fire. They don't know any better."

"Thanks a lot," Eric said as he watched the four walk away.

Evert turned back and waved for Eric to follow. "Come on, Eric! Let her go. Let her refry someone's else's beans."

Eric waved Evert off and watched her run to catch up to Little Cane John, Earless Dwight and Burned Butt Bran.

Evert nodded to the beer tap at the bar. Her father caught Sebastian's eye across the table and approved with a nod.

"Knock yourself out," Sebastian said.

Evert got up and walked behind the bar, took a glass mug,

watered the inside to keep down the froth and studied the four choices on the tap. She picked one, then filled a second from the worn beer nub for her father.

She returned and sat with Nelson, Sebastian, Henderson and her father. She nodded to the burned hull of the sailboat out on the dock, its mast limping off kilter. "That ever going away?"

"I hope not," Sebastian said. "I'm double billing the cops and Captain Kirk four bucks a foot per day!"

The men laughed.

Evert smiled.

Nelson spoke first. He looked at her. "So?" he asked.

"So they were at the boat."

"Thee boat? *Southern Cross*?"

Evert nodded.

"They get inside?"

Evert shook her head.

"Why?"

"She broke his heart," Evert said. "And it's a perfect, beautiful, wonderful world we live in."

# LOG ENTRY 17

5:45 am—abeam Grand Traverse Light
Bright Red East. Too red.
Waves 3-5—choppers off stbd beam
Heading NE
9 knots under reef head and main.

Texas Tex Vanderdyke became the prime leader of Bay View City Council in 1982, and she inspired (or conspired) the Chamber of Commerce to change the town's name. She didn't despise the city founders who coined their town with a non-industrial name. She just wanted to use industry to drive her bandito thorn out of her country as if I was a disease in her flesh. She didn't care if she had to sink the town to do so.

"What kind of name is Bay View Valley, anyway?" Texas Tex, the first female mayor, had said. "Any valley by the bay has been filled with swamp long ago. It just doesn't make sense! And by Lady Luck we have found a factory that wants to move in!" she said and paused to accept the applause.

"What's the factory?"

"It builds boxes," she said. "Metal and wooden ones."

"How many will it employ?"

"Two hundred and fifty. It's a coffin factory, okay, but it's still two hundred and fifty jobs!"

"Fantastic!" they all said, beaming.

"But the factory has an odd request," Texas added. "Two requests actually."

"We'll never make budget without industry," the City Planner said. "One. They want to build atop the city park. They need ten acres with water access. They'll dredge."

"You want a Coffin Factory inside our city limits?" one asked.

Another leader's face flushed red.
"Industry," he said. "We're dead in the water
without it!"

"There's more," the mayor said. "They want a
hand in renaming the town."

"Like what?"

"The factory wants to rename Bay View
Valley to Morguetown!" Texas said and watched
their chins all lower in defeat.

But in the end, the vote had come down to
something as simple as money.

**E**ric returned to *Southern Cross*. Alone. He took up the ladder and was soon in the cockpit. Taking up the crowbar, he frowned, then gripped the top of the companionway hatch and pried the lock from the soft, rotted wood.

In the blue light of his phone, he stepped down the hatchway and settled on the floor. A blast from stale, stagnate water stung his nose and he dropped the light to the floor. Symmetric lines ran across the dark wood where hatches had been set into the floor.

Something was wrong.

It was an old boat, sitting dead on land for decades. But it was not abandoned. Underfoot were rags and wire fragments.

Using the bar, he lifted a floorboard. Seeing wires, he followed them until he found the lowest part of the vessel. The bilge smelled. Stunk awful.

Eric squinted at a battery system and followed wires from the batteries down to what looked like a pump. Below the pump was black water. He was now looking far below the floor in the deep guts of the vessel. Then he put the boards back and stood up. Someone was draining the water from this old boat. He jumped lightly on the floor.

Solid.

This boat had been exposed to the rains of decades but it was dry and the inside wood structures were still strong. Something didn't fit.

*Why did Samantha come here?*

*Why did she bring him here?*

But he knew these answers. *It was the boat on which her father had died. The boat that had been sunk and wrecked out.*

*Then why am I here?*

Bad ventilation and an extensive mildew harvest messed with his sinuses and he looked out the hatchway at the night sky, envious of the fresh air above. His light blacked out to conserve energy. Closing the phone, he opened it again to see the exit stairs and then he saw the photo.

He stepped to it and saw a girl in a bathing suit. Because of time, the gray tape had become one with the wall, but despite the years, the image on the photograph was clear.

He leaned closer.

*Samantha!*

He looked around. He touched the picture but it was held fast to the wall.

Something didn't fit. The picture was wrong.

He smudged one edge with his grime stained finger and he tried to pull it from the wall. He leaned close and held up his light.

The picture captured Samantha standing in the surf. Dark, soaked hair blown over one shoulder onto the top piece of her bathing suit. Her body temperature seemed to be boiling the waves. A small gold sailboat hung from a leather necklace, and drops of water covered her rich skin. Eric swung the light and saw a corroded butter knife near the sink. He slid the blade along the tape under the photo. It hacked through the gray tape, gouging the wood underneath. The photo came free but for the tape on the top of it.

He flipped it up to look at the back. Seeing print, he stepped up on a bench, tilted his head and held his phone close. He read...

*Hey Allister,*
*Come back! Don't*
*forget I'm*
*pregnant! Stay*
*safe. Don't*
*trust that Sebastian*
*or the woman!*

*Do you really,*
*really still*
*think I can be*
*a good mother?*
*I know you'll be*
*the best father.*
*-Your Love!*

Eric lowered the picture and looked closer. *It wasn't Samantha! It was her mother!*

His fingernails were lined with dirt and his shirt seemed too tight. Inhaling the thick trapped air somehow felt wrong; a violation.

What happened a long time ago just happened again.

He sat, stunned.

*We murdered her father!*

Eric balanced on the iron rim of the pier under Coffin Light, the beach fire reflected off his unblinking eyes. Wind chilled his perspiration and his breath calmed. Stripping off his shirt and shoes, Eric jumped far out into the channel.

The bitter cold water tried to crush him but he swam on, stroking hard for the north breakwall. The hard-pumping blood forced friction and heat through his body, but when he reached the rocks his arms only wanted to wrap his chest. He was pulled up onto the Mexico Pier by some gringo fishermen.

If he stopped moving he would freeze. Eric started running it toward the beach fire.

*Fire or die.* He pounded it into his head. His life became simple. The cold was getting a start on him and he dared not look at his feet, which had gotten sliced up by those foreign invading zebra mussels on the rocks.

Eric came out of the night and went up to the fire.

A big Mexican and Samantha turned to him and jumped. Samantha went behind a man twice Eric's size.

Eric went past them, took up an armload of wood and dropped it on the fire. The knifing, cold north wind was burning his throat and chest. He dropped to his knees before the flames.

"Eric!" Samantha cried.

He nodded in a herky-jerky way.

The Mexman took the blanket off Samantha and approached Eric as if he were trying to catch a seagull. He let his foot drag sand over an axe head. As he wrapped it over Eric's shoulders, he sunk and re-sunk his fingers deep into Eric's arms and back, using pain and pressure to stir the blood and bring warmth.

"Thanks," Eric uttered between the finger gouges of the Mexman. "*Gracias.*"

"Eric, this is Leñador," Samantha said as Leñador sat beside her.

Eric nodded to the Mex, noticing for the first time his blue-jeaned shirt had no sleeves. He saw thick, knotted bi's and tri's forcing the arms of the man out away from his chest.

"You the guy who broke Dwight's arm?"

"Dwight?" Leñador asked, as if he broke arms daily.

"The blond-haired scum."

Samantha looked at Leñador then turned to Eric and nodded.

Eric thought over the list of trouble he had caused Samantha. He looked at Leñador and pondered his fate as he saw the strong face, thick black mustache and dark-hardened eyes beneath a tassel of black hair.

Leñador would break him next.

And Eric also knew he had it coming.

"Snow is coming, Eric. Are you loco?"

Blood oozed from the sand-clotted slices on his feet, and they howled nonstop in pain as he thawed by the fire. Eric looked up. Lake Michigan was giving chill in the soft north wind. His jeans, soaked and dripping, were now giving off steam from being near the fire. Watching flames eat the wood down to coals, he moved closer to the fire for warmth and settled for another patch of silence.

"*¿En serio quieres arreglar el Southern Cross?*"* Leñador asked her.

"*Sí.*"

"*¿Por qué?*** He took a worn stick with a blackened tip and stirred flame, ignoring the visitor.

She held her fingers toward the fire.

"Samantha is rebuilding a sailboat," he said to Eric.

"I know."

"Are you going to help her?"

"Do you not know me? I'm the one who brings all the *problemos* to Samantha. I have no *solutiono's*, just problemos," Eric said.

Leñador smiled. "Ahhh! *El Chico de espárrago!*"

Samantha turned so sharp at the man that her hair flung over her shoulder. Her eyes snatched the grin from Leñador's face.

"I've been called a lot of things. And I probably deserve them all. What's that mean?"

Samantha shook her head but Leñador spoke on. "The lawyer list. The list given to us by the police who say that Señor Bendolly is guilty because it was his rifle."

"Not true," Eric said, thinking back to the dinner at Sebas-

---

*Do you really want to fix the Southern Cross?*
**Why*
***The asparagus boy*

tian's and what he did and did not agree to. He didn't remember disagreeing with too many things. But he didn't sign anything either. He looked at Samantha. "I'm not them. I'm *not* scum."

"¡*Me frustras,*\* Eric! You brave me to enter the boat that killed my father, but *tu pueblo invitó a esta oscuridad.*"\*\* Samantha smiled. *Un minuto quiero besarte. ¡Luego quiero apuñalarte por el corazón mientras duermes!*"\*\*\*

He smiled back. The tone of her voice sounded pretty cool. "When will you be back to the boat?"

"*Mañana.*"

"I saw something in the boat. Something that is yours."

Leñador and Samantha became still and calm.

"You were inside *Southern Cross?*"

"*Sí,*" Eric said, exhausting his linguistic skills.

"*Vámonos, Eric.*"\*\*\*\* It's time to go, Eric," Leñador said and stood.

Samantha took Leñador's hand and he lifted her up. Then they stared down at Eric.

Eric stood and pulled the blanket tight over his shoulders.

The three of them walked up through the sand dunes. After a steep climb, they reached a sandy shelf of forest and saw dozens and dozens of trailers. Window lights winked out at them from behind thick tree limbs of ancient oaks. Lines in the sand had been carved through the dune grass, but Eric saw no cars. A few had laid down planks on the sand to walk on. He also saw color bands of pain when he blinked, but said nothing as he limped on his cut feet.

------

\**I'm frustrated*
\*\**your town invited in this darkness*
\*\*\**One minute I want to kiss you. The next I want to stab you in the heart while you're sleeping!*
\*\*\*\**Let's go Eric*

Leñador led them up and across another dune and then into a second patch of forest with dozens more trailers. Before descending, they passed a large pavilion-styled barn where maybe fifty adults were gathered with countless small children running about.

Eric pulled the blanket tighter around his shoulders and relaxed as his feet numbly surrendered to the cold sand. *I'm barefoot and blanketed*, he thought and smiled. *I fit right in.*

Samantha edged him a look as he adjusted the blanket.

"What? I fit right in," he smiled.

Tears welled in her eyes.

He looked away. *Swing and another miss.* He peered under the shelters and saw fires glowing in and among the cement blocks where grates crossed hot coals. Then he smelled the hot, sizzling food.

It smelled so good that it made his frozen feet sting.

Eric saw tables and stores and crates of tomatoes, peppers and apples. A small radio hung from the ceiling by a bent metal clothes hanger and blared music of a faraway culture. Everyone inside was talking at once.

"Party tonight?" Eric nodded without stopping.

"No."

"What are they doing?"

"Having dinner."

"For who?"

"This is the Calentos family. They eat dinner here," she said. "But we can't stop. They would talk to us for hours." She took a fistful of Eric's blanket and broke off his stare as Leñador pulled her by her other hand.

Several small girls were carrying wood and Eric smiled to them.

They smiled back.

Samantha was holding his elbow and steering him as if he

was blind.

They came to a road. It was hard and worn underfoot. He saw that one could drive to the Calentos picnic area, but he saw no cars. "So they're making dinner for one family?" Eric asked.

"*Sí.*"

"It's dinnertime?"

"*Sí.*"

"Well, how many families live on the farm?"

"Many," she pointed north. Talientas, Savanas, Olicias and," she thought for a moment, "and Santanas live up there. These are the big families on the west line."

"Are they all big families?" Eric asked.

"What?"

He nodded back to the barn and shrugged. "Like them?"

"The Calentos family?" Samantha smiled. "About the same. But some are bigger. The Sanacho family is much bigger. The biggest right?" she asked Leñador.

Leñador smiled teeth in the darkness and nodded. He seemed proud enough.

They rounded the bend and came to a ragged, rusted excuse of a defeated truck. Eric felt now, as before, utterly stunned that it still worked. It looked like it had spent the last decades rotting in the surf in the Pacific ocean with some WWII tanks. It did have tires. Hearing the driver door snap metal when it opened confirmed to Eric that it was the truck that fetched Samantha from the boat. The cab had no windows and the back frame had ragged, wooden walls that were screwed into any metal on the truckbed that wasn't rusted.

Leñador lifted a double-bladed axe he had been carrying, looked at Eric and hung it on the gunrack behind the only seat.

Eric realized that Leñador had been carrying it the entire time, holding it as if it were just a part of his arm.

"*¡Apuesto que mi madre esté preocupada porque llego tarde!*\* She said.

Leñador smiled at her and looked to his truck.

*¿Así es? Pensé que él sería más grande.*"\* He looked at Eric and winked.

Samantha stepped by Eric and smiled hard and true at the lumberjack. "*¡Estimado Leñador, sé agradable! ¡Y no quiero enterarme de ningun otro hueso quebrado!*\*\*

Uneasy, Eric peered at him as indifferent as possible. "Nice truck," Eric said, and waited for her to translate.

"*Mentiroso.*"\*\*\* Leñador lifted three fingers to salute.

Eric smiled weakly and saw the man's skin tighten from corded muscles as the arm lifted.

"*¿Puedes llevarnos en el camión?*\*\*\*\* Samantha asked the driver.

Leñador smiled and Eric followed them to the truck.

Samantha climbed in and Eric did to and rested his bare, sand-chilled feet on the bar along the gaping hole where most trucks have a floor.

"*Gracias*," she said to Leñador and leaned up and kissed his cheek.

Leñador stared forward.

Eric looked out the gaping hole where a window should have been. Air from behind, below and all around evaporated his jeans and shivered him. Squinting in dust and wind, he peered into the bright patches beyond trees every now and then where Pebble People were feasting. Even the dust

---

\* *I bet my mom's worried because I'm getting home late!*
\**Is that it? I thought he would be bigger*
\*\**Dear Woodcutter, you be nice! And I don't want to hear about any more broken bones!*
\*\*\**Liar*
\*\*\*\* *Can you take us in the truck?*

smelled good.

The farmers all waved at the passing truck from where they fussed and seemed to be fighting as they crowded around outdoor fires in rusted 55 gallon barrels.

Eric shook his head. *Backwardness exemplified! And what heck does "mentiroso," mean?*

"Where are you going?" Leñador asked.

"Will the truck make it to town?" Eric asked.

"Careful, Eric, this is Leñador," Samantha said and elbowed the driver in the chest.

Leñador flashed his bright smile of white teeth at Eric as if the city kid was something that should be on a menu.

*He seems proud enough!* Eric squinted out the window into the open air and tried not to cough as dust swirled the cab.

"*¿Nos puedes dejar en el pueblo? ¿Tienes suficiente gasolina?*\* she asked.

"*Sí señorita,*" he said.

Nelson and Texas Tex Vanderdyke were alone at Sebastian's. Every once in a while, despite the rage it caused to his wife, the two of them lingered on and locked the place up when they were done.

"I don't like it," Texas said.

"He'll be fine," Nelson said.

"Henderson and Stompson both fell for a Lazzair. Remember? Lazzair's got Mojo."

"I know. But I didn't fall. And he's *my* son."

"I want to talk to him."

"You want to bring him in and it's not gonna happen. He's too young. His bowling pins are still wobbling."

---

\**Can you drop us in town? Do you have enough gas?*

"All right. I won't talk to him about *that*. But I want to talk to him."

"All right. He's at the pier."

As Nelson and Texas walked out to Coffin Light, the soft wind blew her hair back and pressed her clothes against her body.

It was like old times.

"I can't believe the Coffin Lid is still there after all these years," she said, taking his hand. "It took some serious mustard for you to stick that there, I must admit. I'm impressed." She looked at him, smiled and rested her head on his shoulder for a few paces.

He nodded.

"And right after. I never knew you had it in you."

He smiled.

"That'll teach him for calling you the 'Asparagus Man!'"

They walked out over the water on the chunked out pier, glimpsing each other only in flashes of red as they entered the darkness over Lake Michigan. They stopped at pier's end and looked around. They were alone.

"Hey…" Nelson stopped and looked at his son's shoes, shirt and phone alongside the iron support wall. He felt Texas next to him, and together they looked at the fire blazing beyond the channel.

She knew enough to stay quiet.

The man reared back and kicked the shoes and shirt into the channel. If he had been able to think right then, he would have known his anger didn't come from Eric swimming to his sweetheart. Or the reminder of being the Asparagus Man.

No.

None of that scared Mr. Nelson.

What scared him was that he didn't put the coffin lid on the lighthouse.

*If she thought he did?*

*And he thought she had Sebastian do it! Then someone else did it!*

But Coffin Light was *their* history. The coffin lid is what changed them from being common killers and helped them become friends and lovers.

But right then he watched his son's clothes drift out to sea. Then thumbed through the phone but didn't see anything.

Texas moved her soft hand into his, rested her head on his chest and felt his crashing heart. She liked being able to create that effect.

# LOG ENTRY 18

6:50 am Abeam: Fisherman Island.
All waves of Grand Traverse Bay are capped
Red by sunrise!
Winds dropping to 18 knots
The shoreline is back!
Red East. Swollen red sun. Too big.
Waves 0-1. NNE at 10 knots

In 1984, when the Coffin Factory needed to
renew its military contract, the Coffin Factory
Union went on strike. The CFU had the company
locked over a casket, so to speak.

The factory investment group countered by
offering to move all CFU workers to their sister
factory in Mexico.

The CFU didn't flinch.

Next month three hundred unemployed workers
and Morguetown got handed the body bag.

I told my investment group the factory was too expensive to demolish, so we let it go to rot.

Sebastian's Yacht Club had a shipyard and marina by then, but they didn't know that a 1980 volcano eruption made for some snowy winters.

Lake Michigan resumed its normal depth and shallowed Morguetown's inland lake. Without money to dredge, it became but a gas station on a shallow island. With bad water, a derelict coffin factory for its western neighbor, and an empty paper mill to its east, club members sailed off for bluer horizons and then the bank took the shipyard.

Then a Louisiana oil investor resurrected the dead paper mill.

Morguetown, desperate for business tax, allowed the reek station of Southern Way Paper to smolder smokestacks three shifts a day!

My paper mill soon clogged the nostrils of Morguetowners as I layered stink, haze and asthma over their town.

Texas Tex bribed a health inspector, who closed my produce stores along the northeast side of the lake because of the factory. She claimed a victory.

Morguetowners now had to drive twenty miles to buy food for twice as much because the store up the road had to truck it in from me.

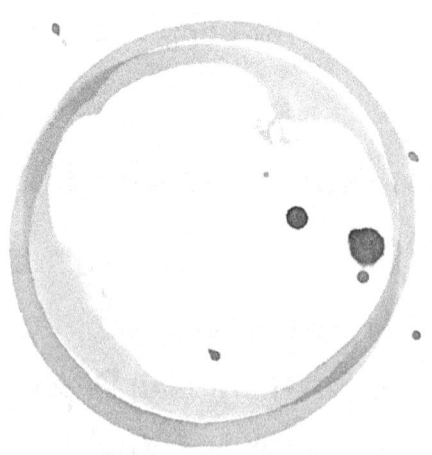

amantha wept bitterly. Her picture in her hands got wet. Eric knew her sobs were drifting out of the cockpit and down the ladder into the darkness and he kept a wary eye. He didn't dare scratch scalp as he stressed over Leñador's fingers tightening around his axe back in the shadow of another boat.

It was Leñador whom Samantha had huddled against on the way to town, letting him freeze.

She cradled the photo like Madonna holds an infant, then brushed her face with a sleeve. She lifted heavy eyes to Eric. "*Ya nos vamos.*"* She nodded for him to help her out of the boat.

He took her elbow and guided her up the companionway steps and into fresh air. As they made their way out, he watched her treasure the picture in her hands as she locked her fingers over it.

They went down the ladder entered the shadow under the hull and huddled until the stillness settled. The only movement was Leñador's head as his eyes patrolled the area.

"It's all real now," Eric said.

"*Sí,*" she said. "*Y es una realidad tan encantadora en que nos encogemos de miedo.*\*\*

"What?"

"It'd be easier if this boat was at the bottom of sea," she said.

"Don't say that," Eric said.

"So much pain," she turned to him. A wave of hair covered half of her face. "Do you think my father made a sailing mistake and lost the boat and drowned?"

"Dunno," Eric said.

Leñador puffed some air out his nose and turned away.

---

*\*It's time to go*
*\*\*And it's such a lovely reality we cower in.*

"What?" Eric asked him.

Samantha stepped between them and looked to Eric.

"*Que después de todo este tiempo. Después de todos los alardes de tus mentores borrachos y después del hundimiento de la ciudad!* \* Then she walked into the blue light of the moon.

"What?" Eric asked the man.

"Death is heavy here. Death and hate are clear and heavy." Leñador said.

Samantha turned, her silhouette hazed in blue. "I can't believe it's real, that's all."

"What? The boat?"

"Coffin Light, Eric. Coffin Light."

"But…?"

"Do you want to know what it means?"

"Coffin Light?"

"*Sí.*"

Eric looked away. He knew and didn't want to hear any more. He felt the sky roll clouds in and saw her fade into shadow. Then his eyes blurred at the drifting gray clouds. He felt Samantha turn and look farther away from him.

The three of them stood, both young men waiting on the girl. New stars kept appearing every few minutes and red radio tower lights flickered to warn planes. Breath hazed white among them and the ground stirred up fog as it cooled.

Eric brought his hand to her shoulder but it was shrugged away. "Okay. Tell me. Please?"

She faced him. Her cheeks were wet. "It means Leñador is right. Pirates kill. They kill families and dreams. They poison children. They suffocate towns."

"What would Leñador know? I mean, he's never really off the reservation?"

---

*\*That after all this time. After all the drunken boastings of your mentors and after the sinking of the town.*

She looked towards the edge and there was metal in her voice. "You're glass in my eyes, Eric. Acid in my ears. You're an insect in my throat."

Leñador looked around as if this was old news.

"But I got those pirates. I sunk their boat. It was you who saved their lives! I wanted to kill them!"

He pointed to her scar. "It wasn't right what they did to you." His brow broke a sweat and he wanted to hold her tight. His cut feet stung bad.

"Bad memories are breathing again," she said.

The fullness of night came upon them.

He realized his legs were numb with cold. "What are you saying?" he asked.

"You *told* me the truth once, but you didn't *hear* it. It's in your head but not your heart." She looked up at the rigging hanging over the topsides of *Southern Cross*. Wires and spars were not only a nest worthy of nasty birds, but also a reflection of her soul.

"What?" he pressed.

"Our first sunrise?" she asked.

"My headache," he smiled.

"There's a part of me that says I'll never see one again. There's a part that says the monsters of Morguetown have caged the sun, and that they torture all and bind me to my father's fate."

"Dwighto and his pirates are gone. They can't hurt you," Eric said

"They're not pirates. Just big *niños* pleasing their little *padres*."*

"What?"

"*Los adultos son los piratas.*"**

---

*parents
**The adults are the pirates

"What are you talking about?"

She outstretched a hand and caressed *Southern Cross*. "Do you think this sailboat will really float?"

"What? Why?"

"It's going to take me to Coffin Light."

Eric pointed at the channel then turned to her, looking confused.

Samantha shook her head and pointed north. She pointed to the far north, arcing her finger as she did so, marking the Coffin Light well beyond the horizon. Marking the Coffin Light where the town leaders had murdered her father.

Eric looked away. Confused and dazed, he knew it would do no good to ask more questions.

Leñador stared Eric's eyes into the dirt.

Whatever she had said wasn't news to the Axman

Two dozen men from the Calentos and Talientas families arrived at the shipyard at dawn in four overflowing trucks. Armed with ladders, sandpaper, scrappers, acetone, Interlux 2000 E Epoxy and VC 17 Red Bottom paint, they entered the shipyard, bounced over to *Southern Cross* and attacked the outside hull.

Before they were underway, two more trucks came. More hombres hopped off the truck beds, unloading tools, a generator and more ladders.

The mechanics went to the rudder, bearing shaft and the wheel slide sprocket. Others took balance zincs for the shaft, and exposed and greased the insertion hole on the propeller.

Inside the main salon, men took up the floorboards, exposed the diesel and started tearing it down. They soon had the oil and coolant pumped out. One man opened a box of voltage testing gear and installed a new regulator.

Four men formed a line, unhooked the house battery system and the engine batteries, and handed them out. No sooner were the old ones out than five new ones came aboard. By then an engine hoist had been reassembled in the main salon of the boat and a massive red hunk of rusted generator was lifted from the deep belly and rested on a rubber mat on the salon floor. Through sheer muscle and shouting, the red hunk was lifted, pulled and hoisted up and out the companionway and heaved overboard. It thudded hard on the blacktop and did not bounce.

A man sat down with a bucket of 12-volt bulbs and followed another who started tracing and testing wires, leaving trails of junk wire in his wake as he clipped and snipped away.

On topsides a man named Regio worked on the windlass, chain cables, anchor line and coils of rope.

Men like ants opened hatches, unplugged hull valves, drained antifreeze out of the bilge and cleared away bird and rat nests.

All this was being accomplished with a myriad of shouts, grunts, whistles and relaying orders in various levels of Spanish slang.

Then a smallish, Grove RT-58 all-wheel-drive crane traveled in, forcing men to move some trucks and gear. Soon the masts and all topside stays and wires were off-loaded and laid out on the ground. Men dove into untangling the lines and were soon cutting and re-cutting stays from a heavy coil of stainless, matching-gauge wire.

Officer Belt, recently off suspension, was relocated from school to third shift patrol officer. He was first on the scene. He parked outside the gate, which was closed and locked, and looked inside the shipyard and scanned the dozens of boats along the first line. Nothing looked out of place and he wondered why he had received the call. He stepped out of his cruiser, stroked his nightstick with one hand before sliding it into the slot on his belt.

He approached the locked gate. He took a hold of the chain and lock around the gates.

Both were heavy and new.

He tongued the inside of his mouth and lowered his eyes to the tracks that were grooved in the placid mud puddles in the middle of the yard. Then he noticed the humming sound coming from deep inside the shipyard.

"LBG's?" he asked and frowned at the memory of the new chain and lock. Pulling his hands from his pockets, he rocked back on his heels, then spoke into his shoulder microphone. "Officer Belt on scene of trespass at the shipyard. Doing a perimeter check, over."

"Roger, Belt. Proceed," dispatch came in clear.

He pulled his stick and started along the sidewalk, dragging it along the chain links. At the corner of the property, he turned away from the yard and saw the tall, skinny Sebastian. He nodded to the owner, who was in front of the door wiping his hands on an apron.

Belt then turned inland and followed the fence up a slight grade. The trees got older and he started sinking in sand. His shoes filled with sand and the buzz of a generator grew louder as he approached the older, original area of the shipyard.

He went to a clearing and saw Tower of Babel II. He looked down at the dozens of men who were all shouting wetback yak. Staying hidden in the trees, he choked his voice into his shoulder mic. "Dispatch, this is Belt requesting back-up!"

"Your nature?" dispatch asked.

"Nancy! Just get Morgan and another car to the old shipyard and pronto! Mexico North is in Morguetown!"

Belt walked back to the road, crossed into Sebastian's and waited for other protectors and servants of the peace to arrive.

"You're not going to arrest them?" Sebastian asked.

Belt finished speaking in his shoulder mic, giving HQ his new twenty. "You the one who called?"

"I sleep upstairs. They woke me up."

"How many you figure? I figure thirty."

"Bout. Trespassers! Plant-Pissing Trespassers!"

Belt walked to the door. He heard the sirens coming. "Who owns that over there, anyhoo?"

"Dunno. I thought the city repoed it after the drought."

"Doubt it. We're broke. Maybe some stupid bank."

"Well, that ain't the point. They're trespassing on the boat and that's for sure! The boat they're beavering belongs to Bull's old lady."

"He's married?"

"His Ex. She went south in '81. It's Evert's mom, stupid. The one from Wisconsin, somewhere."

"Where?"

"Somewhere over there," he pointed west across Lake Michigan to narrow it down.

Belt's mic chirped. He nodded to Sebastian and turned and spoke into it. Cop stuff. He crossed the street to his cruiser and waited for the others to zoom up.

Soon three cars and four officers were outside the gate. One was Chief. "What's up, Belt?"

"About thirty," Belt nodded inside the shipyard.

"They try to lynch you or something?"

"No."

Chief went to the locked gate and lifted the new chain and saw the lock. "How'd they get in?"

"This gate."

"What are they doing?"

"Fixing a boat by the look of it."

"Any boat in particular?"

"Yes. Sebastian called it in."

Chief turned to Sebastian's. He saw the ice crystals in the shadows of the yacht club's lawn from last night's frost. "You know Sebastian used to own this boatyard?"

"Really?"

Chief walked back to his car and opened the door. He smiled and shook his head. "Sebastian done lost the yard to a bank back when the water fell. I might as well be the one to tell him that it's time to let 'er go."

Belt lingered after Chief broke the news to Sebastian that someone besides a bank owned the yard. By then he saw a heavy equipment loader coming his way from way down the street.

With thousands of hours in the seat of the Terex TX7745, one of six '45 degree rotating reaching forklifts used in Mexico North, Johnato Calantos idled down the diesel and turned into the boatyard. He stopped the machine next to the police cars, hopped down and walked to the gate.

He pulled a shinny key from his ragged trousers, unlocked the gates and shoved them open. As he returned to his machine, the police officer met him by the big front tire. Johnato smiled, showing a front tooth that was half decayed and pointed at his wrist.

"What's this?" Belt asked.

"*Ya es tarde. ¡Tengo que irme ahorita!*"*

"What? No habla Engla?"

"*¡Sí!*"

Johnato Calantos scooted around Belt, climbed his

---

*The time is late. I have to go right now!*

machine and high idled through the gate. He looked mainly out his right side as he passed the police car within inches of its bumper. Once inside, he dismounted, closed the gate and dragged the chain. "*Adiós!*" he said to the policeman as he locked the gate between them and turned away.

Maybe it was the presence of the big machine. Or seeing such a small man driving it. But Belt then found his voice. "Get back here LBG!" he waved the man to the fence.

The man stopped, climbed back down and came back.

"Who owns this property? I don't know what you're doing with this in town!"

"*¿Su pueblo, Sr. Cerdote? ¿Usted piensa que Bendolly sólo posee este varadero? Él posee sesenta de estas propiedades pequeñas. ¡Está cambiando todo! ¡Pronto será el pueblo de Bendolly!*\**

"Hey! Don't start giving me the jabber jack! I don't speak Wetback Jack!"

"*¡Gordo! Sin esposa. Sin niños. Sin amor. ¡Estoy de acuerdo, usted no se parece a uno de* nosotros!*\*\** He gave a small, Jap bow and turned and scooted back to his machine.

Officer Belt stood and watched a minute. Then he turned back and went to Sebastian's. If he didn't have authority to slip a greaser, there was no point in trying to squeeze one. *And every oiler here seems to know that better than me!*

He knew then that they were being coached.

*Bendolly's back!*

He ran to his car, closed himself inside and pulled out his cell phone.

---

*\*Your town Mr. Big Pig? You think Bendolly only owns this boatyard? He owns sixty of these little properties. Everything's changing! It's his town soon!*
*\*\*Fat! No wife. No children. No love. I agree, you do not look like one of us!*

By the time the welders, deep down in the belly of the old sailboat, had finished re-enforcing the mast step, the reaching forklift had extended itself to the sling around the main-mast below the spreaders. With the topstays secure and untangled, new wiring to the mastlight probed and tested and new bulbs in the spreader lights, the 4x4 crane grunted and lifted the mast vertical.

From the windows of Sebastian's, several men and a woman started laughing.

Henderson, after handing everyone a cigar, clipped his tip and flamed it. "Here's to the dumbest group of Mexicans north of the Mason Dixon!"

Others joined the cigar toast.

Sebastian was having a good time. He couldn't help it. "Let me get this straight! Again! You have to hear this again!" he turned to Texas Tex, the most recent arrival. Thompson had joined them for his mid-morning break and had yet to return to school. He still had four young men chipping away at a mountain of community service.

Texas looked at them.

"They're working on Stompson's ex's 25-ton Irwin Ketch that draws six and a half feet! It's sixteen feet wide! And they have it in a shipyard without a hoist!"

Nelson laughed out loud.

"But wait!" Sebastian said, wiping his eyes. "They have a lake across the street that is three feet at its deepest and! And! They're raising the mast so they can't put it on a truck because the town's wires. Even without the mast it can't get under the train bridge! And that's the only way out of town! See? It's like they're getting instructions from a coloring book!"

"How many have come?" Texas Tex looked out the front

window.

"Sixty. Maybe a bit more."

"They have water running over there?"

"Don't know. Why?"

"I hear a boat engine running."

Henderson laughed and watched her inhale her cigar. "Don't worry! They can't drive the boat away!"

"Would you look at that?" Nelson pointed to yet another truck, overloaded with women in the bed.

They watched another six or eight women drive through the gate, which was now manned by a pretty good sized Mexican with no sleeves on his ragged, denim shirt.

"What's this?" Nelson asked. "The in-out traffic warranted a gate-keeper? I thought they only knew about tunnels and ladders!"

"Lunchtime for them," Sebastian said. He walked behind the bar and filled their mugs. He gave orders to his kitchen rat to knock up some Chub Tums.

Bull was getting hungry. Good times were coming back.

Dozens of men climbed off the sailboat. They were a sawdust, engine oil, grease and sweat covered lot when they reached the ground. From inside the hull, five or maybe ten others were just finishing up.

The two bow anchors, their windlass, chain and rode locker were new and working. New heads were installed and new, thick white hoses had been threaded through bulkheads so all sewage could run downhill into a thick plastic fifty-five gallon barrel which had been secured under the floor where the generator used to set. The mast was stepped and being tweaked. Its stays were strung. Stanchions re-done. Hatches had been removed, sanded, had had their aluminum fired by torches, and were newly painted and drying. The entire teak had been sanded, cleaned and was now stained with brown oil. All the exterior stainless had been polished and buffed. The through hulls had been removed, recaulked, replaced or recleaned. The engine shaft had been removed and taken back to the farm, where it had been straightened at the machine shop. It had just been reinstalled and repacked.

The engine had been unseized, stripped and re-built by a man who could fix five or six of them on any given day off. It sparkled with all new hoses and belts. The bleeder valve and primer valves were painted bright orange. Alongside a fuel tank, stenciled against the bulkhead under the flooring, the Federal Identification Numbers had been painted onto a beam. Both fuel tanks had been pressure tested and re-filled with pink farm fuel. All essential wires had been tested and the two battery systems had been up and powering various supply systems. And they had only started two small fires in the process.

The massive hull, its bright, clean white gleam above the sharp red waterline, flashed and bragged. Below the line was a new layer of bottom paint. Six men sat hard with heavy arms from burning the abrasive Perfect-It III™ into the hull with heavy polishers. They where exhausted from grinding away on the hull while balancing on the hoods of their trucks.

All men dove into lunch, speaking of the progress like any other project on their day's job list. They all seemed to speak at once, scooping food from any one of twelve steaming, cast iron, Dutch oven pots and over-spilling it into tortillas. Across blankets spread on hoods of trucks were piles of cut tomatoes, peppers and other essentials.

As they ate, the ten women climbed aboard. Toting rags and cleaners, they split into three groups and removed all dirt, grime, sawdust, oil, spilled fuel, grease, calcium and about sixty types of mold from the interior of the vessel.

One woman looked out after a half hour and saw the thirty or so men on siesta in the sun under a blue sky. After two hours the women had cleaned down or up to the main floor of the vessel. Soon they had it stripped of all its scum. Old cushions had been removed and thrown overboard to where an old woman was seated. She manned a pre-WWI sewing machine with her feet and stitch coverings over new foam.

Soon the men were stirring.

Another truck had arrived with bags and boxes of sailing gear. Tired, sweating and wiping their faces with the last of their clean rags, the women descended ladders and stood on the ground, joining the circle around Señor Bendolly.

# LOG ENTRY 19

7:30 am Abaft: Charlevoix
Winds East at 25 knots.
Waves 0-1
Heading: North at 8 knots

The 1988 Town Council of Texas Tex, Peter Nelson, Bennet Sebastian and John Henderson celebrated my ruination. Gloating, they paraded by my sinking, rotted produce buildings and showed their kids how to throw stones at them.

The Council all got canned two weeks later by the broken town, but they partied on!

They had wrecked out many businesses across town in their strike against the produce stands and Morguetown was all but dead. Maybe they thought you have to make a ghost town to ruin a farmer.

I believe you have to ruin a town to drive away the ghosts.

The 1988 election drew a record 712 voters. The new mayor rode a ballot of change.

Name change and image change.

He didn't know what to do with those looming, putrid factories around the lake. Some looked like death. Others stunk of it. Bad for business; bad for growth. He vowed to think of something.

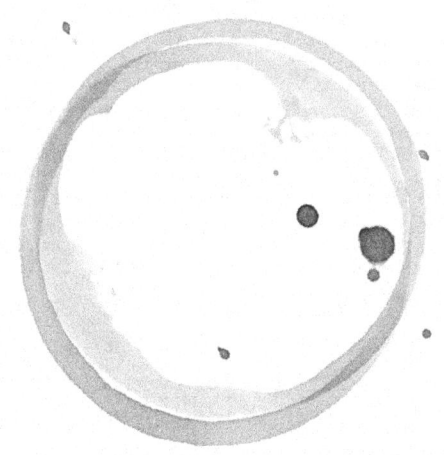

Mr. Puke became more unemployable than ever. He had accomplished what millions have tried and failed. Despite the teacher's union (the strongest union in the state besides the state employee's union of course), he had gotten himself fired. So in a way he had become a winner. But for sure he had become a walking man.

Then something happened. He was offered a job to stroll around Morguetown so to speak. It was not a high paying job, but it had given him purpose. Being a literature teacher, finding purpose had always been something akin to a quest.

After he had listened to the entire proposition, he adamantly denied financial compensation for tasks that only someone like him could do.

Something so beautiful could only be done for free!

They didn't stay at Sebastian's all night. But Nelson, Henderson, Stompson and Texas stayed long enough to wreck out tomorrow's morning.

Bull was as bad as the rest. He made it to school early enough to scrub in, which was good because it was Wednesday and his community service mice were available until noon.

The boys of piracy were shined and bright, lounging in their orange suits and ready to shave more time.

"Why can't you give us two for one on our hours?" Dwighto asked. "I got that last weekend when I cleaned my church."

Bull looked at them red-eyed and weary. His head cold made his face itch and he backed them down with a grunt.

All the school's gum had been chiseled off the nether regions of desks, and the toilets of the sports teams were still clean from their efforts of the night before.

Scrap metal thieves had just pinched off the visitor side bleachers from the football field, and three Mexicans hadn't reported to work. With no Mexican Moes, tasks were starting to pile up. He turned from the computer and looked at the four boys.

The one-armed bandit was useless. John and Bran didn't know squat about the custodial arts. Eric at least knew what end of the broom to hold. Bull nodded to the refer in the corner and John retrieved a Pabst for Boss Man.

The day had started.

"Can we have the rest of the six-pack?" Bran asked.

This got Bull thinking. As he motioned them to join him for a morning brew, he finished his and dropped it in the can return barrel. "You boys ever think about getting paid to do this stuff?"

They looked at each other and shrugged. Becoming professional had never occurred to them.

Sebastian awoke with a late morning sun on his face and the clothes from last night on his body. He had seen worse. Neck stiff from dozing six hours on the couch by the pool table, he sat up, worked on a kink for a minute or so and frowned because the lights at the bar had been left on.

His watch said 11 a.m. He nodded. He'd seen much worse.

He stood and the buzzing got way louder in his head. Habitually walking to the front door of his joint, he opened it to the world and realized the drumming wasn't coming from inside his head.

He closed the door and went back to the couch. The guys were counting on him to keep them informed. He put his head on the sofa. A few more minutes wouldn't hurt anyone.

Corporate hours are a strange, wonderful, weird and beautiful thing. If the group is bored or misdirected, the hours become multiplied addends of wasted time and money and can ruin companies. Like Detroit's car companies for example.

But when persons are moving in a unified effort, compounded hours create a reckoning force.

One person working on a minimally maintained, 52-foot sailboat that had been sitting outside in the elements for fifteen years, faces a daunting task. But if seven join him, then every hour is a work day. If 39 join him, and the boat is big enough for them to section off jobs and keep from stumbling over each other, then every hour the team works equals a 40-hour-work-week.

When a leader can influence groups of 40 people to work around the clock, and they can work without much of a break, then they can accomplish about a thousand man hours of work in a day—especially when they have access to a support team of machinist and unlimited tools.

*If* they know how to work and how to sweat, and if they feel the passion of a project, the power of such effort can be incredible. The team can do as much in a day as one man can knock out about a year (counting therapy sessions).

*Southern Cross* was resurrected in two days.

A huge mass of scrap soon piled up off its stern. Empty bottles and cans of cleaner and solvent formed big mounds. Dull drill drums and polished sand belts. Scrap wire and aluminum. Hoses and more wire. Nasty cushions. Rotted bulkhead plywood glazed in fiberglass and an entire pile just for rags.

A bobcat came in and scooped the crap into a dump box and it went away. Them two Terex forklifts situated themselves on each side of *Southern Cross* after moving off two neighboring boats. A Grove RT crane with two thick straps under the ship's belly did the initial grunt work. But then a KS truck crane was fitted into the mix and provided the primary hoist.

Enfadala and Santo had been deformed by farming accidents decades before. So since they couldn't walk much, they just drove and ran the cranes for the farm. It was their first time lifting a boat, but weight is just weight and they all but shared the same brain. And *this* was the Señor's sailboat, the one his son was sailing when he had been murdered. So they united their telepathy and did the job right.

*Southern Cross* cleared the ground and a hundred or so Mexicans shouted as if they were Jews around Jericho.

Then Terro got the call and rolled into town, perched high on the crushed seat of his 1978 Freightliner Cab over. His head bobbed like a prairie dog getting shot at, as he peered out the truck's cracked windshield. He ducked instinctively as he went under the town's low-clearance 12' 2" train bridge. Behind him rattled a flatbed with a full underbelly of bare tires, each protruding enough wire to spark on the roadway. It was the rig used in delivering and retrieving stuff around the farm. It didn't get off the range too much.

Kissing the gate, Terro nodded to Leñador and dust followed. Without a pause he went to the far end of the shipyard, away from *Southern Cross* and dropped the diesel into reverse.

Through the crowds, around boats and trash cans, over bumps and potholes he brought the trailer back without stopping once or re-cutting his line.

The sailboat went up in the air and his trailer slid under it. Terro watched the lifters work together and lit a cigarette while men lumbered in thick, squared beams and rested them perpendicular to the flatbed. Then he felt the 25-odd tons come down and creak and settle on his trailer. He waited and looked at his watch.

A man named Danstan came up and unhooked the trailer and slapped on his door. Terro inched away from the trailer and bob-catted out of town.

He looked at his watch and smiled. He could still run some apples to the Wal-Mart hub before the highway filled up.

Eric Nelson held the gray waste can to the wheeled dolly in the cafeteria and made sure no students trashed their trays as they dumped food, wrappers and plastic. Except for his orange suit, he was a Moe. By his feet were a half dozen milk cartons which had escaped the net, but he chose to wait until the place emptied before picking them up. The next stooge who said, "Hey Moe!" was going to get clobbered.

His low point came when Samantha dropped her trash and picked up the cartons by his feet for him. "What are you doing?" he asked.

"Picking up the cartons," she said as she rose and dumped them in the hopper.

"Why?" he asked.

"Why not?"

At this he nodded. "I guess I can't change the order of things."

"What?" she stared at him. "*Olvídatelo.*"*

He looked away. Across the cafeteria her kind were leaving out the far door and he watched her walk over to join them.

Eric wondered why she had come to *his* can. It did seem like she had something to say.

"Wait!" he called out. "*Arret!*"

---

* *Forget it*

She stopped, turned and came to him. "French?"

"What?"

"You told me to stop in French!"

"What's the difference?"

She looked at him.

"Why did you come over here? To me?"

Her eyes went a shade deeper and her cheeks flushed. "You still want to take me to Coffin Light?"

"Really?"

She nodded.

"Sure."

"Be ready. When I call, you'll have to come fast."

"Why? When?"

"I don't know. We wait on the wind."

He nodded and she smiled.

He watched her walk away, wishing there was one thing about her that was normal. *Wind? How do you wait for wind?*

It was high noon and the shipyard was still. Dust settled. Oil fumed gas had cleared out and the air was crisp. A lone lock and chain hooked the gate, and no cars were on the roadway between the yard and Sebastian's.

Henderson looked across the table at his life-long friends. "Something's wrong!" He held up his hand for them to listen.

"Nothing," Nelson said. "I hear nothing!"

"Must be siesta time," Henderson said.

"What *are* they up to now?" Sebastian asked himself. "Bringing in a dredger?"

"Belt?" Ms. Texas looked at the cop.

"My hands are cuffed."

"Well unlock yourself from the bedpost and do something!"

"What? The yard is owned by the Sentala brothers. You

want me to go up to Mackinaw and ask them why they bought it? It's deeded to S&B's something or other. We called and left messages but no one's really doing nothing wrong. There's no crime."

"You sure?"

"Sure. They just fixed up Bull's former squeeze's boat."

"Get her on the horn, Bull," Texas said.

"Why?" the janitor asked. "She sold it."

"To who?"

"Didn't say."

"Ask her?"

"No."

"You have to."

Bull looked at them. He looked at them hard. "No. Don't forget it was her yacht we sunk halfway to hell! Don't forget why she done up and left this town and took her money folk with her. You all's acting mighty forgetful lately. We best start remembering what true crime looks like! And it's not fixing up some dead boat!"

"So what's with the boat?" Henderson asked.

"Think it through, numbnecks," Bull said. "They have free labor. They fix a boat a week and sell them off. They're sitting on a lot of boats over there."

"Maybe we should take a look at it then. Maybe we're in the market," Henderson said.

"Suit yourself," Bull said. "But boats that big don't sell overnight. Ebay or not!"

A few of them frowned and nodded. Hatchet head Sebastian grunted. "Putting the mast up may help their pictures, but that there trailer it's resting on raised it to nigh 20 feet. Ain't a bridge in Michigan they can get under. Heaven help them heathens if they ever want to move her!"

❀

A few days passed. Then the better part of a week. One lone Mexican hung out in the yard as if it needed a guard all of a sudden.

The men of Sebastian's took watches. Sebastian found a way out of Morguetown through back streets if they hauled the boat through a couple of vacant lots.

"They'll do something like that," he said. "They can Mexrig nigh anything."

Another day passed. Dusk fell.

Then, in the dark of deep night, deft hands unhooked the lock and lowered the chain along the gate with almost no sound.

A big Mexican cracked the gate and slipped out of the shipyard like a shadow. He walked west.

Leñador went toward the beach. He stopped near a telephone pole on the dead end road to Coffin Light and looked at the houses.

He knew it wasn't so much the presence of sound that woke people up, but rather the absence of it. He had to be quick with has axe.

He looked up and down the street. All was still except for the last of summer's bugs, surfing the heat below the arc of streetlights that hugged the shoreline of Morguetown Lake. Over on the water side of the street was a lone string of poles running electricity that powered a dozen or so houses.

He looked long and hard at the Henderson house and took up his axe.

Going straight at the target, he sunk the blade home with all his force. He struck low and hard several times.

Soon the deed was done and the normal night sounds of crickets were again chirping. The one thing that stood in Señor Bendolly's way had been toppled.

Sí. It was a crime. But sometimes it has to be done.

Leñador was sweating despite the cool.

Nelson had called the group after midnight. "Tonight is Eric's lucky night!" he had said. "He got the call a couple of hours ago."

"Why now?" Bull had asked.

"Dunno. I really don't."

Bull had taken first watch. He waited in the dark room until the shadow came and the glint of the axe passed Sebastian's as if were Grim Reaper Night. Then he nudged Bran and Little John awake. It was 4 a.m.

"What? Now?" one of them said from the couch.

"Shh!" Bull said. "He's gone! We go quick!"

The two boys and the man ran to the shipyard and went to *Southern Cross*. Near the back of the boat was the mound of rusted chain.

"It's like a pile of poop!" Bran whispered.

"Shh!" Bull hushed. "Eric's up there with his Beanie Baby!" He took up the end of the rusted chain. "You ready?"

Bran nodded, but as the chain wrapped around him he started to squirm. Then he withered and felt his heart flopping from pressure.

"I can't!" Bran uttered.

"Shh! It's only for an hour. Quit your whining!" Bull said.

"I can't!" Bran hissed louder. He was ready to blow.

"You yell out and I'll thump you! We can't Frame-a-Frank without this!" Bull whispered.

Bran inhaled to scream in claustrophobia.

"I'll do it!" Little John volunteered.

Bran nodded.

Bull unwound crusted chain back off Bran and John took the spot.

"Will it hurt my guts?" John asked.

"Probably a little."

John nodded. He could do it. He let the layers of chain wind around him as he sat. It was heavy. Very heavy.

"Imagine it as armor," Bull said.

"You should have told me that," Bran whispered.

"Shh!"

"Ready for the tape? It's gotta be done!"

John nodded.

High above the hissing squad, beneath a thick blanket, Eric watched the girl sleep next to him. They were bundled in gortex and fleece jackets as if they were Mr. and Mrs. Noah waiting for the flood.

Soon the soft movement of crusted chain was still and two sets of footfalls thumped off into the night. Eric looked at the diamond stars across black sky. He knew the Mexicans had a plan. But now Sebastian's had one too! He thought again of a road that could take the boat out of town to the gaucho ranch. He knew the farmers had gotten him involved and needed him in their plan. But surely they would have known that he would rally his faithful. Well... Maybe not. They did do everything backwards.

The grind of the gate caught his mind and he turned to the sound. From across the yard, the movement of new chain brushed aluminum.

Eric knew the yard was again locked. It was happening!

# LOG ENTRY 20
9:20am—abeam Good Heart
Raising Dahlia Shoal to port
Winds East at 25 knots.
Waves 0-1

The new 1988 town council soon grew their own black sacks for their own eyes.

It was because of me.

Three were fighting bankruptcy. One, a banker, had just sold out to avoid foreclosing on the other two. The only secure businessman in town was Sebastian, and he was no longer a member.

"I think the town is officially dead!" the new mayor said in public. "Unless we change our name with the mandated 80% majority vote. Let's vote in the name change then we'll find a way to lure business back!"

They voted. The polls said it would happen.

But five hundred Mexicans must have missed the math. Registered voting Mexicans that is.

Morguetown didn't change its name.

Rut became their constant.

I heard the new city leaders convened at Sebastian's with the old ones. They all left drunk.

"This town gets what it deserves!" A man named Bull Stompson said at a public town meeting the week before. "I say we let those Spicles have their nickels and get on with it!"

He got fired from his office as clerk and barely got into the school system as a janitor. I guess you can't be a free-speeching public servant. Not even in Morguetown.

As far as tractors are concerned, the red Internationals of the 1980's were a little heavy but had the staying power of a waterfall in a rainforest. The farm favored the 4786's. They had a half dozen or so, and except for some compaction issues, they did just fine.

One of them pulled out from the gravel road of what used to be CR-141 and turned onto the blacktop that led to Morguetown. Despite the limited slip differential, asphalt cracked and pulled apart as it went up onto the road. The workhorse had left the farm at predawn on a cloudless, starry night. Soft east winds, laden with smells of pooh and swamp, drifted over and carried off the scent of winter-tilled dirt.

At the edge of Morguetown, four homes slept. Their ceiling fans gave off a slight shimmy and then a full-blown wobble as the crushing tractor rumbled by. Inside the town limits, homes warned of the beast by rattling dishes inside their cupboards.

Some Morguetowners woke and grumbled, but none were rousted enough to rise or even flip on a light.

The 4786 lumbered down Main Street, enlarging every pothole and deepening those that had been repaired. It passed more foreclosed homes than occupied ones as it tremored onward. It slipped under the 12-foot bridge and its tall air intake above the cab, demon-screamed as it sucked in all the spiderwebs from the underbelly of the concrete overpass.

Carlos of Corn slowed at the blinking yellow light and passed it, looking at the thing just up from eye level. He took up speed, bouncing sound waves from the massive diesel off buildings and down streets and alleys. He rattled the cage of the empty Coffin Factory, then inhaled the stink of the paper mill before chunking out more roadway as the heavy tires took the turn into the shipyard.

As the gate closed behind him, Carlos reversed the machine, passing the bows of many old sailboats from his high, glassed-in perch as if he was seated inside an old telephone booth. He backed toward the bright red and green running lights that reflected the gloss and white sheen on the port and starboard sides of *Southern Cross*. He looked up at the spreader lights as they glowed high in the air, illuminating the decks. All interior lights seemed to be on and the portholes beamed bright, displaying the full radiance of *Southern Cross*.

The diesel roar seemed to hasten the first wave of dawn as the tractor hooked up to the trailer and lurched it forward, twisting and groaning the strained tires. The massive red machine seemed to smile at the ease of rolling something over the ground rather than grinding the soil up with thirty-six plows.

High atop the decks of *Southern Cross*, Samantha, Eric and Señor Bendolly sat in the backblast of tractor engine concussion. They held fast as the sailboat pitched some and rolled out of the yard on the trailer. Eric saw Leñador, who was but a shadow with white teeth holding wide the gate.

The smile left when the tractor stopped. Leñador darted behind *Southern Cross*. In a moment he was atop and in the cockpit, and Eric heard him mumble some jumbo to the old man.

The old man nodded and pointed forward.

Leñador swung himself back overboard and the huge machine revved hard and brought its load to a roll again.

Eric watched for Leñador from his perch but saw nothing. Then he turned to look behind him but all was dark. The tractor hurt his ears as the trailer straightened from its left hand turn. *Left?* Eric looked to the Yacht Club and saw old man Sebastian framed in the door of his place. Someone else was behind him. They looked confused too.

One of Sebastian's hands held a phone to his ear, the other clamped his boxers. His eyes followed the roll of the huge, six foot tires. He seemed lost.

"He's trouble," Eric yelled toward the old man over the roar of exhaust. "You watch out for them!"

"*¡Ellos no valen nada!*"* Old Señor Bendolly said. He said it loud.

Sebastian darted out like a rabbit, signaling them to stop.

The machine turtled onward, showcasing the rabbit's futility as well as a law of physics. The topside decks of *Southern Cross* were five feet above its waterline. The cabin top was higher still. The keel was some six feet below waterline. The boat rested on four 18x18x18 foot beams and their jackstands. Below the braces was the truckbed that was over five feet high.

As near as Eric could figure, his head was twenty-something feet off ground and aside from firing a rocket propelled grenade, there was nothing little Sebastian could do. He peered down at the roof of Sebastian's and saw where the moss had darkened the slope. He saw the bald on the Sebastian's head and watched the bartender yell against the roar of the tractor. Eric was close enough to see Sebastian's mad, twisted face.

It wasn't difficult.

Sebastian was freaked.

Tips of tree branches scratched and strummed the stays as if they were violin strings. Leaves and twigs fell on the deck. The tractor weaved *Southern Cross* down the middle of the road toward the dead end at Coffin Light pier.

Señor Bendolly pointed to the downed telephone pole that once supported an arcing line of electric wires.

---

*They are nothing!*

"Leñador!" he yelled to Samantha.

She smiled.

Eric turned away from her and saw the beaver-gnawed end of the downed pole. A snarl of twisted wire nested next to it. It was still sparking some.

"How is this going to happen?" Eric yelled towards the ear of Samantha, feeling her hair brush his face. His picture was as foggy now as his first day under the captainship of Mexican Mo. He leaned behind Samantha, masking his glance in the flow of her hair and looked at the old man, who now, fully seemed to be every ounce of the feared patriarch Bendolly of the ranchero.

She pointed west.

That was big help.

Then Samantha held still as the smell of sand along the roadway dusted up to them.

Eric recalled how the jackstands beneath the boat had braced the hull from atop the square-hewn beams. The stands were attached by chains passed under the keel. He looked fore and aft at the thick straps that circled both trailer and boat.

"I don't get it," Eric yelled over the roar of the tractor, whose damper had been upright since increasing speed. "There's no boat ramp down here!"

Samantha turned to him. As the dawn grew brighter, her face was no longer gray but was tanning before him in the pink light.

Then the damp smell of Morguetown Lake bit their noses as the east wind rolled it over them.

They topped the rise and the power and vastness of the flat, gray-blue expanse of Great Lake Michigan seemed to stop the procession. The driver paused.

Eric felt alone. He looked behind him as he remembered the strange inquiries of his father the evening before.

"News from your Spic Hick?" the man had asked.

"No. Not really."

"Tell me about the not really."

"She asked me to sail with her to Coffin Light in the morning. But that doesn't make any sense."

"Those people never make any sense," the man had said. "That's why they're different. But going to Coffin Light seems harmless enough. Your mother and I used to walk the pier every sunset. Most of the town did back then. Back when there were real people around. Say anything else?"

"No. But the way she said 'Coffin Light' made it seem far away. Far away and different."

"Really?" he had answered quickly. Too quickly.

"Is there a different one?" Eric asked.

"You never know with them. If she wants you to sail off into the blue this time of year, you better think twice before joining that crew."

"Well, I'm gonna hang out with her tonight. I wonder what'll happen?"

"Don't get your hopes up." Mr. Nelson had said, then watched his boy pack some clothes.

The man paced. "So you're gonna be on the boat?"

Eric shrugged. "It looks to be all fixed up."

"Eric, you stay on that boat no matter what."

Eric had nodded and watched his father scroll and code up a group text on his phone. Whatever he had said seemed to have made sense to his old man, but what his father had said, didn't make any sense to him.

Leñador become a pondering Mexican. He stared at the squirming bundle of chain and listened to the nasally mum sound coming from behind the tape. He had dragged the teenager wrapped in a hundred odd pounds of chain into the center of the gravel parking lot of the shipyard. He didn't have time to deal with it now, so he left it in the open.

Whoever had made the package lived in the world of risk. They had chained it to the boat for some reason and it took two swings with his axe to cut the links.

Leñador hated risk. His passion for order is what attracted Señor Bendolly to him.

He listened to the fading roar of the tractor.

It was making good progress.

He jumped into his truck and left the shipyard following the tractor.

There was nothing in the yard worth value now.

*Except the chained up boy in the gravel!*

It had been chained to the back of the trailer, so someone knew the plan. *Eric.*

He relaxed but a little. *If they knew the plan, they would have already foiled it! But someone beside the players knew the plan.* At this he thought. He contemplated.

If only he had more time.

He thought back to the package. The boy had been awake. Globs of snot were stuck over his mouth like chunks of dried caulk. The tape had been wrapped around the head. But he had been bound by someone who knew him.

Yet the hate was obvious. It wasn't an attack on the chained teenager, it was an attack on *Southern Cross. Who could live with such a murder?* Was he to be drowned? *How did they know we were going for the water? ¡El soplón de Samantha! ¿Que tal el viejo mexicano poderoso que hizo que su nieta estuviera dañado y que su velero hundiera?**

That would fit. That would make sense.

---

*Samantha's stooge! How about the old powerful Mexican who had his granddaughter harmed and his sailboat sunk?

It would make sense to the murderers. Maybe the town. It did not make sense to him. It was not the Bendolly he served.

Dark wind blew his hair as he trucked by the old man standing outside his little cantina. Reaching the tractor and the massive boat on a very small road, he passed by in the dirt and went on ahead.

*Si algunas personas fueran a lastimar al capitán hoy, ¡tendrían que ser muy valientes!\**

From atop *Southern Cross* Eric looked down at the town. He stared at Little John's house. *No lights?*

Eric sat next to Samantha and Señor Bendolly himself and could only look forward. His phone burned hot in his pocket, telling him to text the others.

Beyone the square red roof of the tractor was the sun-warped, beach parking lot. Beyond the lot, two hundred yards of soft, bright sand, glowed in the coming pink light. The sand seemed but a small thread of golden hair compared to the seemingly endlessness of the expanse of one of the world's largest freshwater lakes.

Mere distance again separated *Southern Cross* from the water.

Eric looked behind him. No one came. He knew they were checking the obscure roads that led out of town.

White rocks and a red lighthouse caught the sun and glowed atop the dark blue water.

Birds by the thousand covered the beach as if it were a trash mound. Some stretched their white and gray wings to the sunrise as they walked. Most just faced the breeze or dozed.

---

*\*If people were going to harm the captain on this day, they would have to be very brave!*

In a united squawk, all took flight as the sound of the tractor scared them into the air.

*Southern Cross* lurched as the Tractor crossed a section of sand so as to avoid turning. It reached the empty parking lot and held course, folding over a "No ATV's on Beach" sign like a weed.

Before the tractor was Leñador, standing on a pile of yanked up concrete curb guards. He waved the tractor forward and nodded to Carlos, perched high up in the cab.

The interior lights on *Southern Cross* went out as it they were candles in wind when sunlight burned the hull into bright white.

Black smoke blew from the exhaust as the engine powered up to meet the challenge of soft sand. The trailer was off the parking lot and sinking in the thick.

Momentum became an issue as Carlos of Corn went up the grade, counting off the seconds until he reached the slope. Speed dropped to two miles an hour, but they were still plowing.

The long, protruding snout of the red International reached out to the blue expanse of water like a thirsty dinosaur on a leash. It crested the shallow dune and drew the trailer and the 25 ton vessel overtop, churning up golden sand and leaving deep brown ruts.

The trailer, balancing *Southern Cross* high above, sunk into some soft sand beach. Its axles became plows as the tires sank into the tractor ruts.

The tractor slid straight sideways and Carlos let her. She found foothold and carried on. At water's edge, where the surf had compacted the sand, the red beast climbed atop and entered the clear water with a powerful burst of unexpected speed.

The boat and its crew followed as if pushing.

Eric said nothing. He sat there, dumb-founded by the screaming diesel power. No phone text was possible.

The old man clenched his granddaughter's hand, then pointed. On the northern shoreline of the channel, beyond the red Coffin Light, the masses had crowded the northern breakwall alongside the cane polers.

They all stood.

The under-chasse of the International was now in the water and its black, gleaming tires were enjoying the swim like elephants. The soft sand, cushioned *Southern Cross* on the trailer as if it was afloat.

They deepened.

The eight tires were now submerged and the water made the faded paint on the tractor sparkle bright red. The dark blue keel and hull of *Southern Cross* was partly in the water and the flatbed appeared more like a surfboard.

Eric turned to the old man. "Won't the air in those tires float, Captain Bendolly?"

"Bueno. Air floats, but these tires are filled with Chloride."

"Chloride? Why? Cavities?"

"It doesn't freeze," Samantha said, not framing the answer because it was common knowledge.

The machine kept sinking. Water was alongside the cab and they could see the driver sitting in it as he turned the train toward Mexico North.

Coffin Light came close, the east wind had cleared the water visibility and brown, mussel-covered rocks were visible below the surface sparkle. The east wind had calmed the lake waters.

In the shadow of Coffin Light a fat woman sat in a mobility chair. She was a big woman and she sat very still.

Wind now rustled the freshly fallen leaves along the gunnels of *Southern Cross*. It pooled them by the scuppers below the midship steps and they looked wrongly out of place.

Rich silt and mud mushroomed to the surface from far below as the tractor neared the entrance of the channel, blurring the water. But the driver kept bearing to sea, going deeper. Carlos seemed relaxed for good reason. He had checked and had sealed all the fluid caps himself.

Eric stood and leaned over. The squared beams were deep in the water as well as the back of the jackstands. The waterline of *Southern Cross* was sinking toward the water! Looking ahead, Eric saw the tractor roof but two feet above water and the smokestake alongside was but a periscope.

Noise ended sharp.

Bubbles roared up and around the cabin as the exhaust sank below the surface.

But the tractor pulled onward. In this new silence of no exhaust, they now heard air being sucked into the intake.

"No smoke is coming from the stack," Eric said. "Are we going to make it Captain Janitor-Mo-Bendolly or whoever?"

Bendolly pointed ahead and down at the tractor. *"¿Así que usted no sabe nada de tractores, pero sabe que soy Bendolly? ¡Usted es el Niño del Espárrago!*

---

*So you know nothing of tractors, yet you know that I am Bendolly? You are the Asparagus Kid!

# LOG ENTRY 21

10:10 am Abeam: Dahlia Shoal to port
Winds East at 25 knots.
Waves 0-1

Deep in my language is the story of Derecho.

Gringos first heard this from Señor Gustavos Hinrichs of Iowa in 1888. He tried to tell our secret. But he knew only some of its mystery.

For this they will struggle.

Derecho lives atop the waters east of my homeland. It is the haunt of pirates and thieves in the Caribbean.

But Derecho can come north too. Like my people, it comes with the harvest.

We and Derecho are one.

We love to eat and breathe in passion.

If you live in the dust like the farmer, inside the dirt with the taste of the ages, you can feel Derecho.

"No Señor, No. It's not too cold!" he says. "It builds. It builds very tall and moves very fast!"

I know his heart and what he wants for me. I know this may influence his calling me on the telephone. But I listen for his voice for he calls from South Dakota.

I do nothing with his call, for he is only one voice.

But then they call me from Minnesota and I know Derecho has heard my hardship.

Derecho knows of my journey?

Of this I cannot be certain for Derecho is untamed.

But now the farmers say he is coming; that

he screams like a woman in childbirth. They say that life is coming.

"It is too cold," I say to Minnesota.

"No Señor," he says to me over the telephone. "The harvest is big. Very warm is the air. Very high it builds! The echo of Derecho's birth may cry out. He is coming."

Derecho!

The frost-pitted concrete below the dull, red, paint-flaking Coffin Light was black with dew. On it balanced the woman on an electric personal scooter.

The three sailors fixated on the woman as the tractor ahead of them chugged away in silence under the water. It exhaled bubbles like a soda bottle stuffed with Alka-Seltzer. With only a torrent of fizz from the output of air, loud pounding could now be heard from the lighthouse.

The tractor arched around the pier head to stay in the hard-packed sand as long as possible. A large woman came into view.

Her thick arms were a blur as she smashed at the black coffin lid bolted to the red door of the lighthouse with a metal baseball bat. At the same time she was belting out holler. She shouted north to the fishermen, the mass of crowd and even out to us. "¡Lo siento, Señor Bendolly! ¡Estoy tan arrepentida! ¡Estoy muy arrepentida!*

Eric lowered his head.

Samantha and her grandfather watched the big woman banging on Coffin Light.

"¡Lo siento, Señor Bendolly! ¡Estoy tan arrepentida! ¡Estoy muy arrepentida!" The fat woman yelled as she splintered off the coffin lid and let it slam onto the concrete. She kept striking it like a reptile hater would club a withering snake.

She stopped when Southern Cross moved into its closest orbit. The hull glowed white in the sunrise against blue water. Rich dark teak sparkled under a shine of new oil, and the stainless steal stays glittered to a silvery pink in the sunrise.

The baseball bat fell from the woman's arms and she staggered to the edge of the pier when the boat was closest. Her foot stubbed the coffin lid and it spun. "¡Lo siento, Señor Bendolly! ¡Estoy tan arrepentida! ¡Estoy muy arrepentida!"

---

*I'm sorry Mr. Bendolly! I so sorry! I'm so very sorry!

Señor Bendolly stood and stared at her.

She focused the projection of her voice to the *Southern Cross*. "*¡Lo siento, Señor Bendolly! ¡Estoy tan arrepentida! ¡Estoy muy arrepentida!*"

The old man lifted a hand to her."*Usted es una mujer buena. ¡Usted es un BMW bueno! ¡Entre en paz!*\* His voice went to her clear and calm over the open water.

She fell to her knees. Her arms clasped her heart.

Eric shook his head at the woman and put three fingers over his right eye. He wished the boat would move faster. He also felt bad for Mr. Bendolly and Samantha. Dwight's blimpo mom was blubbering some blabber from under her mop of greasy hair.

"Don't worry, Samantha," Eric said, "she don't know any better. She's just white trash floating out to sea."

Samantha looked to Eric. Tears welled in her eyes.

He put a hand on her shoulder to share the hurt.

She shrugged it off.

He didn't blame Samantha for her anger. Getting heckled on such a morning was awkward even for him.

Leñador flipped the concrete curb markers back into place, watching only a moment as the high sailboat and its tall mast rocked across the beach on the hugh trailer, like a vulnerable youngling just hatched from an egg. Turning, he stepped into his truck and drove away.

This was no place to be.

The wind blew through his truck as he reached the speed limit. By the time he rounded the bend and passed Sebastian's, many cars had gathered, including a police car.

---

\**You are a good woman. You are a good BMW (Big Mexican Woman)! Enter in peace*

He drove on. He knew who they were and they knew who he was.

Enemies!

He turned sharply into the yard and blew through the open gate. Before him was the mound of chain around the little ball of fat. He gunned his heavy truck toward the ball of chain and circled it twice, throwing stones and dust everywhere as the back of the truck tailed and bounced so hard that it nearly came apart.

Then Leñador stopped the truck beyond the little ball. He jumped out and ran east. He looked at the security camera at the roof line as he darted into an old building. He dropped down into a vent in the floor and ran along the storm drain that passed under the road toward the paper mill.

"Carlos of Corn!" Samantha pointed.

The driver heard her because sound travels over water. Water was ebbing in and out of his control room. He smiled at Samantha from where he stood on his seat, only his shoulders and head were above water in his cab. He assured her with a wave. He looked cold.

The captain stood and went back to the cockpit. He turned the key and the sailboat's engine fired. Tuning his ears to the engine, he relaxed and straightened the neutral lever to a steady idle.

Eric and Samantha followed.

"Go below, Eric, and see if we're taking on water in the bilge."

Eric did.

Samantha looked to the east at a sunrise igniting fire diamonds across the outflowing swamp water between the piers. Coffin Light was fading behind them. The stacks from the far away factories dropped shadows on houses.

She got the nod from Eric, who returned with a lifted thumb from down below.

Movement at Coffin Light caught their eye.

The big woman whizzed and wiggled her cart up alongside the light and stopped at the edge of the water.

"Dwight's mom is up to something," Eric said.

"I know," Samatha said, and nudged the captain.

Bendolly looked.

By then the big woman had taken out a handkerchief. But instead of wiping her oily face as Eric had expected, she pinched two corners and held it up in the air.

"What's she doing?" Samantha turned to her grandfather.

The old man nodded to the big woman. He rose and went to the huge ratchet straps and popped the tension on the thick, dirty yellow bands holding *Southern Cross* to the trailer. They released and he threw the heavy buckles that held the straps into the water and watched them sink.

The quiet tractor chugged on.

The boat held still but a moment. Slowly, it began to pivot on the trailer as it sunk deeper still. Then the jackstands to port shifted as the logs on the truckbed adjusted from weakening pressure. The stands fell away. The hewn logs splashed up to the surface and *Southern Cross* floated.

Ahead was a floating square of red roof and the hissing, open end of a coffee can that had extended from the air intake. Bubbles spewed up from far below as if the tractor was geothermic. On the back window ledge on the tractor balanced Carlos of Corn, steering with his feet.

"He's like a Cuban on a raft in the Gulf Stream!" Eric smiled.

Samantha turned from him.

*Southern Cross* floated alongside the bubbling, sunken tractor and Carlos, who was now knee deep on the roof, watched the gunnel and rubrail drift by him. All bubbling then stopped. The intake had gone below the surface and water had officially drowned the engine. All was still and quiet. Even the squared beams were still as they floated behind the tractor above the trailer.

Carlos stood still on the roof. In his hand was the looped end of a thick cable that led down to the tractor's snout. Eric walked along the boat and reached for the cable.

"Come on! Quick! We'll tow you!" Eric pointed to the stern cleat.

Carlos held the loop and watched *Southern Cross* drift out of reach.

Carlos and Bendolly nodded to each other.

*Southern Cross* was now abeam the north breakwall and passed a small man in a tiny boat puttering out with a heavy cable from the pier. It was attached to his bow, but soon the weight of the cable forced the boat to spin in a half circle. The old man in the small boat engaged reverse and continued progressing toward the sunken tractor.

Eric walked into the cockpit. "Backwards. Why is everything is backwards?" Eric questioned Samantha with a whisper.

Her deep, dark eyes looked at him from behind a wave of black hair, but she held her chin steady.

*Southern Cross* passed the north pier and approached the beach. The white sand was covered with dark people in bright clothes. They stood still. Even the small children were still. They watched the white hull of *Southern Cross* ghost forward and idle over the calm, cold blue waters. They were motionless as the boat approached them.

Back in the deep brown river water off the pier, Carlos lifted his loop and took the end of the man's cable from the boat. He carriage-bolted them together, clipped the pin into the horseshoe shackle and splashed the connected cables into the water in front of the sunken tractor.

The small boat left Carlos atop of his metal reef.

Several hundred yards away, *Southern Cross* drifted to a stop as Captain Bendolly turned abreast to his beach, showing off the white glow of the full hull to the crowd.

A united roar of sound blasted *Southern Cross* as the Latino crowd, thousands strong shouted cheer.

The captain nodded to Samantha and she dropped the anchor. Her dark hair caught the offshore breeze and blew across her yellow coat. She looked into the golden dunes and saw her mother high up on a hill on her Widow's Walk balcony. She smelled the wind carrying scents of land. She detected stables, orchards and the fall harvest. She smelled home! She lifted a hand to her mother, but the widow held still.

Señor Bendolly saw Samantha wave and watched his daughter-in-law with concern. He felt alone on the boat in a sea of people. It had been 18 years.

The widow still walked.

Coffin Light still talked.

The ghost still stalked.

Bendolly squinted into the sunrise, punching pink red light through his trees of his sand dunes. When he felt the applause coming from the crowd, he smiled. He was on the water, in a boat, before a mass of people. His people. He pushed a dry tongue alongside his tired, worn teeth and felt the emptiness of his lost son. He again looked at his people.

The little dingy with its old captain puttered up to Southern Cross. Bendolly stepped down into it and was motored toward his cheering crowd.

✶

Officer Belt became inspired by the words of last month's report. That big-ole woman had said, 'The Pepper Belly who popped my son drives a blown-up truck!' These words now flashed into his thoughts as the distinctive truck rolled by Sebastian's. Panic, his own personal quest for outstanding police work, and the presence of Texas Tex, all motivated Belt to dive into his police machine and punch it. He had to get one Mexican in custody in order to grease the fittings of the Law Enforcement machine!

*I got the missing piece right here! Stakeout payoff!* Belt's siren sounded good and loud as he juiced his tires in white smoke, banked hard to the right and jammed the wheel left to hold speed through the turn into the shipyard.

It was hot pursuit. He did his power-drift just like in training on wet pavement and saw the truck dead ahead beyond the dust. As he landed back in his seat from the bump at the gate, he stomped down on the gas to put the truck out of its miserable life once and for all.

The truck was a suspicious vehicle and near a crime scene from the night before. The criminal always paid for the damages. He T-boned the truck and, catching some debris in the parking lot, careened it all into a standing sailboat, which toppled onto the truck.

Belt stepped out of his cruise and drew his pistol. Then frowned at his smoking hood and the off-kilter, angled mast hanging overhead from the beached sailboat.

On shore, the 19 main families of the farm formed a long line. About a hundred men from each micro family, each shouldering a 30-foot trucking chain, hooked them all together. Several hundred yards of connected chain formed.

The chains hooked the cable. The cable hooked the tractor and its trailer.

A man brought an old wooden stepladder to Bendolly, opened it and braced it with his arms as it sunk into the sand.

The distinguished Señor Bendolly stepped up onto the low rung of ladder and all lifted their arms together.

The crowd roared.

Along the south breakwall and the northern green beacon of the channel came the fishermen, clapping. They went near the water and took hold of the cable.

Señor Bendolly climbed the ladder and stood before all. "¡A la una!" he shouted.

"¡A la una!" the mass yelled as they took hold the chain and stepped back, raising the links from the sand.

"Dos!" the leader shouted.

"Dos!" the massive gang followed, stretching the chain taunt as the women joined the line.

Young and old now took a grip. Short and tall. Strong and weak.

"Tres y tira!"* The leader lifted his hands.

"Tres y tira!"

Jóvenes, pequeñines y niños pequeños* were lifted off the sand and started to swing on the taunt wire.

As a unit, the leader started the chant and the long line of people heaved ho and stepped back. Then heaved again.

Up and down went the niños.

These people pulled as if Gulliver himself needed to be hauled from the depths.

Alone at sea, Carlos of Corn appeared to stand on water as he balanced on the roof of his sunken tractor. As it shallowed, he entered the cab and cranked (to little avail) on the steering.

---

*Three and go!
**young ones, little ones, and small kids

Shouts came as the red leviathan surfaced out of blue water. Screams came when it was beached, as if they were starved Eskimos dragging in a harpooned whale for the winter food stock. The International sloshed up onto dry land. Its trailer followed, dragging the logs and jackstands and the thick straps.

"They going to drag it over the dunes and back to the farm?" Eric asked Samantha.

Hearing sound, she looked at him. The wind had puffed when he spoke and took the clarity of his words out to sea.

"What?" she asked.

"Where are they taking it?" he spoke this louder, despite her being close because the freshening east wind.

*Southern Cross* was now pointing right at land as the east wind pushed her back on her anchor rode.

On shore, the water-gushing tractor and trailer had stopped.Eric followed Samantha's point and saw a man walk to the tractor with a long, wooden box of tools along his waist. A thick leather strap over the man's shoulder held up the box.

The mechanic stepped up, lifted a wet hood and exposed the engine. He took spray cans from his box.

Eric saw Samantha expressionless as the shouting increased to a roar and was blown out to them. He looked at the tractor and to Carlos who was now facing *Southern Cross*.

The old captain faced the applause.

"What now?" Eric asked Samantha. "What the heck are they doing?"

"They are thanking him."

"Why him? They just did all the work."

"All the work isn't done. *Ni casi terminamos.*\*

---

*\*Ain't near done*

# LOG ENTRY 22
10:40 am Abeam: Le Aux Galets Light
Winds East at 25 knots.
Waves 0-1

When I launched Southern Cross, I expected a splash. Since small towns don't like surprises, I knew I was double-dipping my corn shells into some spice.

But spice is good. If it's hot enough, it reminds you that you're not dead.

The money or the mixins didn't bother me none. I was more than ready: just waiting for the wind so to say. I picked up a good man that the town discarded. I've always been a sucker for men who can put pieces together. I don't care if they assemble engines or Lincoln Logs. If they can think on their feet, I put them to work. That's why I like Mr. Puke.

He didn't need much incentive. Matter of fact, if he had come to me first, I would have challenged his motive.

Motive is the heart of a man.

I liked that in Mr. Puke.

He was motivated.

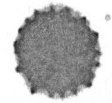

Sebastian's was locked and the shades were drawn. Cars were strewn about its parking lot. An angry east wind rattled the window panes that faced the foam-flecked lines of spindrift on Morguetown Lake.

All was still at the bar except five slamming hearts from lugging the chain-wrapped Little John across the street on a sheet of old plywood. Two men wiped their brows as the group looked down at Little John stretched along the bar.

His eyes were open and moving. The tape had been stripped from his mouth but he was quiet. The clinking of chain sang off a discordant song as it scraped on the wooded bar. They looked at the raveled boy, searching for a loose end.

"Let's not call the cops on this, okay?" Officer Belt advised.

Faces nodded around the bar, then glared down at the boy wrapped in chain.

Little John's head turned. "Can't breath!" he mumbled.

"Get the weight off his chest!" Henderson yelled.

Someone pounded at the front door but no one moved as their hands grabbed chain and lifted it off the teenager's chest.

A crashing sound came and Sebastian winced.

Bull rounded the corner with his four-foot locker snips. He parted the bodies and hooked links into the teeth of the giant shears.

Metal pieces clinked along the bar and floor as the chain was clipped.

With every strap lifted, Little John felt closer to freedom.

Mr. Henderson was turning from fear to rage before them as his son was resurrected. "I'm gonna git those people if it kills me! That farm is going to burn!"

"Ouch!" Little John uttered. "My guts!"

As the chain and rust fell off the teenager, the group tightened their circle around him.

"Belt!" Texas said. "You're a first responder with some EMT. What do we do?"

Belt was sweating hard. He was a big man who could really pump it out. "Um. Well the first rule is to make sure you don't make anything worse."

"Too late for that," she said. "You already done ran him over!"

"Okay," Belt said, holding his hands over the boy on the bar. "Then next is to keep him stable in case of a spine injury!"

"Oh! Come on, Belt!" Nelson yelled. "Give us something we can use!"

Belt lifted a finger. He ran it along Little John's legs. "Feel this?"

John kept nodding.

"That's good," Mr. Henderson said. "His spine's okay!"

"The chain protected him, if anything!" Belt said, whiffing a smile.

"We gotta get his shirt off," Bull said, and pulled out a utility knife. They cut it off.

Midway, Dwight and Bran backed away.

Bull used a strip of shirt to cover Little John's eyes.

Mr. Henderson's face went alive in a whirlpool of horror and anger.

"Turn some tunes on," Bull nodded to Dwight.

"What's wrong?" Little John asked.

"Quite a lot," Nelson said. "But you're fixable."

The men looked at Nelson. He sounded believable.

"What happened?" Henderson asked. "We agreed Bran was going to be in the mound!"

Bran was backed up next to Dwight now. He looked to the door. *These people are going to eat me!*

"They're coming!" Sebastian hung up his phone and they tuned their ears to the silence, hoping for the sirens.

They nodded at the owner.

"How're you hanging, son?" Henderson asked. There was no movement.

They lifted the rag and saw that Little John's eyes had dolled back to white.

"He's in shock," Belt said. "We gotta keep him warm and get his feet up." His training was coming back.

The ambulance siren was heard for the first time.

"Belt, you gotta come up with something fast," Sebastian said.

"You saved him!" Nelson said. "You rammed the truck and knocked him off the back!"

"You saved him, Officer Belt!" Texas said, looking to Nelson.

"Come on, son!" Mr. Henderson tapped the cheek of his boy.

Once Bull had cut the shirt off, the talking had stopped. Little John's shoulders were touching each other in front of his chest from being rolled under the cop car.

The chain had worked as armor to some extent, but the dragon had still stomped him.

Belt looked at Nelson and Texas and nodded. *It would work. I saved Little John! But saved him from what? What were those people going to do to him?* Belt looked up and around. Instinct beaten into him from his days at the high school took over.

"Bull, you get Dwight and Bran back to school. They were never here! You neither!"

Bull nodded. Not being around for this one sounded good.

Mr. Puke, once labeled a creative thinker, marveled that he didn't hear more sirens as he walked along the decrepit houses of Cherry Avenue. Looking through yards, he glimpsed Shoreline Drive and its hulking factories that cancered the shoreline of Morguetown Lake.

Shoreline Avenue had been taken care of, as had Apple Avenue, Peach Street and Pear Boulevard. They were easy. On those streets there had been some seventeen vandalized, empty, locked down HUD houses that had been repossessed by the Department of Urban Housing. He never knew there were so many, but when he started counting the orange stickers on the padlocked doors, they started stacking up.

Puke had nothing to do with the HUDs. Or the houses listed with a realtor. Both of those markets had laws and contracts that gave power to the purchasers.

He looked at his watch and slowed down. Being early wasn't good. After a spell in a rare patch of sun among the oaks that lined Cherry Avenue, Puke thought a moment about the street's name. Shaking it off, he went up and knocked on 515 Cherry Avenue.

The door opened.

"You can come in if you want to," a bathrobed man waved him in with a Wal-Mart brand soda. "You want a glass of water?"

"No thanks," Puke said. "I'm not too early am I?"

"You're fine," the homeowner said. "You still want to see around?"

"Why wouldn't I?"

"It's been slow. You're the third and it's been a year. But the first two were Latrino's looking for a place to piss."

"Why you selling?"

"Dunno. Just sick of Morguetown and them circling our town like desert buzzards."

They entered the kitchen and the man pointed out a few features. "The smell doesn't bother you?"

"No."

"So you're a schoolteacher, huh? Why you looking at such a small house?"

"I just got fired."

"Why? Because you can't speak Dozor? Or does Goya make you sick?"

"No. I'm an English teacher. Too many essays! Too many paragraphs!"

At this the man smiled. "How's the price look?"

"What's your best offer? I'm not much for haggling."

"I can do forty grand. She was worth twice that at one time. But that ain't news to you if you're in the market."

"I was thinking something around twenty," Puke said, pulling out a contract from his attaché. "But I can put ten grand down if we can close next week."

"You can do that kind of down payment?"

Puke took out a pile of bills and a sheet of paper. "This is just a standard contract. You good with twenty?"

The seller paused. He knew he wanted fifty, but he knew he would take an offer in the thirties. But now money was on the table. "Well, I don't have any realtor bills. I guess I can do twenty-five, since you're not a Sexican trying to overpopulate yourself where you don't belong."

Puke smiled. "That I'm not," he said and signed his name. He counted out ten thousand dollars in Ben bills, making ten stacks of ten as he helped another For-Sale-By-Owner sell his home.

The man signed and they talked.

Puke let him. He listened to the man's dreams for the next year or so and where he was thinking of moving. Puke heard the man emotionally detach himself from the home on street downwind from the papermill.

He did take the owner up on that glass of water. After a bit he excused himself. He didn't want to be late for the next appointment up the street with a woman who was selling her house. As he stood, he noticed his attaché case was getting lighter. Relieved, he smiled.

This was not the neighborhood for carrying a lot of cash.

The thick hedge of old forest trees lined the pastures where four horses grazed in knee-deep grass. Bright white fences lined the different corrals of the Wisconsin dell, and a red barn helped balance the expanse of green.

Across the table sat a girl who had been trying to spoon a lone strand of spaghetti for the better part of three minutes.

The mother looked at her sulking, miserable shell of a girl. "How's dinner?"

"Slippery."

"You get but one life, Evert. You must engage it."

"There's nothing to do here. In Morguetown I have friends."

"Bran?"

"So what. I know you don't like him. But you don't know him!"

"I know him. You and him got kicked out of gym class for rollerblading on the treadmills, right? What do you expect me to say?"

"Dad thought it was funny."

"I'll bet."

"What's that mean?"

"It means the town's so busy laughing at him that he chooses to laugh at himself too."

"Well, I like him. He's the only Bull in town who's standing up to the Dozers!"

"Dozers? The Mexicans are the town, Evert."

"Ya, right. When's the last time you were there? We got it

back."

"Is that so?"

Evert put her fork down and fingered the strand of pasta. "A trip to Morguetown won't kill you."

"It's you I'm worried about."

"Maybe I'll just go myself."

The mother looked at her daughter. "Maybe I'll take you halfway, but just for the weekend and you'll have to take the ferry back."

"Okay."

"And your father will have to pick you up. From what you told me of Bran, he's still having a hard time sitting."

# LOG ENTRY 23

11:00 am Abeam: 82 foot SGRP Lighthouse
Entering Grays Reef Passage
Winds: East at 25 knots.
Waves 3-5

Southern Cross takes a turn to the east for the first time and our speed is cut. The waves are now against us as we near the top of Michigan.

I think of home. I see the trees wave among our dunes. I smell the last fields of drying corn and hear their soft songs. I know all is well for the familiar smells assure me.

I remember my first nod that I gave only yesterday and watched able hands pull halyards and lift unstretched sails to the tops of the masts. I hear the passion of my people cheer out from the shoreline. I recall the new white sails clapping as they danced unstrung. How I nodded to Leñador, for he is my strength in these late days. How his muscles ripple as the cold anchor rises from the water and clangs up into the bowsprit.

I remember my smile at Samantha who is my hope as she sheets the sails. How we shot off northward from anchor.

And I recall my nod to Eric Nelson who had joined us as of late. I made sure he received many affirming grins, for Eric Nelson, The Asparagus Kid, is my memory.

Southern Cross sails for Coffin Light! Only yesterday we departed. Or has it been the journey of the decades?

I still don't know. Time has been unsettled since the murder of my son.

I do know this. Our bow has finally turned from its north track and our sails groan tight in anticipation as we tack in the last few miles to Coffin Light.

I know many will remember these times. Many will dread the decisions of Derecho. For he comes.

For he is the teeth of the wind!

I feel him in my bones and I hold fast the wheel.

We must hasten.

He comes!

The EMT's huddled around Little John. "I can't find a vein," one said. "Oh, wait. Now I got it!" The IV began to flow. Others stepped atop the links as if they had done their training on a pile of tangled trucker chains.

"Why's triage here?" one asked.

"Wasn't safe there," Belt said.

They asked a few questions about John's history and allergies.

"His guts are messed up," Mr. Henderson said.

Then they took Little John away.

"You're not coming with us?" one asked the father from the ambulance door.

"In a minute."

As they bounced Little John down the stairs, one saw the shattered doorjam and looked at Belt. "What's going on here?"

"It's under investigation," Belt said, hiding behind the badge.

The teenager was loaded and secured. Within five minutes, they were gone, siren and all.

Nelson, Henderson and Texas bellied to the bar. Behind it, Sebastian took out four shot glasses and a black labeled bottle.

"You know I can't come with you," Belt said. "But a unit said she's still out there."

"Anything else? Any charges? Coast Guard?"

"Dunno. It's never been done before. Maybe an ORV fine."

"Wow!" Sebastian said. "That'll hurt 'em!"

None moved as they drank.

"It's gotta be done," Texas said. "She blabbered to Bran, for Petro's sake!"

They knew.

No Coast Guard sounded good.

Cops came.

Belt took them over to the crime scene in the shipyard and

they started taping it off.

Under a full electric charge from the night before, Homer had amps to spare from his new batteries. He took on the bumps of the pier full speed as the woman balanced on the seat above him and started scolding him for going too fast.

Homer lived in a challenging mobility cart world.

But when she recognized the men coming to her, she U-turned and headed back out to the lighthouse. "Go Homer! Go! It's the three amigos!"

Sebastian, Nelson and Henderson walked toward her like gunslingers on some dusty street in a no-name town.

"The Mexicans are off floating their boat!" Sebastian yelled to the woman, who had powered away from them and was fleeing toward Coffin Light.

"You're too done late and all the dollars short," she hollered back over her shoulder.

They came to her.

"Perfect," Henderson whispered.

"So Big Momma is the the tiny little mouse that ratted us?" Nelson asked. "What next?"

"That's what I'm gonna find out!" Henderson said.

She had seen the sand beach and empty parking lot beyond them but she knew she couldn't break their ranks. Coffin Light now loomed. She looked over her shoulder.

They were coming.

At the circle of concrete at pier's end, she stopped. Looking hard at the dented baseball bat on the pier, she reversed toward the men and turned sideways as if to block them from going to the light.

"You done banging on your bongo like a chimp pansy?" Henderson asked.

"Stop right there!" she hollered.

They walked on toward her.

She gripped her steering bar. "Whatta ya gonna do? You gonna kill me like you killed that beautiful boy?"

They walked in.

"And in front of all these people?" she looked north and saw the crowds on the far beach. She also noticed them all facing away from her as they cheered a man on a ladder.

The three men kept coming to her.

"Then I'm going with Erilick the Derelict and his Squeeze Tease! I'm going up to Coffin Light. I'm going to see the bones for my ownself!" She flipped them and gunned Homer toward the lighthouse.

Her scooter banked the turn and darted over the shadow of Coffin Light. She looked behind her, oily hair blown out of her eyes by an east wind. She saw the red sun. Turning back to the west, she buzzed under Coffin Light and bumped over the potholes in the last circle of cement. "We can do this Homer! Leñador will find a place for us!"

Homer couldn't.

His front tires jumped the two inch rim of iron but her weight made his frame snag.

The three men stopped. Between them and the woman, rose Coffin Light just off to their right.

The back of Homer started to rise as the woman leaned forward. Rear tires spun free from lack of tension, and then the machine dumped her headlong into the river.

She saw the deep water beyond the shallow rocks at the base of the pier. Leaning to it, she reached out her arms as any Olympic diver and shouted. "Mexico North!" The boarder was in her sights.

Homer slid toward the water but his revenge came swift. The inside of a back tire caught the rim of steel. It griped as if it were a hook.

Snagged on the handlebars, the woman felt herself lose momentum. She bent the steering shaft and then felt herself dead-falling straight down.

Homer's wheel broke loose and the heavy cart flipped over and went belly up as it drove the woman onto the rocks under the shallows. The few inches of water didn't offer much cushion and her head struck a clam-covered rock.

Her head hit hard.

Then rained down the heavy, lead-acid batteries. Those new batteries from the Welfare Wench helped finished her off by crushing the back of her neck.

Nelson, Henderson and Sebastian lingered in the shadow of Coffin Light.

"Not much we can do now." Nelson looked north at the tractor getting pulled out of Lake Michigan and all the people cheering at man on the ladder.

"Hey. Some women just need to be free," Henderson said.

They turned from the dead woman and walked back to town. The wind felt good on their faces. The red sky felt soothing.

"Who's Leñador?" Nelson asked.

The east winds held and the new crew of *Southern Cross* hoisted the sails to the cheer of the crowd. They then sheeted them down on the port side and jumped the vessel northward on a starboard tack.

All the beach faces watched the vessel leave.

Shapes held and vacuums were strong, and wind force pulled the heavy cruising hull through the water. Dust and the sharp smells of warm sand and dry trees weakened as fragrances of home gave way to the scents of fresh water.

Samantha looked at her grandfather and saw him smaller and calmer. Yet a fire of phenomenal heat burned behind his eyes. "You okay?" she asked.

"It comes," he said.

Looking ahead to the north, she nodded.

But he was looking to the west. He let his eyes settle somewhere beyond the far horizon. "It comes," he said to himself.

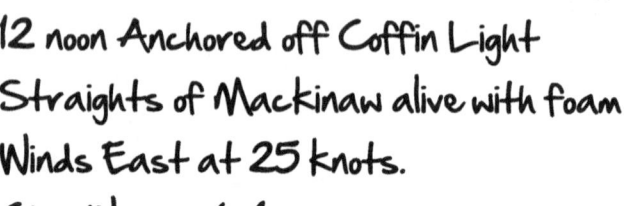

## LOG ENTRY 24

12 noon Anchored off Coffin Light
Straights of Mackinaw alive with foam
Winds East at 25 knots.
Chop Waves 4-6

Home at last. Whether by fortune or fulfill-
ment, the breath of the deep west is inhaling air
off the big lake and we are alive and taking a
beating in the chop. Waves surge and boil under
our dolphin striker and keel.

In these shallow waters we enjoy little shelter
or calm from the power of wind and wave. Our
sail north along sheltered shoreline is over. Now
the east winds funnel power between the Michigan peninsulas. They are both friend and foe!

Southern Cross thunders on anchor.

Off our stern, beyond the lighthouse, the
rollers march to Wisconsin, following the echo
that is summoning them.

We will soon learn if Coffin Light and the
waters of Grays Reef will avenge their dead.

For too long we have been sleeping.

But now the horizons are calling out.

Be warned.

**B**ull stepped out of Bran's Yugo and stretched. He looked at his watch and nodded, pleased that he was an hour early.

"Does Pop's have a swirlbucket?" Bran asked. "My Mackinaw dump was just the cork."

Bull walked the stiff out of his legs and went toward Evert, who was sitting on the curb. For a moment she looked like the cute little mushroom from long ago. Bull scratched his beard, sat next to her and gave her a hug.

"Hey, Evert," he said.

"Nice ride?" she smiled.

Bull rubbed his knees. "A Yugo ain't meant for the likes of me. It swerves when I sneeze!"

"Back in ten!" Bran said and went by them fast, fanning the outside of his sweats as he headed into Pop's.

"Sure they're coming?" Evert asked. "I mean, you want us to stick around and wait to be sure?"

"They're coming," Bull said. "Can I bum a smoke?"

"Sure," she joined him.

Bran returned. He shook his keys at Evert and she jumped up.

Bull waved them off. Pleased that they were driving away. He smiled at them and hoped they were going to Wisconsin. His ex was going to love Bran. He was the gift that kept on giving.

*Southern Cross*, anchored with sails lashed, kept her engine powered up to take pressure off the ground tackle. She was being thrashed, but she held firm in the cut of deep water between land and the crusted, storm-chewed, colossal abandoned lighthouse.

Sturgeon Bay was all but asleep off their starboard beam.

It looked very quiet and still on the other side of Waugoshance Island where the water was sheltered by mainland.

But *Southern Cross* and its crew were in the stew. They faced the full bash and wrath of the 25 knot rip wind that was funneling through the Mackinaw passage.

Far to their north, across many miles of the Straights, the dark treeline of Michigan's Upper Peninsula seemed to enjoy watching them suffer. As did the two pillars of the Mackinac Bridge miles ahead of them in the east. Below them, the shallow shoals of Grays Reef boiled every wave into a breaker.

But it was the haunt of crushing waves, busting themselves upon rock and lighthouse that ate the resolve of the crew.

Here, *Southern Cross* settled into its violent pitch as the waves rolled in. The low islands of Wilderness, becalmed in the lee of the nearby point, teased them. Less than a two hundred yards away was the tip of land and the calm water.

Samantha followed her grandfather's gaze as he looked south and measured the deep, vast, peaceful expanse of Sturgeon Bay. The open bay was doing its very best to seduce them into its calm.

"Why not anchor in there?" Samantha spoke over the wind and wave crash and disrupted her grandfather's contemplation.

*Southern Cross* then took two flanks of waves and Samantha watched her grandfather hold fast his resolve as he nodded to Leñador, who now released a third anchor and let its chain pour straight down into the water and pile up on the seabed. The chain was studded together with short nylon cords that had been woven into the links to cushion the tug of the anchor.

Confused, Samantha went up to the foredeck, grabbing hand holds because of the lurch.

The exposed anchorage gave a hard pitch to *Southern Cross*. The sailboat fought its rode, not liking its leash.

Unnerved by the roar, shallows and the gloom of Coffin Light, Samantha retreated below decks. There, she turned to Eric, who was wrapped in a blanket and wedged in a corner of floor space between the table post and the port bench.

Their eyes met.

She saw his white and green face. "Feeling better?"

He shook his head.

"We're here," she held the hand hold above her on the ceiling, and swung to the motion of *Southern Cross* like an arm of a tolling bell.

"Where?"

"Coffin Light."

"Why'd we come here again?" he asked with the back of his head on the hard floor. Next to his face, his arm held a reek bucket of slop from his recent barfing.

"Think," she said without pity.

"That's right. To find your father's remains."

A shadow was in the companionway hatch and then Señor Bendolly joined them. "Anchor three is down," he said as the rattle of chain on metal plates finished echoing inside the main salon.

She nodded and the old man turned and stood before her. He looked at her spray dampened hair and the strands that clung to her eyes. Then he looked into those eyes.

"Is it coming?" she asked.

Placing both hands on her shoulders, he balanced himself against the pitch of the surf.

Peace and fear were in odd unity inside his gaze. He leaned toward her ear.

*El Arrecife de Gray hierve blanco.*

*Gemidos metálicos se oxidan por la luz de la mañana.*

*Los dientes del fantasma de Derecho vendrán esta noche.*
*¡El lago Michigan abandonará sus muertos!*

She looked at him. "My mother taught me that. She sang it to me since I was a baby. It is a strange..."

He let her travel to the place. He knew where it was.

In the background, Eric wretched a dry heave into his stink bucket.

Samantha stared at her Grandfather. "When she sang, she always cried. It is her saddest song. It is strange to hear it on your voice. When she sang she was young. Younger than me. She was infant. How could that be?"

"It is a song of life and death being together. A song of mystery."

The wind puffed down the open hatch and made an announcement. Cold came with it and took heat from them.

Finding it difficult to stand in the lurch, Samantha sat with her feet by Eric's head and huddled in the corner of the main salon. Bright daylight from the open hatch, glared shine on brass fixtures. Mahogany walls glowed rich and clean. Samantha took off her coat for the first time in 22 hours and huddled under a thick blanket. Across the cabin she saw the one spot of the wall that had not been stripped of flaking vanish, mold or dirt. In the circle of smuk hung the picture of her mother.

Eric looked up at her, then followed her gaze to the photograph. "It's you," he said.

The decks above sounded the footfalls of Leñador.

She looked at the ceiling and smiled.

Eric saw this.

---

*Gray's Reef boils white.*
*Metal groans rust in the morning light.*
*Ghost teeth of Derecho will come this night.*
*Lake Michigan will give up her dead!*

She felt Eric's gaze, turned and faced him. Not long ago they were in this position. Back when she was bleeding from her face and he was defending her with a rifle.

Now she bled from her heart and he was puking.

*Southern Cross* lurched on the chain like a leviathan on a hook. In foreboding waters on the eve of winter, the sailboat didn't like being in shallows.

She stared down at Eric.

He knew they were at a place where his father had murdered hers. He felt the heat of the horror in his heart. He wiped a chunk of chew from his chin.

Señor Bendolly walked back into the main salon, brushing his hand along her shoulder as he passed. He was dressed in layers to face the topside wrath.

"Why here?" Eric asked and rolled to his back as *Southern Cross* heaved again.

Samantha envisioned the keel just below her, fanning silt from rocks as it pitched.

"Why not anchor in the calm? In the calm on the other side of Coffin Light?" he asked. "Why does everything have to be…?"

Samantha looked at the Captain. A mild interest was in Eric's question.

"*Los dientes del fantasma de Derecho vendrán esta noche,*"* he said.

"What?" Eric asked and looked at her sitting very still despite the pitch of the vessel.

Señor Bendolly climbed the ladder and stepped out into the wind.

"You okay?" Eric asked Samantha. "Looks like someone just walked on your grave!" He looked up at her white face and felt the cold breeze pour down the companionway. He

*Ghost teeth of Derecho will come this night

chilled. It felt clean. Clear of fever, he inhaled. Maybe it was the fresh air. Or laying still for the last few hours. Or that his guts were empty. Either way, he felt better. Actually, he felt good.

Samantha adjusted her look as she peered down at him. She felt that they weren't a part of her Grandfather's scheme. For the first time she felt this, and she then knew it to be true. Maybe Señor Bendolly wasn't even doing the plan. That what was happening went deeper than the connive of any person. That they were in the makings of the code of mystery itself. And that the innocent involved at this juncture were in equal danger as the guilty. They were near the Untamed.

"You okay?" Eric asked again.

"No, I'm not," Samantha said as she turned to him. "And neither are you."

They stopped at Pop's Boat Rentals near the entrance to Wilderness State Park. Shutting off the truck, they got out and stretched.

"We're just going to make talk," Henderson said.

"If he'd wanted a war, he'd done something long ago. Something big and mean," Sebastian said.

"What if he's really getting the bones?" Nelson asked.

They stopped and looked at each other, then they entered Pop's and a woman smiled at them.

"We need a boat," Nelson said to her.

"Little late in the year to be on a boat up here," she said.

"I'm just coming for my son," Nelson said. "He done sailed off with some Mexicans."

"I haven't heard that one before."

"What's the weather going to do?" Henderson asked.

"Sammo. But it's still fishing season," the woman said,

glancing out the door and into the back of their truck. "I see you got some rods. Once the smallies get in the frying pan, it always looks better!"

The door of Pop's dinged and they turned.

Bull was there.

"I thought you had go get your kid?" Nelson asked.

"Halfway," Bull said. "Exis agreed to dump her here."

"They ain't around, are they?" Sebastian asked.

"They bolted."

"Good." Henderson said.

"Where?" Nelson asked.

Bull shrugged. "They were supposed to go back to my place, but I think Evert's gonna take him to meet the Delly!" He smiled.

Nelson backed the truck to an aluminum boat and hooked up. The others loaded boxes of gear. Bull stuffed lifejackets under seats so they didn't blow away.

Sebastian looked at the two, massive windmills spinning on the horizon. "Wind is still east. Won't catch much."

Henderson smirked at him and the other two shook their heads.

"Cold," Nelson said.

The four men were still trying to convince themselves it was a fishing trip.

"*Capitán?*" Leñador handed the binoculars to Sr. Bendolly and pointed toward Waugashance Point.

The old man focused the lenses. "They should not have come," he said.

"But you have his son," Leñador said.

The old man looked tired and spent. He was ready for some sleep. "And he has mine."

A wave came through the maze of rocks and shipwrecks from the north shoal line and slapped the side of *Southern Cross*, sending a cold spray over the two men. It shook the sailboat to the keel and tested the new ground tackle and standing rigging.

Sebastian landed another smallmouth bass. It was his fifth in as many casts. He looked at Nelson and Henderson. Both of the men were taking a break. Their arms were tired. Bull sat in the stern of the rental boat and smoked.

"I never dreamed we'd actually catch fish," Nelson said.

"That's what makes it good!" Sebastian said. "We're catching fish in the lee of the islands and being entertained by their stupid boat out there in the open taking a beating!"

"They sure anchored in the stupid! Those people never have made any sense to me!"

"Lotta drift wood on land." Bull said. "We'll be warm tonight!"

"They got fish luck. I'll say that. Dunno why they didn't bring on their canepoles!" Henderson said.

"Any news of your boy?" Nelson asked Henderson.

"He's good. Collapsed lung. He'll be fine. Pissed at me!" Henderson said. "Serves him right for sinking my boat."

"You?" Sebastian looked at Nelson.

Nelson shook his head and checked his phone again. "No. And we got coverage too."

"She's got Mojo," Henderson said. "Just like her old woman. You might not hear from him until morning!"

"It's just them and us again," Bull said. "Been a long time."

This brought the men to a quiet.

"East wind is fading." Bull said after a bit. "Let's fry fish!"

"What's up with Evert?"

Bull closed his phone. "Hanging out in Mac City. It looks like they're going to mess with the Ex after all!"

"That'll go over well."

"Life's good!" Bull smiled.

"Let's roar a fire and get behind some cover. Wind is getting to me," Sebastian said.

They puttered around the rocks on the west end on Waugoshance Island and then beached their rental. Each one took a gunnel and dragged the boat up and over the rocks and onto high ground. Then they tied her down to a big rock and set camp out of the wind as best they could. They didn't go too far out of the wind. They still wanted to watch the sailboat take a pounding.

Each looked at the sky and the wind direction again.

They still knew they were in the Straights of Mackinaw.

# LOG ENTRY 25

12 noon Anchored: Coffin Light
Straight of Mackinaw alive with foam
Winds None.
Waves 2-4 and confused

I am here and so are they, but neither of us is alone.

Is not this but another day atop disturbed seas?

Southern Cross is groaning and lurching in the boiling waves. She remembers her pain. In this she is not alone.

They want to hurt her and she knows it. They have a wood fire on the shoreline and the oil of fried fish drifts in the fluke wind. With the smells of Waugoshance Point come the memories.

I am breaking.

The lighthouse. Though long abandoned and soundless, it is calling to me. It is tapping at my soul. I am weary from the sail and the weight of this story. But it is never easy to visit the tomb of a lost son.

Wait! The air is from the Straights again. The wind carries a the scent of land. But it is from the north!

Coffin Light appears to be moving because the windshift. It stands brown against gray rock in a dark blue sea. I see large patches of white birds in the bright sky!

The wind is confused.

It is taunting me.

The waves have no rhythm.

Now I smell the birds, cement and rotted iron of Coffin Light!

Southern Cross is drifting to anchor two! I feel her hull shifting as I write.

The rank of the nesting birds is upon me. The songs from their bleeding throats scream overhead and cut into my ears. They are all aflight!

They know something!

They are leaving.

The coffin of my son is breathing!

Derecho!

The old man closed his log and stuffed it behind the cushion in the backrest of the cockpit gunnel. He latched the little teak door over the logbook. It must survive! Taking a heavy winch handle from the sleeve, he struck hard the ship's bell to warn his crew. Thumps echoed below decks as he took the helm and fired the diesel.

Leñador surfaced first. Dark hair disheveled from sleep gave way to eyes of fire and war. He snapped his lifejacket around him and looked to the blazing fire on the island now off the stern. He looked up into the clear sky and squinted at the sun.

"They come?" Leñador asked and was thrown to a seating position in the lurch.

"Wind shift!" Bendolly looked north into the wind but nodded eerily to the west. Waves rolled in from the east.

Leñador looked and went a shade white. "The birds are gone."

*Southern Cross* caught a wave on the starboard beam and pitched hard to port. Thumps were heard down below.

"What's it mean?" Leñador asked.

"The love of God is leaving," Bendolly said.

Samantha climbed up and Eric followed. Both were shrugging on their gear and lifejackets.

"Wow!" Eric said. "You sure brought the boat close to them!" He lost his balance as the east rollers struck hard at midships.

"You are not safe here," Bendolly told Eric. "Call your father to come and get you."

"How? I don't have a phone."

"Call your father."

"Will I be safer with him?" Eric asked.

The old man looked west. "Only Derecho knows!"

"You really don't know?" Samantha asked her grandfather.

"Know what?" Eric asked.

From the fullness of the bright, livid blue sky, Señor Bendolly turned to the teenager and pointed to the north.

Eric looked straight off the bow of *Southern Cross* and saw the massive precipice of the Abandoned Lighthouse.

"Tell me the truth of the lighthouse," the old man said.

Leñador looked away.

Samantha stared at her feet.

Eric looked directly at Señor Bendolly.

It was real.

It was true.

"It's where my father killed your son," Eric said.

Samantha whipped her eyes up to him.

Eric met her gaze. "My father killed your father."

Señor Bendolly reached out his hand and took the shoulder of Eric.

Eric stared at the feet of old man, who had pulled him to his chest. "Let me stay here," Eric uttered.

The gnarled, withered hand went to the chin of Eric Nelson and lifted the lad's face.

"Let me stay. No matter what. Let me stay!" Eric said.

The old man nodded. "*¡Usted escogió bien!*"* Then Bendolly pushed hard on the fuel throttle.

Leñador pointed. He pointed hard and he screamed! His howl split the sky as terror erupted from the bowels of his soul. One hand clamped into the hair of Samantha while the other looped Bendolly and Eric, and he drove them all down.

Still screaming, cowering for shelter behind the companionway hatch Leñador held them down.

But Bendolly knew he had to look. He had to stand. He had to see Derecho

And he did.

He rose and saw the white wall engulf the lighthouse in what looked like a blizzard of snow. Within the surging wall

_____

*You chose correctly*

of white water lingered the lone, black figure of Coffin Light. Then the white cloud of lathered water swallowed it in its grip as if it was a fog bank.

But Derecho is not fog.

Fog cannot rip off an iron rooftop that had sat against the ages. Had anchored itself against the power of the Straights of Mackinaw for the decades. Derecho launched it into the air and crashed it into the water by the sailboat!

Derecho!

The old man saw the wind lance the water and lift its waves into the sky.

*¡Derecho es dientes en el viento!*

Tucked in behind the glacial polished rocks of Waugoshance Point, four men clung to barren fingers of tree trunks as the shriek of violence screeched overhead. Their boat, tied around a big boulder on the face of the peninsula had just torn free and flown overhead as if it were a tinfoil tumbleweed.

Talking was impossible. As they clawed, shrank and wormed deeper in the shelter of the biggest bolder, they stared at each other, blinking lake spray and sand from their eyes. Each word was ripped from their innards the second their lips parted. The vacuum of windfoil curling over the rock tried to lift them away.

Sebastian had the most urgent message. After several repeats and with his forehead bleeding from some beach shrapnel, he finally got them to lean in. Mere inches from the ears of the others he yelled again. "He tried to Farmer Almanac us!"

They showed him that they heard with a quick flash of

---

*\*Derecho is teeth in wind!*

teeth and then they dug their grip deeper into earth and crevasse as the flat line wind raged its war.

Seven of the ten, half-inch nylon lines that had been woven into the chain snapped the moment the third anchor hooked seabed. Acting as shock absorbers, they saved the entire bow of *Southern Cross* from being sheared off. But the shudder of teak splintering and chain sawing deep into fiberglass froze the expressions of the crew.

"We grabbed!" Captain Bendolly yelled from deep inside the cockpit of *Southern Cross*. No one heard him in the thunder of ripping air. He pushed more fuel into the engine. "We're safe for the moment!" His words flew out of his mouth with spit. He was trying to convince himself.

Eric looked out the open companionway hatch at the swirl of wind-driven water. The dark howl of the monster was horrible. "What of them?" he nodded to shore.

From inside the boat, Samantha looked at him, but she was more worried about her own survival.

Waves were chewed down to mere inches of effervescence as the air became streams of lake water. The teeth of the Straight Line Wind tore at everything they touched. All stuff on the deck of Southern Cross had been cut, ripped and shredded away but for the lashed sails, standing rigging, helm and lifelines.

For endless minutes, the roar of winds exceeding one hundred miles an hour, screamed out of the west end of Lake Michigan.

Wet heads peeked out from behind dripping rocks. The men clamped their eyes shut to save their sight. Hair was plastered to their blood droplet foreheads and all their skin was numb. When they did dare peek, they looked beyond the surf coming higher and they focused on the sailboat. Tucked in snug behind the lighthouse, they saw the wind buffet the hull something fierce as the boat rode through the blast in the relative calm and lee side of the shoal. Coffin Light was now its shield.

Then the wind weakened eighty percent in force and dropped to a gale. ·

Sebastian wrung out his shirt tails and looked at the island, stripped by the wind of all but rock and stumps and yelled, "Camp's gone!"

"He tried to Farmer Almanac us all right!" Henderson repeated. "He knew!"

As fast as it had come, the fluke rage passed over them like a death angel and then it left.

They could now think and talk.

"We need a boat," Nelson said.

"It's gone and so's our deposit!" Sebastian grumbled.

"There's a boat!" Henderson pointed to *Southern Cross*.

Nelson walked to the water's edge. "How far is the swim?"

"Closer now because the wind."

"They're not going to just let us board, you know," Bull said.

Henderson and Nelson lifted their shirts and showed their pistols.

"You're going to murder all those people? What if he doesn't even have the bones?" Stompson asked.

"We're not going to murder them all," Nelson said. "One of them is my son."

Henderson, Sebastian and Nelson walked to the edge of the water. "It's cold," Sebastian said.

"Sissy," Henderson said. He took off his wet shirt and

slammed it on the rocks. He looked back at Bull. "So you're not coming? We can end it! Right here we can end it!"

"Nope," Bull said. "I'm staying on land. Walking Wilderness back to Pop's. I'll come and get you with another boat." Bull looked to land.

"I'll walk with you to waist deep to give you some cover," Sebastian said, locking a round into his chamber. "I can't swim all that good."

Nelson and Henderson took to the water. One carried a boat cushion that somehow survived the storm.

The old man watched them walk out into the water. When they were chest deep, *Southern Cross* stopped lurching hard against its anchor. Bendolly then looked into the clear water. The ground was alive and passing quickly below them as if Southern Cross was adrift in a fast moving river.

Leñador rushed to the bow, never letting go of hand holds as he did so.

The anchor rode was slack and then he too saw the rocks below move quickly under keel. He looked to Coffin Light. It seemed adrift. His eyes went to the captain.

"*Seiche!*" Señor Bendolly yelled.

Eric saw Leñador dive for Samantha and drop her to the deck. They grabbed hold of all they could. He went to his knees as he realized the vessel was swirling back into the wind. *Nothing here makes any sense!* He thought.

Then the crew was crunched to their handholds as more pieces of the bow splinted. The bowsprit dipped deep into the water as it came about on its first anchor like a charging dog snapped back by the end of its chain.

Water gurgled and foamed at the bow as if anchored above a waterfall. A maelstrom somewhere seemed to have opened.

"¡*Tierra!*"* the old man screamed. "¡*Seiche!*"

The crew of *Southern Cross* held fast as the surge of countless cubic miles of penned up water poured out of the massive Sturgeon Bay! It funneled out, overflowing across Wilderness Point, sinking the entire peninsula of Waugoshance.

Two men, clinging to one float cushion, jetted by the sailboat as if thrown from a kayak in whitewater. A third followed and the sailors aboard Southern Cross watched three men get sucked along the huge pressure ripple around Coffin Light and get flushed into the Straights of Mackinaw.

Freed from the wind pressure of the Derecho, Sturgeon Bay had released its backlash flood.

On the tallest rock, churning white with foam, a lone man stood out. He lifted a hand and waved.

The captain of the sailboat waved back.

"Who's that?" Samantha asked.

"That's Bull Stompson. Scum of the earth," Eric said as he turned to the sea and looked for his father in the current.

She looked at her grandfather. "Who is Bull Stompson?"

Alfred Bendolly turned from Coffin Light. "*Eso es el conserje Bill Thompson. Un amigo. ¡Un amigo muy valiente y muy bueno!*"*

Then the old man smiled.

Then he wept.

---

*Land!*
*That's Janitor Bill Thompson. A friend. A very brave and very good friend!"*

## Final Entry of Captain Bendolly

From Samantha's widowed balcony, I smile at my daughter-in-law as I look down at Southern Cross, my new beach front home. Terro and one of his dozers dug away some sand and sunk me into my beach. And he built some steps up into my stern. High up on the high beach, her and I can now sit in peace. We will endure the winter cold together. Me and Southern Cross will stay warm with an iron stove and some of Leñador's wood.

As we breathed life into Southern Cross, so we have given life to Bay Valley. I placed Señor Bill Thompson as mayor. He dismantled my factories and made big fields for soccer! He and I are one. We both lost children in the Straights.

Coast Guard divers found Bran's Yugo which had been blown off the Mackinaw Bridge. No bodies were found but we know the truth. The lake does not give up her dead.

With my shadowy factories now but a memory, the Evert & Bran Boardwalk circles all of Allister Lake.

Many now picnic on the town boardwalk, and inside Allister Forest Park. Bill's manager, Señor Puke, is good with money and very shrewd! All commercial properties are under his influence. No cars can come into downtown Bay View Valley. People walk among the stores and farm markets and let their niños run wild in the streets and open areas as all niños should.

Many new people are citizens of Bay View Valley and they live together. Police ride my horses and show no weapons. Horses have a calming effect.

I have forgiven Texas Tex. She asked it of me and I gave it to her. As promised to her mother, I returned her to her homestead. I have given her back the house of her parents and the ten acres of grass within the farmland. My argument was never with her. May she find freedom in the structure her parents once believed in.

As to my granddaughter and me, we still have burdens. My families are now among and within the town. I hope she loves them and helps them live in peace in this new land.

As to the hate that once fueled the White Fight? May we prove that hard work is a gift, and that hate, in time, destroys itself.

As for the division of all those worthless commercial properties that I purchased along the way, I thank the 47 students of the high school who showed kindness to all of us Mexican Mo's who mopped their slop. Their properties are not worthless now. I give their Government and Economics teachers the responsibility to work with Señor Puke and instruct these students as to how best to own business and manage the commerce of Bay View Valley.

Dwight and John, the new janitors at the school, remind us all of how difficult it is to clean away hate. They show that working in the dirt is an act of citizenship, as every farmer knows.

As to my foremen. As they inherit their four corners of the enstancia, may they govern it well for their children's children. To Santasa, I gave all livestock. To Carlos of Corn I gave all fields and fruit. To Terro of Trucks I gave all transport rights. And yes, I am pleased that many in their families, when offered homes in town, chose to stay on their farm.

To Leñador I gave him Samantha's hand in marriage, and my blessing. At the wedding of all weddings I said, "Be strong and of courage. Turn your cheek to violence and not your axe!"

But in secret, Leñador, I implore you and

Samantha to be very wary of Eric Nelson.

Eric is a great and lethal enemy. From inside his little restaurant bar, he will scheme your demise and the ruination of all people of Bay View Valley until his hate matures. In his heart is only bitterness, and many hard decades await him. Eric's evil is blind to Derecho, and he will ever try to avenge the drowning deaths of his father and his father's friends.

As to Dwight?

Leñador, embrace him as your brother and remember it was his mother who sacrificed much of her life to be among the hateful in order to bring me the information I needed. At one time she was a special friend to your father.

Keep bright the memorial of her bronzed electric mobility cart in the shadow of Allister Lighthouse. May all the climbing niños keep it polished and pristine as they sit and pretend to drive Homer into the sunset while their parents enjoy walking on the pier.

May we always know the inscription on Homer's seat:

In the last days of Morguetown,
Big Momma was killed in the line of duty
as she sent hate to the grave
in her fight to resurrect the hope that is
Bay View Valley

Remember, one and all, that it was Allister Bendolly, the first Mexican sailor on Michigan's West Coast, who once had such hope.

# The End

## Author's Note:

I want to thank Torrensen's Marina of Muskegon, Michigan for keeping their gates unlocked back in the early 1980's so a landlubbing teenager from Wayland could stroll among the sailboats and fall in love with the water. I implore the readers of Coffin Light to believe that none of the darkness of the different hatreds within this novel came from Torrensen's Marina.

To the sailors of the Great Lakes and those who boat Michigan's West Coast. Don't try to find the town of Morguetown or Bay View Valley. This town, and all of its struggling people on both sides of the channel are a reflection of the battles between good and evil that co-exist in the my own heart. As to the accuracy of the Ship's Log of *Southern Cross*? Well, in all my sailing voyages, miles and times always seem to get tossed and tangled on the water.

I want to thank my brother Dave, who kept a log of racial slurs he heard along the highways when he trucked about half of Michigan's factories down to Mexico between 2006 and 2009.

I also thank the dozens of friends who volunteer every spring and help me prepare my old Irwin 52 sailboat for another season. May they be rewarded with many good winds!

And for the families and friends who share the loss of the six people killed in The Southern Great Lakes Derecho of 1998, may they realize that there is no link between the punishing Derecho of Coffin Light and the fateful '98 Straight Line Windstorm. Nature's judgement that I leveraged upon

three of the dark triangle characters in this book is solely a cre-
ation from the author's imagination for the purpose of fiction.

As for family members who lost loved ones from high
winds blowing cars off the Mackinaw Bridge, may they know
that the Derecho in Coffin Light and the fatal punishments it
delivered to Evert and Bran and their Yugo is solely from the
author's imagination. If anything, may they be less saddened
by their loss and better sympathize with Bran and Evert. Bran
and Evert were pretty cool characters and they would have
lived well either in Wisconsin or in Bay View Valley. In my
book, Evert and Bran are America.